Getting down to business...

"Kiss the next man who falls into your lap." When Mia Diaz agrees to the dare, she doesn't expect it to happen so literally. But suddenly, there he is—stubble-dusted jaw, sexy half-smile, and lips that make her appreciate the benefits of acting on impulse. Her long-buried libido certainly thinks it's the right move...as long as what comes next is strictly a one-night affair. Mia has dedicated the last few years to building her jewelry store. She's not about to put her heart in a stranger's hands, no matter how skillful they might be...

Ethan has made his fortune by seizing opportunities. So when he finds himself tangled up in long legs, red hair, and satin bedsheets, he doesn't complain—until he finds out the redhead in question is Mia Diaz. The same Mia who's been dodging his emails and calls for weeks, ignoring all his offers to buy her out. The

Ethan is a master of the takeover. Mia refuses to give in. And what started out as a simple dare has become the ultimate challenge, where the only way to win may be to surrender...

Until Dawn

Business or Pleasure

Melinda Di Lorenzo

LYRICAL PRESS
Kensington Publishing Corp.
www.kensingtonbooks.com

Lyrical Press books are published by
Kensington Publishing Corp. 119 West 40th Street New York, NY 10018

All Kensington titles, imprints, and distributed lines are available at special quantity discounts for bulk purchases for sales promotion, premiums, fundraising, and educational or institutional use.

To the extent that the image or images on the cover of this book depict a person or persons, such person or persons are merely models, and are not intended to portray any character or characters featured in the book.

Special book excerpts or customized printings can also be created to fit specific needs. For details, write or phone the office of the Kensington Special Sales Manager:
Kensington Publishing Corp.
119 West 40th Street
New York, NY 10018
Attn. Special Sales Department. Phone: 1-800-221-2647.

Kensington and the K logo Reg. U.S. Pat. & TM Off.
LYRICAL PRESS Reg. U.S. Pat. & TM Off.
Lyrical Press and the L logo are trademarks of Kensington Publishing Corp.

First Electronic Edition: April 2018
eISBN-13: 978-1-5161-0553-3
eISBN-10: 1-5161-0553-2

First Print Edition: April 2018
ISBN-13: 978-1-5161-0555-7
ISBN-10: 1-5161-0555-9

Printed in the United States of America

Chapter 1

Ethan

With a wordless growl, I stepped back on the sidewalk and scanned the row of boutique-style shops, trying to discern which one might be Trinkets and Treasures.

It was an impossible endeavor. They all looked the same. BoHo trendy. Brick fronts with varying shades of trim, no names hanging above the shops. I was sure the last bit was a trick. A subtle marketing ploy. The lack of signage forced the casual passerby to stop and look inside in order to figure out what the hell each store specialized in.

Another damned good reason to do my job from behind my desk.

I *liked* my desk. It had a nice, comfortable leather chair. It was in my office, which had a view. A panoramic one of Toronto. Nice, reassuringly solid concrete buildings as far as the eye could see.

And very few bad omens.

Which seemed to be plaguing me in droves since leaving the comfort of my office this morning.

First came the accident on the freeway, which delayed me so badly that I had to run to make my flight. Literally run. Through a goddamned airport in a three-thousand-dollar suit. Next there was a mechanical issue that forced us to change planes in Winnipeg. The flight in question had zero seats available in business class, which resulted in me being trapped between an asthmatic octogenarian and a woman with a none-too-pleased infant. After that, there was a lengthy stop in Calgary to deice, and a fifty-minute delay at YVR *after* touchdown due to staffing issues. I'd finally stepped onto solid ground in Vancouver a mere six hours behind schedule. My car rental had been given away when I didn't turn up to retrieve it on time. Some kind of job action had the limo drivers running a skeleton crew, which in turn meant the taxi drivers were run ragged, and the wait to get one had been an outrageous hour and a quarter. I'd had to pay the driver double his fare to get him to agree to come back, and even then, he'd refused to return any sooner than an hour later.

Like living in the fucking Dark Ages, I thought bitterly.

So why wasn't I holed up in my five-star luxury suite at the Regent Inn? The answer was simple. Mia Diaz. The thorn in my side who'd forced me to leave Toronto in the first place. I fought a need to curse the woman aloud. After making initial contact three weeks ago—and receiving a flat-out rejection of my offer—I'd tried dozens of times to get in touch with her.

The phone was a total no-go. Her business line was screened by some kind of answering service, and after putting me through just once, they'd subsequently rejected every call after. So I'd switched to email. At first, I'd been triumphant. Ms. Diaz sent polite, personal answers. To start, anyway. Then came the automated out-of-office replies. On my last attempt to get through, my email had been bounced. It didn't take a genius to figure out that she'd blocked my address somehow.

A less determined person—a less successful businessman—might've taken that as a sign to let it go. I saw it as a challenge. My own company, Burke Holdings, hadn't become the third-largest distributor of unique, handmade products in Canada through a willingness to give up. Even if my focus group hadn't told me that they'd be willing to pay three times as much for the personally designed items that Mia offered in her store, just the woman's unwillingness to even consider my offer would've been enough to drive me harder to acquire it.

The last few hours, though, were a real test.

That's what makes it worth it, I reminded myself.

It was true that some of the businesses I took over were parted with reluctantly. The owners knew their product had potential. They fully believed in it. The harder they fought, the more profitable it usually ended up being for me. In the end, the quick buck I offered—combined with the promise of improved distribution and potential popularity—always won out.

Except with Mia Diaz and Trinkets and Treasures.

The mental reminder made me grit my teeth and turn my attention back to the row of shops. I squinted against the dim sky and took a step closer to the buildings. Everything was dark. Which I supposed was to be expected at eight o'clock on a Sunday night. I'd assumed, though, that I'd be able to get a good look at the shop in question. Or at least enough of a glimpse to let me know what I was up against. Having an edge meant no surprises. So far, the edge seemed damned far out of reach.

Then, as if to drive home the pervasive futility of my efforts, a car—the only one I'd seen on this street other than the taxi that had dropped me off just a few minutes earlier—flew by and sent a spray of water in my direction.

"You've got to be fucking kidding me," I muttered.

My gaze turned down in disgust. The mess wasn't just wet. It was dirty. My suit was officially a total write-off, and I hadn't even made it to the hotel yet.

The hotel. My stuff.

"Shit." The whip of a sudden gust of wind carried away my curse as I spun on my heel.

Sure enough, my small suitcase, which I'd yanked out of the taxi and unthinkingly set on the ground, was covered with the same garbage as my clothes. And the bag was wobbling. Hovering right over the edge of the sidewalk.

Sensing its imminent demise, I took a step forward. My reward was a soggy splash as my foot slammed into an ankle-deep puddle. The split second of ice-cold pant leg sucking against my calf was all the suitcase needed to complete its suicide attempt. It toppled over. It bounced. Then it sprung open. A crisp, white shirt tumbled out alongside a pair of dress socks.

I narrowed my eyes at the ruination. "What? That's all you've got?"

The universe decided to respond with a metaphorical middle finger directed straight at me.

A second heavy gust of wind kicked up and sent the top of the suitcase flying all the way open. A stack of paperwork—everything I'd collected about Trinkets and Treasures and its elusive owner, and that I could swear I'd secured—was loose. It lifted into the air, and before I could react, it sailed past me, hit the stream of water that bounced against the sidewalk, and started on a path toward a storm drain a few feet away.

"Shit," I said again.

With my feet sloshing unpleasantly through the water, I dived forward and bent my knees to grab the paperwork. I failed in an epic way. One foot caught on a rock. The other stretched out far enough that it made me close my eyes and groan in pain.

"C'mon, Burke, get your shit together," I commanded.

Yanking as hard as I could, I pulled my foot out of my shoe and drew my sock-clad foot forward, stumbling a little as I did. Both hands hit the ground.

"Fuck."

I drew in a shallow breath, and tried to get up again. My body protested heartily, and it took everything I had just to keep from letting my chin slam into the concrete. All I could do was lift my eyes and watch helplessly as the precious sheets of paper danced over the grate, then slipped inside.

This, I thought, dropping my lids closed again. *This is why I like my desk. It's why I leave the grunt work to the grunt men. It's why I write persuasive emails and drink hot cappuccinos and—*

The silent tirade cut itself short abruptly, choked off by the fact that I lifted my eyes and spied what I was sure had to be a mirage. Or whatever the soaking-wet, rain-induced equivalent was. I blinked, trying to clear my vision. Nope. The mirage stayed.

A perfectly curved, perfectly smooth, pink-covered ass, hanging from a window a few buildings down and a couple floors up.

"What the actual hell?"

I stared up, wondering what I was supposed do. If I was supposed to do anything at all. As I puzzled through my ass-hanging-from-window obligation, the curvy piece in question abruptly disappeared. I didn't have time to consider whether I'd imagined the whole thing, though, because just a moment later, a pair of feet, clad in dangerously high heels, appeared instead.

I gave my head a scratch and watched as the feet inched out to reveal a pair of creamy ankles, then a pair of smooth-looking calves. The knees attached to the calves came next, and they hinged a little as the feet tried to find purchase on the ledge below.

"You're not seriously climbing out there, are you?" I said into the rain.

As if the wearer of the heels had heard me, they retracted back into the building. Not ten seconds passed, though, before the feet came out again, this time bare. They moved faster this time, flattening against the ledge. It still didn't seem like a safe maneuver.

I called out from my prone position. "Hey!"

Even if I'd been upright or closer, the wind would still have swept the word away. I moved again, this time to stand. I couldn't right myself quickly enough to perform whatever heroic move I might've been thinking of performing. The woman attached to the shapely legs slid herself the rest of the way out the window, pressed her back to the building behind her, and rendered me momentarily speechless.

My gaze traveled the length of her body. She had lightly muscled legs that disappeared under the pink skirt, and full hips that pressed against it at the same time. Her slim waist was showcased nicely by the way her cream-colored blouse had been tucked into the wide waistband, and her full chest rose and fell temptingly.

Hell. She was once of the most beautiful women I'd ever laid eyes on, and I didn't even have a clear view of her face.

I took an automatic step forward, trying to catch her features. Were they soft and delicate? Or classical and imperious? Did she have full, kissable lips? For no good reason—aside from lustful self-indulgence—I hoped to God the answer to last question was yes.

Unfortunately, I didn't get a chance to find out. She straightened her shoulders, shook her head a little, then stepped sideways along the ledge on one of her bare feet. Apparently, she was unaware that, A, she was risking her life and that, B, I was standing there gaping at her. Weirdly, the second oversight seemed more important. I had a strange—and admittedly irrational—feeling that she was deliberately avoiding turning her head in my direction. Irritation niggled at me for second. Going unnoticed felt like a slight, especially considering how aware *I* was of *her* presence.

I took another step forward, watching as she disappeared around the side of the building.

What waited for her on the other side? Why the hell had she climbed out there in the first place? I felt compelled to know.

Without even being conscious that I was doing it, I moved to catch up so I could find out.

* * * *

Mia

There were three things that made me a terrible choice as a bridesmaid. One. I hated weddings.

Two. I hated weddings.

And three…

Well. Yeah. That.

But somehow, that didn't stop my dearest—my only—brother from asking me to become one at *his* wedding. Fluffy dress. Boxes of candied almonds. All my most dreaded things.

And it didn't stop me from agreeing, either. And me being me, once I'd agreed, I wouldn't back out.

But if I wanted proof that I was the wrong person for the job, all I had to do was take stock of my current situation. It was eight o'clock on a Sunday night. I was supposed to be at a pre-wedding, pre-rehearsal, pre-insanity dinner with my brother and his merry band of groomsman and bridesmaids.

Instead, I was inching my way along the exterior of a building. In the rain. In a blouse that now felt like a second skin.

Part of it was karma. I had to admit that. After all, I'd created a phony disaster at work to avoid the dinner in question, telling my brother that a well-known fashion blogger had a can't-wait complaint about one of my jewelry designs that just had to be remedied. He'd been understanding. My reputation as a designer was integral to my continued success, after all. Except my brother's sympathy just made me feel even guiltier. But I'd planned on showing up late. Just to grab a quick drink, offer an apology, and smile like I was supposed to. Still. I was going to make an appearance.

But then came the iced coffee. Which didn't mix well with my laptop at all, and which had kind of *sizzled* when it poured over the keyboard then hit the extension cord. Next came the zap of protest from the electrical outlet, the light overhead shattering. And the moment of panic, where I jumped up to save something—anything—and instead knocked my phone to the ground, cracking the screen and turning it a dismal shade of gray-black. I'd tried to make my way to the door, even if it was just to open it and let in some light from the hall. But when my hand got a hold of the metal knob, it'd succeeded only in twisting it straight off.

So.

No computer. No phone. No light.

And no way out.

Except, of course, the window and the two-foot-wide ledge that spanned across my building then around it. On the other side—where I was headed now—grew a hundred-year-old oak tree.

"Perfect for shimmying down in business attire," I grumbled, clutching my heels to my chest as I glared at the tree.

I stretched out a hand to the nearest branch, grasped it tightly, then tried to make my foot follow. It only took a second to realize that as short as my skirt might be, it was still going to get in the way of progress. And so were my shoes, which I still held clutched in my hand.

Sighing, I eased back on to the ledge again. I regretfully set down my Ferragamo heels. I gazed at them longingly. They weren't my newest pair, or even my most expensive. In fact, I'd managed to pick them up for a steal. But they were the first pair of designer heels I'd ever bought, and it just plain felt wrong to abandon them.

"I'll come back for you, I promise," I said to the shoes.

Then—reminding myself that every shop along the block was closed and that the likelihood of being watched was slim to none—I grabbed the hem of my skirt and unceremoniously shoved it up to just below my panty line. I gave the shoes a final look, took a breath and reached out again. This time I was successful in getting both a hand and a foot in place. And with a grunt and a push, I moved the other half of my body over.

"Take that, karma," I said as my toes curled triumphantly against the ridges of the tree's bark.

But apparently karma wasn't overly fond of being called out. Because I no sooner moved to start my descent than my feet skidded. As I threw my arms around the wide trunk to stabilize myself, my purse slid down off my shoulder and landed with a dull thump in the curve of a branch below my knees. It flopped open, and the contents—my keys, makeup, a gazillion receipts for God knew what—all flew out and tumbled to the ground below. Well. All for except one thing. My broken cell phone. It stayed right beside the purse, and from its gray-black screen, rose the disembodied voice of my fellow bridesmaid, Liv Holt.

"Lu?" she greeted, using my family's nickname for me. "Are you there?"

I stifled a groan and answered in my cheeriest voice. "Hey, Liv!"

"What's all that noise?"

"The, uh, rain?"

"Sounds like you're standing in the middle of it."

"Just an open window," I lied. "What's up?"

There was a pause. "You called me."

"Oh." *Whoops.* I winced. "Would you believe it was a butt dial?"

She let out a sigh so loud that I could hear it over the rain. "I'm guessing you're *not* at work with an emergency."

"Not exactly," I answered.

"Oh, God."

"What?"

"It's *regular work,* isn't it?" She made it sound like a particularly contagious disease. "You're sitting up there in that office of yours, beading away, aren't you?"

"Okay. One, I don't 'bead'. I design. And two, I'm definitely not sitting in my office."

"You're still working when you could be drinking and ogling the groomsmen," she said.

Wondering how I'd been roped into this conversation while standing in a tree, I shook my head. "I have zero interest in ogling."

"The whole purpose in being a bridesmaid is to ogle. And be ogled. In fact, it's the perfect excuse to suck face with some hot guys. Maybe even go home with one."

"I don't do that."

"Do what?" She sounded genuinely puzzled.

"Men!" The word burst out in an exasperated tone, and my face warmed even though she couldn't see me.

"Really? I wouldn't have guessed that—"

"That's not what I meant. I don't kiss—or go home with—men *casually*."

"Well. That a given. You don't do *anything* casually," she pointed out.

"Exactly."

"You know what? I'm about to do you a huge favor."

"Great." I infused the word with as much sarcasm as I could.

But she just laughed. "I'm issuing you a dare, Lumia Diaz."

I groaned. "God. My brother told you, didn't he?"

Her response was far too innocent. "Told me what?"

"Don't play dumb with me, Olivia Holt. Marcelo told you that he used to dare me to do stuff when we were kids and that I couldn't say no."

"Maybe. Or maybe he told Aysia and *she* told me."

"Great," I muttered again.

"Are you going to say yes?" she wanted to know.

"No."

"You don't even know what it is."

"I know that you came up with it, and that's enough."

"I'm daring you anyway," she said.

"Fine," I replied. "Give me your useless dare."

"The next attractive man you see...kiss him."

"What?" I don't know what I'd been expecting, but not that.

"Drop whatever you're doing, walk up, and kiss him." Liv said it like it wasn't an insane suggestion.

"I can't do that." But my never-back-down mind was already narrowed in on the logistics. "What if he turned out to be married?"

"Then he'd push you away pretty quickly, wouldn't he?"

"Or his wife would punch me."

"Check for a ring before you do it then."

I rolled my eyes. "Who decides if he's attractive?"

"You do, of course." She paused, then added, "And that doesn't mean you can just decide that no man is attractive from here on out."

"And if I decided—hypothetically—to kiss this unknown but attractive man...what then?"

"Then at least you've kissed a man sometime in the last decade."

"Hey!"

She let out another laugh, and I swear to God it was a cackle. "Please, Lu. We both know you've basically got the Fort Knox of vaginas."

"That is *so* not true."

"When's the last time you got laid?"

"I'm *not* answering that."

"That gives you away right there."

In spite of my best effort to keep it under control, my temper flared. "I don't need to disclose the details of my sex life to you—or anyone else—just for the sake of proving that I have one. So, no. I won't take your stupid dare."

Liv didn't seem to be fazed. "Whoa. I wasn't trying to hit a nerve."

"It's not a nerve. It's a choice."

"I just thought you needed a push."

"Yeah. Well. I don't."

She let out another of her noisy sighs. "I'm going to take a wild leap here and say that you're not popping by for a drink?"

I surveyed the tree. And my abandoned shoes. And my hiked-up skirt.

"I'm a little…indisposed," I told her.

"Okay," she said, "but if a good-looking man happens to fall into your lap…"

"There won't be any laps." I looked down. "And no falling, either. I hope."

"Just think about it."

"Bye, Liv."

"Bye, Lu."

I stood there for a minute, staring down at the still-black phone. I had no way to tell if the call had actually ended, and I couldn't stop myself from imagining Liv—and maybe everyone else too—being treated to the oh-so-pleasant sounds of me clambering down a tree.

"Not happening," I muttered.

One slow knee at a time, I bent down. I kept one hand secured to the tree trunk and stretched the other toward the phone. My fingers tapped the edge of the purse, and I tried to pull it closer. I didn't even bother celebrating. Which was a good thing. Because in keeping with the last half hour of my life, all the contact between my hand and the purse did was send the phone flying out of the tree.

My eyes started to close in frustration, but a thump and yell from beneath me—"Shit!"—made them jerk open again.

Startled, I flipped my gaze toward the source of the curse.

For a second, a pair of eyes so dark that they looked almost black and framed by thick lashes stared back. They were the kind of eyes that begged to be drown in. Faintly exotic. Almost enthralling. And just distracting enough that I forgot about the rain and the tree and the bare feet. But those three things didn't forget about me. The moment my hand slipped from the tree trunk, a gust of wind sent a slap of rain my way. My feet skidded over the bark, and I yelped at the sudden scrape. I lost control.

I plummeted straight from the branch directly onto the man below, effectively knocking the dark-eyed stranger to the ground.

I had to grudgingly acknowledge that Liv had been right after all. There was falling. And a lap. I'd done the former and landed with my head in the latter. And worse than that, there was no getting around a few small, very important details. The man who I'd more or less flattened was very definitely attractive.

The lines of his face were chiseled and distinct. Prominent cheekbones. Thick, stubble-dusted jaw. Straight nose and dark, even eyebrows. His features belonged on a model. His don't-give-a-shit curve of a half-smile—almost a sneer—fit the bill perfectly too.

And slight sneer or not, his lips were as seductive as the rest of his face. Firm-looking. And they *had* to be warmer than the wind that blasted through the air. They were the kind of lips that made Liv's dare seem a little more realizable. More desirable.

But I can't really kiss him. Can I?

Except maybe I could. And maybe I kind of wanted to.

I released my lip and sucked in a tiny breath in its place. His gaze flicked to my mouth. Hung there. Like he could read my mind. Then his eyes came up again and locked with mine.

It should've been weird. Sitting, gazing into the eyes of a total stranger for such a long, silent moment. Instead, it was…intense. And a little hot.

More than a little, I acknowledged.

Which is why, when one of his hands came up to brush away a loose strand of hair, my fingers moved all on their own. They reached forward, snapped closed around his overpriced tie, and tugged. Hard.

At the last second, common sense reared its head. I tried to stop the trajectory. Tried to yank myself backward. And I almost succeeded. Maybe I *would* have succeeded, if the dark-eyed stranger's hand hadn't come up just then to cup my cheek. Or if it hadn't been warm and pleasant, and tugged me forward as it sent a startling thrill through me. Maybe then.

But maybe not.

Chapter 2

Ethan

I don't know what the hell possessed me. Jet lag? Too much rain in my ears soaking into my brain? The insane certainty that the look in her eyes—this unknown, unnamed, red-haired woman—said she wanted to kiss me? Or maybe just sheer, reckless stupidity. Probably a lot of that last one, actually. Either way, the result was the same. I leaned forward and brushed my lips to hers.

I had a heartbeat of sheer enjoyment. A heartbeat of mouth-to-mouth with a total stranger. A beautiful, rain-wet stranger, who clung to me. Whose mouth was butter soft. Warm. Responsive. Fulfilling a fantasy that I didn't even know I had. Reminding me that it'd been far too long since I put pleasure before business. It was long enough to decide that there was at least one good thing about Vancouver and its shitty weather—it drove the women within its borders insane. In a hell of a good way. And it was by far one of the best damned heartbeats I'd ever had.

Then a bang echoed through the air, and she jerked back with a soft gasp.

In some ingrained reflex that came from God knew where, I became a wannabe hero. I pushed myself up. I pushed her down. Then I leapt on top of her to cover her body with my own, careful to keep from crushing her while still shielding her. A few more, rapid-succession bangs filled my brain with the idea that shrapnel could be raining down on us at any second. I braced for it. Instead of being hot with incoming weaponry, though, we were assaulted with color. Blue. Then red. Then blue again. And I clued in.

So did the redhead. "Is that…"

"Fireworks," I confirmed, rolling off her.

"Literal fireworks?" Her voice was soft and pleasant and a little breathless as she pushed to a seated position.

"Think so."

"I kiss a stranger and fireworks go off. What are the odds of..." She trailed off, her eyes going wide. "Oh, God."

I stared at her, so distracted by the way a pink blush crept up between her freckles that I almost forgot to answer. "What?"

"I'm so sorry!"

"You're sorry?"

"I just...this is so embarrassing. It was a dare, and I...God. I can't even... if it weren't for the stupid coffee...ugh..." With each awkward sentence, her skin grew redder, her breathing a little more uneven.

Damned if I could tear my eyes away from her.

Her words faded to the background as I watched her talk. I was mesmerized by the way she sucked in one breath after another. Held captive by how the air made her lips tremor. My eyes hung on those quivers. I wanted to taste her mouth again.

Not just again...more thoroughly.

I wanted to run my tongue over her lips, then slip it between them. Slowly. To kiss the unknown, unnamed woman breathless.

The need was so intense that I had to forcibly rip my gaze from her mouth. It didn't help. My eyes stalled on her freckled chest and ran over the peachy spots with interest. Some were spread out, others close together. I couldn't help but search for a pattern, thinking that they brought to mind one of those connect-the-dots games I'd liked to play as a kid.

Except in this case, I'd choose to play it with my tongue rather than a pen.

The errant, dirty thought slipped through before I could stop it. Once it had come, I couldn't pretend the idea didn't have appeal. I could even see the freckles I'd call One, Two, and Three—all just above her ample cleavage—and I had no problem imagining just how high the number would get before I finished.

I was so distracted that it took me a minute to remember that in polite circles, it was better to focus on a woman's face rather than her other assets. So I dragged my gaze up from her tempting chest to her eyes instead. The shifted attention did nothing to ease the distinct tightness of my pants.

On first glance, I'd thought her eyes were hazel, but now I saw that I was wrong. She had warm, light brown irises. Like melted caramel. It made me want to lick my lips. Which brought me back to licking her body.

Jesus, Burke, I thought. *Get a hold of yourself.*

I forced my attention back to the fact that she was still rambling, and I tried to focus on what she was saying.

"So if you could *not* call the police, that'd be—"

"Wait. What?"

"The police. I mean. If the roles were reversed..." she said.

"If I'd fallen out of a tree and landed on you, we'd be calling 911," I replied dryly.

"That's not what I was talking about." She sighed. "Look. I really *am* sorry."

My mouth twitched with a suppressed smile. "So you said."

"Yes," she answered.

"Can I ask you something?"

"Okay."

"What part are you most sorry about?"

She frowned, the freckles on her forehead creasing together. "I'm not sure I..."

"There're a few things to pick from," I said. "Dropping a phone on my head. Falling out of a tree and landing on me? Or—"

A blush spread out under freckles. "All of it!"

"All of it wasn't bad," I said. "Or at least not apology-worthy."

She blinked those honey-browns of hers at me, then shook her head. "I swear I don't normally do this kind of thing."

"I would never have guessed."

She winced. "It was pretty bad, wasn't it?"

"Bad?" I echoed. "Not the word I'd use."

"What word *would* you use?"

"Adult-film-star-esque?" I teased.

Her nose wrinkled. "I don't think that's a word."

"Is now." I pushed to my knee, stood, then held out a hand.

She took it and let me pull her to her feet. "Thank you."

"You're welcome." I held her fingers in mine for another second before releasing them and adding, "Can I ask you something else?"

"Sure."

"Why did someone dare you to kiss me?"

"Not *you*. Not specifically."

"Who?"

"Who dared me?" she asked, sounding puzzled.

I fought a laugh. "That too. But I meant who were you dared to kiss?"

"Oh." Her blush became crimson. "My friend dared me to kiss the next...uh...guy that I saw."

The admission disappointed me. *Well, what were you expecting to hear, Ethan? That a complete stranger would* want *you to play connect the dots with her freckles and your tongue?*

Still. When I met her eyes again, I got the feeling that she was leaving something out. There was a palpable heat in the air between us, and I could barely feel the rain.

"So..." I said slowly, and took a step closer. "I could've been anyone. A troll. Or someone's grandpa. A one-legged, one-eyed pirate."

She exhaled but didn't move away. "No. There was a condition."

"I'm all ears."

"You don't really want me to tell you."

"I really do."

Her eyes dropped down, and her cheeks went almost crimson. "He had to be good looking."

The statement made me itch to touch her again. "And was it a success?"

Her gaze flicked up. "What do you mean?"

"The dare. If your friend were to have witnessed it, what rating would she give it on a scale of one to ten?"

She hesitated. "Honestly?"

I nodded. "Definitely."

"Probably not more than a five. At best."

"Ouch."

"What?"

"Even handsome strangers have bruise-able egos," I said.

How she managed to get even redder was beyond me. "I wasn't calling *you* a five. The performance—*my* performance—was a five."

I lifted an eyebrow and repeated her words back to her. "At best."

"I fell from a tree," she pointed out.

"And broke a cell phone on my head."

"Well. To be fair. It was broken before it hit you. But yes."

"What about the kiss itself?" I asked, my eyes flicking to her mouth.

Her bottom lip disappeared between her teeth for a second. "It was... quick."

"Too quick to earn a stamp of dare-approval from your friend?"

"Probably."

"So you can't very well go back and tell her you did it, can you?"

Her caramel gaze met mine. "What are you suggesting?"

I reached out and dragged the back of my hand over hers. "That you try it again."

"Doesn't it ruin the dare if you know about it?"

A vision filled my head, then, of the pretty redhead and her soft lips being thrown at some other man. As unreasonable as it might've been, I hated the thought.

I had to force an even tone and a casual shrug. "I'm still a stranger. And presumably still attractive."

"Yes, but..."

"But what?

"You're serious?"

"As a funeral."

She shifted from bare foot to bare foot. "So should I just—"

Suddenly impatient, I stepped forward and moved my fingers up to clasp her chin. I tipped her face up, and she pushed to her tiptoes, her breasts brushing my chest as she leaned in. I could feel the heat of her lips. Almost taste their softness. And God how I wanted it to happen. Didn't want to wait a single damned second more.

So I was sorely disappointed when she pulled back a little and gasped, "Wait!"

"What?" My reply was almost a growl.

"Are you married?"

"What?

"Married."

"Uh. No. Never been."

"A psychopath?"

"Not that I'm aware of."

"If you *were* a psychopath or married, would you tell me?"

"I don't know. Probably not."

"Dammit."

Her mouth was still maddeningly close.

But not close enough.

"If you knew if I was married or a psychopath," I said, "then I probably wouldn't be a stranger."

"Oh. Good point." She leaned up again, but stopped just shy of kissing me, her brown eyes wide.

I stared down, somehow annoyed at the delay and amused at the same time. "More questions?"

"Just one."

"Which is?"

"Am I going to regret this?"

"Only one way to find out."

She nodded, and her nose bumped against mine in a way that made me want to chuckle. The urge to laugh didn't last long. She pulled back once more, shot me the sexiest, half-lidded stare I'd ever seen, then slammed her soft, sweet mouth into mine.

* * * *

Mia

Kissing a stranger sounded like a weird thing to do. An insane one.

Except as my body sank into the hard planes of the dark-eyed stranger, it just felt natural. Better than natural. It felt amazing.

Erotic.

Yes. That was the word. Dangerous and forbidden. Charged with heat and a passion that I was sure I'd never felt before. Maybe *because* I didn't know him. No strings, little forethought, zero emotional connection. Kissing him sent a shock wave of uninhibited want through me, and I pressed harder against him.

His mouth was firm and just the right kind of insistent. He tasted like clean rain. Like heaven. I wanted more. So much more. And my hands came up on their own to take it. They slid up his arms—and oh, my *God* were they covered in thick, roped muscle that made my heart beat faster just by virtue of its existence—then moved over his shoulders to clutch the back of his neck. My fingers found the edge of his thick hair and dug in. He groaned in response. The noise vibrated against my mouth, and my lips dropped open.

His tongue took immediate advantage, diving in to tease and explore. I gave it back as thoroughly as I received it. I ran my own tongue over every inch of his mouth, then pulled away so that I could drop my teeth to his lower lip. I nipped it hard enough to make him hiss. For a second, I thought I'd taken it too far.

But then his hands moved. They landed on my hips. His wide, strong palms gripped me tightly, and he pushed me across the lawn. The urgent motion made my bare feet slip on the soaked grass, but he didn't let me fall. He was too sure and too strong. And in seconds, he had me pressed to the tree trunk.

I was panting as he grabbed my wrists, lifted them over my head, and pushed them just shy of roughly against the bark. His knee found its way between my thighs, which reminded me that I still had my skirt hiked most of the way up. The fabric of his suit pants rubbed over my sensitive skin and the resulting sensation was a heady sting that made my legs drop open even farther.

Like he had with my lips, the dark-eyed stranger took immediate advantage. He thrust against me—possessive and demanding—in a delicious circle. I could feel the length of his erection through the fabric between us, and my hips jerked forward, trying to draw him closer. He responded by driving himself against me even harder.

Heat was building inside me. A quick spiral winding up tighter and tighter.

And he's barely touched you.

Then, like he could read the thought, his hands started moving again. They released my wrists and dragged down my forearms in a sensuous dance. They paused at my elbows and gave a light squeeze before making their way down to my sides. There, they paused again. Each of his palms rested on the outside of my breasts. Not hesitant. Just as though he was looking for a sign that he wasn't crossing a line. But the wait was excruciating. And I wasn't sure that there *were* any lines or rules for this kind of scenario anyway. When his fingers started a slow slide inward, I couldn't take it anymore.

"Touch me!" I gasped.

As soon as the words were out of my mouth, a wave embarrassment fought to overtake my more carnal needs. But it didn't last long. He dipped his mouth to mine again, and as he gave me a deep, lingering kiss, he also obeyed my desperate command. His thumbs stroked my nipples. Back and forth, then around and around. In seconds, he'd drawn them out into needy points. And each insistent touch drove my desire higher. I couldn't stop myself from moving against him. I didn't *want* to stop. I didn't want him to stop, either.

And he didn't.

His mouth dropped to my throat, and one of his hands slipped between us. As his tongue and lips and teeth worked over my goose-bump-covered flesh, his fingers worked their way up my skirt. For several seconds, they rubbed along the lace of my underwear. It was exquisite torture. My arousal became a deep ache, begging to be soothed.

It was the sexiest moment of my life.

A stranger, with his hands on my most intimate parts.

A stranger, claiming my skin with his mouth.

A stranger.

And I'd never been more turned on.

"Please," I said.

I didn't even know what I was begging for until one of his long, strong fingers pushed aside the lace of my panties. Then I knew what I was craving. And there was no time to think it through. No time to question again if I'd lost my mind, to wonder if I should be asking his name, or to consider a single, other thing. I was too busy drowning in pleasure. Moving to the rhythm he created, thrusting forward to drive his fingers in farther as his thumb circled my clit. And the spiraling heat continued its ascent, higher and higher, so that when his voice filled my ear—"Come, baby."—I couldn't have stopped myself from sailing over the edge if I tried.

I shuddered against his hand, my whole body letting go of a tension I didn't realize I was holding. I clung to him, riding the wave of release, while he just held me, one hand pressing firmly to my pulsating sex, the other running gently over my hair. He stayed that way for a minute, letting my ragged breathing calm itself before he pulled back enough to meet my eyes.

His gaze was like liquid obsidian.

"Okay?" he asked, low and raw.

"Okay?" I repeated with a headshake. "That was…"

"Don't say a mistake."

"Definitely not a mistake."

A sexy little smile curled up his lips. "Good."

"Yes." The word came out breathless, because his hand had started up again, its motion slight but undeniable. "Good."

He bent to run his tongue along my earlobe. "Not to be presumptuous. But I have a hotel room."

His finger was distracting, and my reply was a stammer. "A h-h-hotel room?"

"Uh huh. Not that we have to go there. But I have a cab too."

"A cab?"

"He's waiting around the corner. Or he will be in a few minutes, anyway." His teeth gave my ear a nip.

I fought to retain control, wondering how I could possibly be getting turned on again so quickly.

Really? said a little voice in my head. *That's what you're worried about in this particular scenario?*

But it was true. My insides were warming again, and it was already getting harder to think. I had to work to focus on our conversation.

"A hotel and a cab," I made myself say. "You're from out of town?"

"Mm. Here for a little bit of business." His finger slid into me once, then pulled out again. "Do you wanna talk about that right now?"

"No," I gasped. "Which hotel?"

"The Regent Inn."

That was enough to bring my attention away from my increasing need. I suppressed a groan that had nothing to do with desire. My brother's wedding was being held at the Regent, and I'd spent far too much time there recently to be guaranteed anonymity.

The dark-eyed stranger picked up on the change in my mood right away. His hand ceased its movement, then slipped to my thigh. He met my eyes again.

"No pressure," he said sincerely. "At all. If you want to walk away and pretend you never met me, that's okay."

I couldn't quite stop a laugh. "I don't think I *have* met you."

He smiled. "Right. I'm—"

I pushed up and cut him off with a swift, firm kiss. "You don't have to tell me."

He studied my face for a second. "I don't have to tell you, or you don't want to know?"

"I don't *not* want to know, but…" My face heated.

"But what?"

"I don't want to, uh, ruin this?"

His sexy little smile made another appearance, and his hand tightened on my thigh. "Ah. You like the mystery."

"Yes," I admitted, distracted again by the way his thumb stroked my thigh.

"So. The cab and the hotel?"

"Not the Regent."

"Got something against the Regent?" he asked.

"No. The Regent's actually really nice," I said. "But it's a twenty-minute ride."

"I'm sure we could come up with something to do during that twenty minutes." His fingers tapped teasingly over my leg.

"We could…"

"Or?"

"Or we could take a four-minute ride to the Memory Motel and find something to do *there*."

"The Memory Motel, hmm?" He quirked a dark eyebrow in amusement, and it made me want to grin.

I covered it by making a face at him. "It's not an hourly place, if that's what you're thinking."

"Did I say that?"

"You didn't have to." I reached up and gently touched his eyebrow. "This gave you away."

"Damned tell. I guess my chances of beating you at strip poker are pretty slim."

"Was that on the agenda?"

"Were you hoping it would be?"

"Maybe I was."

"Don't be disappointed." He bent to kiss me again, then snagged my purse from the ground and handed it over. "You wanna know what's on the agenda now?"

"What?"

"Any damned thing you want."

The words sent a renewed wave of heat through me. And when he threaded his fingers through mine and tugged me across the grass, the warmth fanned out, and a laugh bubbled up from my chest and carried out over the sound of the rain.

Chapter 3

Ethan

It took about thirty seconds in the cab—which had pulled around the corner just in time—to decide that forgoing my nice, cushy room at the Regent Inn was an excellent choice.

With her eyes still on me, the redhead told the driver our destination, then dropped her hand onto my knee. Her fingers kneaded their way up slowly, and I had to clamp my jaw shut to keep from letting out a growl. Every drop of blood in my body was already repositioned between my legs. I had no chance in hell of making it twenty minutes.

Thank God for the Memory Motel.

I didn't give a damn whether it really was a pay-by-the-hour place. I didn't give a shit if it had saggy, threadbare sheets. Or a bed powered on quarters. All that mattered was getting the woman beside me into the room. Stripped down. And satisfying her again, because damn had I enjoyed watching her come undone under my attention. After that, I'd take my own, slow pleasure. With any luck, she'd like that as much as I'd liked bringing her to climax.

Her fingers were just below crotch level now, and each movement pressed her closer to my painfully full erection. I held still. If I didn't, I would buck against her. As it was, the moment her knuckles bumped my thick hard-on, a curse escaped my lips.

"Fuck!"

The cab driver shot a startled look at me via the rearview mirror. "Sir?"

"I'm fine," I managed to get out.

The redhead let out a little laugh, and her hand slipped back down to my knee. Disappointed, I tipped my gaze her way. The disappointment slipped away immediately. Her mouth was tipped up a little on one side, her lips parted, and her breaths coming in and out rapidly. She was sexy as all hell. Her hand was on the move again too, inching up.

My eyes wanted to drift shut, my hips wanted to thrust forward. Her touch was just the combination of giving and demanding. Christ, how I wanted to lose myself in it. My heart thudded against my rib cage in perfect time with the pulse of blood through my cock.

She's not even touching you there.

It was true. She was just shy of giving me the rub I craved, and the second her knuckles *did* brush me in the right place, she dropped her hand yet again. Back to my knee. Back to the slow climb. It was sweet torture. I leaned my head back against the seat and took a masochistic moment of enjoyment as she repeated the tease again. Three more times, she managed to get her fingers just to the edge before dragging them away. Each time, she let herself touch me for a few seconds longer. The fact that I didn't burst right through my zipper was a minor miracle.

"Hey." The redhead's voice made me drag my eyes open.

"Hey," I said back, not bothering to disguise the raw heat in my voice; it wasn't like she didn't already know I wanted her.

"We're here." She nodded out the taxi window. "What do you think?"

I fought an urge to tell her I couldn't care less about the motel, and made myself politely turn and follow her nod, expecting to find a strip of doors in a rundown building. Instead, I was pleasantly surprised by a beautifully restored heritage house. Lace curtains covered the soft glow of orange light inside, highlighting the exterior décor—brown on cream. A porch wrapped around the front, and a small, painted sign hung from it announcing that it was, in fact, the Memory Motel.

"Well?" the redheaded prodded.

I bent to whisper teasingly into her ear. "I don't think this a by-the-hour place after all."

"I tried to tell you," she replied.

Chuckling, I pulled my wallet out and handed a stack of bills to the driver. I waved off his offer to give me change back as I jumped from the car and offered the redhead my hand. I'd already decided his exorbitant, near-extortive cab fare was worth it.

Just like my ruined suit's worth it, I thought as I slammed the taxi door. *And the mud-soaked clothes in my suitcase are worth it. And—*

"Shit," I said.

"What?"

"I left my damned bag in the middle of the street."

"You want to go back and get it?"

The cab was already pulling away. My gaze flicked from the disappearing vehicle to the redhead's freckle-covered face and soaking-wet blouse. Desire leapt back to the forefront on my mind, and I realized that even if I'd thought I *could* chase down the taxi, I had no desire to do it.

"I can buy new things," I told her.

"Seriously?" she replied.

"All I want is to get a room, get you naked, and kiss you head to toe." Her skin pinked between her freckles. "Then what are you waiting for?"

"Fuck if I know," I said.

I started to grab her hand again, then thought better of it, and instead reached down to scoop her off the ground.

"Hey!" she protested.

"Hey," I said back, grinning. "Wait. Didn't we just have this conversation?"

"Possibly. You don't really think you're going to carry me up there, do you?"

"I do."

"You can't."

"I can. And I will."

I squeezed her a little tighter, enjoying the way her very curvy body fit against me. Her round ass hung down just enough to bump against my still-hard cock. The thought that she could probably feel it with each step made me smile.

"Are you *sure* you're not a maniac?" she asked as I stepped up the stairs. "Because you're grinning like one."

I deliberately bared my teeth at her. "Could be."

"You said you weren't—"

"Uh-uh. You specifically asked if I was psychotic."

"That's different than being a maniac?"

"Definitely." I paused at the top of the steps. "Unless that makes you want to leave. In which case, I swear I'm also not a maniac."

"Are you just saying whatever you need to so that you can take me to bed?" she asked.

"Possibly." I kissed her soft, sweet mouth, then sobered to add, "If you're having second thoughts…"

She shook her head. "Weirdly. None."

"Glad to oblige your weirdness," I teased.

She grabbed my tie and pulled me in for another kiss. "Just take me inside."

"You got it." I tightened my hold again, started to push my way through the door, then stopped again.

"What now?" she asked, amusement laced with impatience.

"What's our story?"

"What?"

"Are we illicit lovers, pretending to be husband and wife? Or a real husband and wife, having our first night away from the kids in years?"

"Why? Are you ashamed to admit that I'm a strange woman who fell from a tree?"

My mouth twitched. "It just seems a bit unrealistic."

"Does it?" she replied.

"Yep. But you're right. The truth is always best."

I shoved my shoulder to the door and pushed the rest of the way in, then strode up to the desk and announced, "We're strangers. She climbed out a window and landed in my lap. We're going to do all kinds of kinky things. Can we have a room?"

The redhead let out a choked-sounding laugh. "Please?"

"Please," I added.

The guy behind the counter—twentyish with a heavy dose of tattoos and piercings—barely looked up from his phone. "Got a credit card?"

"As a matter of fact…" I swung my human cargo to the floor and dug into my pocket. "I mentioned the kink, right?"

"What you do on your dime is your business," said the guy.

"It's in your hotel," I said. "So kinda your business too."

"It's my nan's hotel."

"And I'm sure your nan would be thrilled to know you're taking such good care of it. We'd like the best room you've got."

"Best room's the master suite. Six hundred and fifty for the night. Last-minute deal."

The redhead squeezed my elbow. "That's—"

"Perfect," I said smoothly. "We'll take it."

Mr. Pierced-And-Tattooed swiped my card, then handed it back. A printer whirred to life from somewhere behind him, and as he turned to grab whatever it was spitting out, the redhead grabbed my arm again.

"That price is crazy!" she whisper-yelled.

"We'll get our money's worth," I promised.

"I'm not actually that kinky," she argued.

I stifled a laugh. "Trust me. I already feel like it's money well spent. And it's too late, anyway. Kid's run my card."

On cue, the prince of punk turned back to the counter and held out a sheet of paper and a clunky, old-fashioned key. "Head all the way up the stairs. Only door up there. Checkout's at eleven."

"Thanks," I said, then paused. "Hey. You wanna make a quick fifty bucks?"

He eyed me, then the redhead. "Neither of you is my type."

"Ditto," I replied dryly as I yanked a hundred-dollar bill from my wallet. "What I was hoping for was food. And a lot of condoms."

The clerk picked up the money like it physically disgusted him. "I'll get my buddy to bring something by. Should take about twenty minutes."

"Great," I said cheerfully. "We'll try to hold off on the kink until then."

I grabbed the redhead's hand and tugged her toward the stairs, where I gestured for her to go up first. As I followed, admiring the view, I marveled over the turn of events. An hour earlier, I might've said the evening was in the running for one of the worst ever. Right up there with the time I'd decided to spend New Year's in New York, where I'd been mugged, then *accused* of mugging someone else and subsequently spent the stroke of midnight in a cell, fending off a kiss from a very drunk, very big, very hairy man who insisted on calling me Lydia.

My current situation…it didn't really have an accurate comparison. Kid at Disneyland or puppy at Christmas, maybe? Was it fair to say that the grown-man equivalent of those things was unexpectedly taking a beautiful woman to bed? I didn't know for sure. But one thing was for damned certain. Whatever the hell else happened on my trip—even if the owner of Trinkets and Treasures managed to turn down my in-person offer—every shitty moment was worth what was about to come.

* * * *

Mia

I could feel him staring at my ass as we climbed the three flights of stairs. And I liked it. I liked knowing his eyes were on me. I liked having his full attention. I even slowed down to prolong it, taking the steps one at a time. My thighs rubbed together under my skirt, the residual wetness from my orgasm making the movement altogether a little too enjoyable. And it was easy to imagine his hands on me again. I could almost feel them sliding up, up, then up a little more. I had to bite back a gasp as I reached the top stair and his palms really *did* land on my hips.

"You're killing me," he growled.

"Am I?" I replied innocently.

He spun me by my hips, pressed me to the wall, and bent to nuzzle my neck. "I think you know *exactly* what you're doing."

"I really don't," I breathed, relishing the way he made goose bumps rise everywhere.

"Guess you're just at great improvising?" he teased.

"I did climb out a window earlier," I reminded him.

"Ah. Was that an improvisation?"

"I had to get out somehow."

"You locked yourself in?" He pulled away to meet my eyes. "Now I'm genuinely curious."

"So curious that you want to stop doing *this*?" I slipped my hands to his thighs.

"Possibly."

He said it jokingly, but for a second, I could swear that he was genuinely torn. And *his* pause made *me* pause. Wasn't the whole idea of an anonymous encounter to stay that way? If we started telling each other things—even small things—it seemed like a surefire way to change the dynamic.

He reached up and pushed a strand of damp hair away from my face. "We've got twenty minutes to kill. I'll gladly use that time to kiss you head to toe. But I'd far prefer to do that when I know I won't be interrupted."

I stared up at him, momentarily losing myself in his dark gaze. "Sorry. Did you say something after the bit about kissing me head to toe?"

He chuckled, then let me go. "C'mon. Let's go see if Tattoo Dude really gave us a good deal."

I let him take my hand and lead me from the wall to the door, but inwardly I was cringing a little. The cost of the room wasn't out of line with a nice room at a mid-range hotel in Vancouver. But it *was* way outside of my own budget. When I'd suggested the Memory Motel, I'd assumed we'd get the cheapest room. That we'd split the cost. Or that I'd offer to split it, and he'd argue, and I'd give in. Something that wouldn't make me feel like I was about to walk in to the most expensive one-night stand in the history of one-night stands. Although, now that I was thinking about it, my tall, dark, and handsome stranger didn't seem to care much about money at all. He'd tossed a stack of bills at the cab driver, and paid the front desk clerk a pretty hefty tip for his special request. The cost of the room hadn't made him flinch in the slightest. And though I hadn't noticed it before, his suit looked expensive, he wore a designer watch, and his mud-covered shoes were definitely worth more than the heels I'd abandoned on the ledge of my building.

Mr. One-Night is loaded.

Which made me curious about what he did for a living. He was in town for business, he'd said. Where was he visiting? And what kind of business did he have? How long would he be in the city for?

Dammit.

The sudden tumble of questions made me realize where the dark-eyed stranger's look of indecision had come from. I wanted—really wanted—to tear off the buttons of his dress shirt and lay siege to his undoubtedly perfect body. But it was hard to just put aside the getting-to-know-you bit. Especially to someone I was so attracted to.

His hand landed on my elbow, jerking me back to the moment. He'd opened the door and was watching me expectantly.

"I really do need something to call you," he said.

I blinked. "What?"

He grinned. "I tried 'baby' and 'sweetheart' and 'honey'. None of those got me a response."

My face warmed. "Sorry."

"Don't apologize," he replied, gesturing for me to go into the room first. "Just tell me what completely fake name to whisper when I want you to look my way."

"A fake name?"

"Or a nickname."

"Red?" It popped out before I could stop it, and he eyed my hair.

"Really?" he said, and he sounded so surprised that I actually laughed.

"No," I replied, stepping into the room. "Not really. Pretty much every person I've met since I was *born* has called me Red."

"So not Red."

He closed the door behind me. "Mm. But now I wanna try it out."

"Go for it."

"I might."

His arms came up and circled around me from behind. I sank into the embrace and surveyed the room. It was warm and elegant, with wood trim, antique furnishings, and giant bed covered in a sexy, maroon duvet. My gaze lingered on the last item. It was easy to imagine sinking into it. Wrapping myself around my dark-haired stranger.

Your *dark-haired stranger?*

Before I could answer the surprised and slightly accusatory voice in my head, my mouth dropped open and I said something unexpected. "My family calls me Lu."

"Lu?" His voice wrapped around the nickname like a satin sheet.

"Since I was a kid."

"Louise?"

"No."

"Lucille?"

"Nope."

"Luna?"

"No."

"Would you tell me if I was close?" he asked.

"Probably not," I admitted.

He laughed. "All right. What would you like to call me?"

I answered without thinking it through. "Does your family have a nickname for you?"

"Oh, they call me names all right. Nothing I want to hear coming from those pretty lips of yours, though."

Curiosity struck again, and I extricated myself from his arm and turned to face him.

"I can't imagine anyone calling you not nice things," I said.

His mouth twisted into a rueful smile. "Well. It wouldn't be very easy to get you into a hotel room if I told you all my terrible secrets first, would it?"

"Dammit. *That's* what I should've asked about."

"Too late now." He reached up and ran his arms from my elbows to my shoulders, then back down again. "What do you think I look like? A Dominic? A Peter?"

I pretended to scrutinize his looks. "You probably have one of those names that used to be a girl's name, but got repurposed as a boy's name. Jane."

"Jane?"

"Mm. Or...your parents were New Age types, so they gave you something spiritual. Black Forest Cake."

"Black Forest Cake is spiritual?"

"Haven't you ever had it?"

"Yes."

"And it wasn't a religious experience for you?"

He laughed, but I couldn't take a minute to gloat over my terrible joke. I was too distracted by the fact that the back of my knees had just hit the bed. I hadn't even realized he was backing me up.

I narrowed my eyes at him as he kicked off his shoes. "Oh, you're slick, aren't you?"

"Learned it from my New Age parents," he replied.

The sudden, predatory glint in his eyes was all the warning I had before his foot kicked out to hook behind my ankles. And it wasn't enough to save me from being knocked flat onto the mattress behind me. In a heartbeat, he was poised over of me. His hips were between my thighs, his chest flush with my breasts, and his strong arms flexed into a push-up position on either side of my shoulders.

"I thought we were waiting for the...uh...special delivery?" I asked breathlessly.

"We are," he replied.

"Funny way of showing it."

"We're just talking."

"Talking?"

"Yes. Fabricating stuff about each other's lives." He relaxed his arms and dragged his lips along my jaw.

My pulse jumped. "Right. Like how you started your career."

"How did I start my career?" he repeated?

"Well. You were rebelling against your New Age parents. So you decided to start a business."

"And what's my business?"

"Selling scientific textbooks," I said.

"Of course." He slid down a little, put his mouth on my top button, and gave it a tug.

He's not seriously going to—yep. Yep he is.

The button sprang free. Not open. Completely free. He spat it out then shot me a grin.

"Don't worry," he said, "the scientific textbook business is going well. I can buy you a new shirt."

My pulse thump-thump-thumped even harder. "This is why you failed in your hobby."

"Refresh my memory. What's my hobby?" he asked.

"Underground boxing."

"Right. That's how I stay so fit."

"It *was*," I corrected. "Until you kept tearing off your opponents' clothes with your teeth."

"Bad habit," he agreed.

He slid down again, growled, grabbed the next button in the same manner as the first, then ripped it off. My blouse flopped open. My dark-eyed stranger's eyes landed on my exposed skin. His gaze stayed there for a long moment. When he lifted his eyes to meet mine, they burned with intense longing. And his voice was just as raw.

"Those fucking freckles..." he said.

"Scourge of my redheaded existence," I replied.

"They're so damned sexy."

"Really?"

"You have no idea. I want to touch them all. Taste them. Every single one."

"There's a million of them. It would take a lifetime." As soon as I said it, I realized how it could be perceived, anonymity or not.

But he just dipped his head again, this time to press his tongue to my freckles.

One-two-three-four.

"Like a never-ending game of connect the dots," he murmured.

Five-six. Seven-eight.

Each touch made me moan. Each time he pulled away, I wanted to beg for more. I was so busy losing myself in the attention that I didn't notice as he shifted slightly so that he was beside me instead of on top of me. I didn't feel him loosen the rest of my buttons until his hand was already pressed to my stomach and making its way up to the edge of my bra.

"I wanna take this off." His words rumbled against my chest. "Say that I can."

"Yes!" It was a gasp.

With startling deftness—one-handed and with no visible change in his position—he snuck his hand under me, pinched the clasp of my bra, and dragged it off. With a flick of his wrist, he sent the lace-and-satin item flying. For a moment, I felt exposed. Especially when his hungry gaze found my bare breasts again. Then he dropped a reverent-sounding curse and lowered his head, and any hint of self-consciousness disappeared.

His tongue flicked over one nipple, then the other. His mouth lingered on the second one, opening just enough to draw it in. He sucked. Gently at first, then a little harder. Then harder still. It made me ache for more. Ache for *him*.

And it suddenly struck me as unfair that I was halfway to naked while he was fully clothed, tie and all. I really didn't want him stop what he was doing. But I was also desperate to get him undressed. A battle waged in my head for a second before I decided I really needed to touch him too. Skin to skin.

I slipped my hand between us and fumbled to loosen his tie, and when he realized what I was trying to do, he released his hold on my nipple to make it easier for me. The loss of contact was an acute throb. I very nearly dropped his tie so I could press his face back to my breast. Thankfully, he hurried the process along.

His fingers closed over mine. They expertly dug into the knot, and once he had it loosened enough, he let me yank it over his head. The second it was off, I moved on to his dress shirt. Even though my hands shook with anticipation, I managed to make short work of the buttons. Of course, the second his chest was exposed, the world slowed down.

If I'd thought his face was model-esque, it had nothing on his finely sculptured body. Abs for miles. A real honest-to-God six-pack.

No, I corrected as I ran my hands over the muscles in awe. *An eight-pack.*

He let me explore the ridges of his stomach and chest, his eyes closing and his breathing turning shallow as I continued my perusal. When my fingers grazed the edge of his pants, he groaned. I liked the sound of it. The power of it. Knowing that it was me, making him react.

Spurred on by a desire to drive him even crazier, I grasped the button at his waistband and tugged it open. The zipper came free at the same time, sliding down, revealing a pair of charcoal gray boxer briefs. Beneath those, the obvious bulge of his erection beckoned.

I didn't stop to think about it. I reached in by instinct, sliding my hand past the elastic to grip the bulky length of him. The second my palm hit the silky hardness, a wave dizzying want hit me so hard that my entire body shook. My core tensed. My vision blurred. And the next breath I took burned through me.

Holy hell.

As I started to tug—both with a need to satisfy him and to draw him closer—his eyes opened wide, his pupils so dilated that they blocked out his irises almost completely. And his stare pinned me to the spot. I'd never seen such a ravenous expression. It made me wonder if I had the same look on my own face. The feeling raging through me was certainly one that threatened to consume me.

I breathed out, and a surprising need to say something—I wasn't sure what—tried to take over. But before a single word could make its way out, a sharp rap on the door interrupted.

"Shit," said my dark-eyed stranger. "Our room service."

He stared at me for another second, then spun and—without bothering to do up his pants or grab his shirt or even cover me up—he strode across the room. He twisted the doorknob and opened the door just barely a crack, and reached his hand through wordlessly before slamming it shut again. Something flew from his hand to the dresser, but I didn't see what. And it didn't take much longer than a blink for him to return to his spot in front of me. His fingers were clasped around a small, purple box.

Condoms.

I no sooner realized it than he had the cardboard open and the short strip of foil pinched between his teeth. I watched as he pushed his pants and underwear down, my breath catching and the heady, overwhelming arousal doubling as my eyes hung on his rigid manhood. But he gave me an unfortunately short amount of ogling time.

In yet another slick move, he tore open the silver package, drew out the condom, then rolled it on to his waiting erection. I couldn't hold in a moan at the way his big hands worked the latex up. And the moment he had it in place, he dropped one knee between mine.

He paused just long enough to say, "Do you want this?"

"Please," I replied.

"Good."

With both hands, he shoved my skirt up. And for some reason, that was so much hotter than him pulling it down. Even more lascivious than that, as he eased forward, he didn't take off my panties. He simply nudged them aside. My legs parted easily. Eagerly. And when he entered me—slowly, carefully, tortuously—it felt like something I'd been waiting for forever rather than just a couple of hours.

I gasped. Then moaned. Then released a wordless cry.

He thrust forward. Slowly at first, then with increasing intensity. Every push brought me higher. Every plunge made me tighten around him.

His hands weren't still, either. They roamed my body. Smoothed back my hair. Touched my face and lips.

I'd thought his attentive strokes out by the tree had been satisfying. They were nothing compared to the way he felt now. In and out. Sometimes circling, sometimes slowing for a tease that made me want to swear.

Then his rhythm changed. Became less controlled. Wilder. And as he slammed against me again and again, I knew why he'd asked for a name. It was something to call out. Something to hold on to and something to be oh-so thankful for.

"Tell me," I begged as he rocked back and forth.

"Tell you what, baby?" he replied without stopping.

"What to call you. Your name."

"Ethan."

I said it back. "Ethan."

He thrust into me harder. My insides climber higher.

I said it again. "Ethan."

Harder again. Higher still.

And now his name became a desperate moan. "Ethan."

I knew he was close. I was certain I was closer. Any second, I'd come undone around him.

"Ethan!"

"Now, baby?"

"Yes!"

And just like that—like he'd been holding back, waiting for me to give the word—his pace became almost frantic, his movements a rough jerk. He slammed into me so hard that the bed shuddered—once, twice, and a third time. And as my coil of need exploded, so did he. He pulsed inside me, filling me in a way that seemed more than physical. I could feel every inch of him throbbing with release, perfectly timed with my own. And when at last he eased out of me for a final, regretful time, I couldn't help but say his name again, this time in a whisper.

Chapter 4

Ethan

I woke in the morning and found the bed empty. A sleepy stretch and a glance around told me the room was equally devoid of company.

"Shit," I muttered.

I'd assumed she'd be there in the morning. I wasn't ashamed to admit that I'd hoped to drag out the one-night stand to something a little longer. After all, I was stuck in Vancouver until Tuesday, and I was pretty much guaranteed to be in a shitty mood after dealing with the owner of Trinkets and Treasures. It'd sure as hell be nice to have something to look forward to. A second look around told me it was wishful thinking. Her bra was gone from the back of the chair, and I took that as sure sign that she really had left.

With a sigh, I flopped back against the pillow and folded my hands behind my head, half wondering if the night before had been a crazy, jetlag-induced dream of epic proportions. Legs and arms wrapped around me. Hair falling over my face. Running out of condoms and having to improvise with post-sex foreplay, which the redhead had laughingly insisted was some kind of oxymoron.

Not the redhead, I corrected silently. *Lu.*

Remembering that made me smile. It also made me a hundred percent sure I hadn't dreamed it. Not to be totally crude, but my fantasy-mind would've definitely given her a name worthy of a stripper pole.

I closed my eyes and inhaled, and the residual, mingled scent of sex and Lu's perfume filled my nose. Desire stirred up immediately.

Why the hell did she leave?

Christ, had it been good. For her too. I was sure of it. Not in a cocky, God's gift to women kinda way. Not even in a no-one-fakes-it-that-well way. I'd seen the look on her face. Felt her come under me. Then on top of me. Finally, against my tongue. Even if that hadn't been evidence enough, as I'd tucked her body against mine right before we drifted off, she'd murmured a question that made me want laugh a little, but made me ache in a curious way too.

"Is it supposed to be this amazing?"

I could still hear her voice saying the words, and I wondered what the answer was. I'd always been a fan of the pizza analogy. When sex was bad, it was still good.

Last night, though. Shit. It was *amazing.*

It made me wish like crazy that I'd had the foresight to ask for her number. Though judging by how quickly and quietly she'd sneaked out, maybe she wouldn't even have handed it over.

I sighed again. Then froze as the doorknob rattled with the sound of a key jamming into it. I fixed my eyes on the door. I knew for a fact that I'd stuck the do-not-disturb sign on the handle last night.

Anticipation made me sit up and swing my legs over the bed just as the door eased open. I wasn't let down. She backed into the room, one hand on the door, the other gripping a coffee tray and also weighed down by full, plastic bags. Her denim-clad ass greeting me in a way that made my cock twitch, and she filled out the jeans so perfectly that I was actually a little disappointed when she turned around.

She jumped when she spotted me sitting in the bed. "Oh!"

"Surprised to find me here?" I teased.

She shook her head. "No."

"No?"

"Well. No more surprised than I was to find you there last night."

I smiled. "I can always leave."

"Please don't." Color crept up her cheeks. "I mean. Unless you have to. Um. I've got cinnamon buns."

"Now I *have* to stay."

"Good. I have other things too." She stepped lightly across the room and deposited her armful of stuff onto the dresser. "Wanna see?"

"I'll look at anything you like if you give me a cinnamon bun."

She pulled an icing-covered treat from a paper bag, freed a cup from the drink tray, and handed both over. "Tall latte. You're not lactose intolerant?"

"Not at all."

"Two for two. Here's hoping the rest is a hit, also." Her fingers closed on one of the plastic bags, then another, then went back to the first again.

I fought a grin at her nervous flitting. "What've you got in those bags? Plans for world domination?"

"No."

"Drugs?"

"No."

"What is it, then, that's making you make that face?"

"Clothes."

"You say that like it's a dirty word."

"I didn't want to be too presumptuous."

"Clothes are presumptuous?"

She wrinkled her nose. "Maybe? I don't know. Buying some clothes seems like..."

"Like a three-month milestone rather than a morning-after thing?" I filled in.

"Exactly. But—as you may remember—you wrecked my blouse last night."

"With my teeth. Can't say I'm sorry."

"Me, neither."

"Good."

"But when I got up, I realized that my skirt was ripped too. And I didn't have any shoes. Then I remembered your bag and you saying you'd have to get some new things, and there's this little shop around the corner that I knew opened early, so..." She shrugged, grabbed one of the bags, and tossed it to me.

I had to admit that I was genuinely curious about what she'd picked out for me. I made a show of dragging out the items, one at a time. First came a pair of tan, linen pants. Casual and classic.

"Just my size," I said with a wink.

She blushed. "I might've looked inside your other pants for reference."

"You look in my pants all you want, honey."

"Shut up."

I grinned and went back to the bag. Next came a linen dress-shirt in forest green. Not a color I would've chosen for myself, but holding it up, I saw the appeal. Mostly because it would complement Lu's hair. I could easily picture her hair fanned out over it as she leaned her head against my chest. In fact, I didn't want to just picture it. I wanted it to happen.

I lifted my eyes to meet her honey-browns. "Hey, Lu? Do you wanna go out with me tonight?"

She blinked, visibly surprised. "Go out?"

"Dinner? Movie? A stupidly wet walk in the park?"

"Really?"

"Unless you're ashamed to be seen with me in public," I teased.

"No, it's not that. I just thought..." The seemingly ever-present pinkness under her freckles deepened yet again.

I reached out to take a hold of her hands, and pulled her so that her knees pressed to mine.

"If you only wanted one night, and you'd prefer to walk away, that's fine." I paused and shook my head. "Actually. That's a lie. If you walk away, I'll be sorely disappointed. But since I'm truly not a maniac, I'll let you go. Then spend the next three days wondering what you're up to. Thinking about your hands and mouth." I slid my fingers up her wrists. "About your skin and all these freckles." I stroked my thumbs back and forth over her forearms. "Wishing like crazy that I had you under me."

She sucked in her lower lip, then exhaled. "You can't have me under you in a public place."

"You sure about that?" I dropped my hands to her hips, then slid them to her ass. "I think I damned near did last night."

"Well. To be fair. You *had* just saved me from plummeting to my death."

"Ah. So I caught you in a moment of weakness."

"Yes."

"So if I want another public make-out session..."

"You'll have to save me again."

I pushed my hands up under her shirt and pressed them to the small of her back. "I'm going to take that as a yes."

"It's a yes," she agreed. "But I do have to work today."

"What time?"

"Ten-ish until six-ish. Then I'm all yours."

"Perfect. Gives me time to get my shit done." I grimaced. "Or started, anyway."

"Not looking forward to it?" she asked.

"Anticipating a fight."

"Scientific textbook business is pretty cutthroat nowadays, huh?"

"Sure is. What time is it now, by the way?" I teased.

"It was a little after nine when I passed by the front desk."

I couldn't cover my surprise. "Shit. Seriously?"

Lu nodded. "Yes. Do you have somewhere to be at a specific time too?"

"Not at a specific time, no. But I can't remember the last time I stayed in bed past six-thirty."

"I hope it was worth it."

"Completely. In fact, it's a damned shame you have to go."

"I know. Especially considering that I also bought *these*."

She wriggled out of my grasp, grabbed another plastic bag from the pile, and tossed it to me. I stuck my hand in and pulled out a box. My mouth curved up.

"Well, shit, Lu," I said. "Why didn't you *start* with the condoms? Now I'm gonna have to make you late."

She started to protest. She said something about only having eleven minutes. Something about staff. I didn't care. I blocked it all out. And it was easy, because I was so damned busy grabbing her and dragging her back under the covers.

* * * *

Mia

The euphoric afterglow of sex showed zero signs of leaving anytime soon. In the half hour since Ethan and I had parted ways, I'd had to try so hard to not smile like a fool that I was giving myself a headache. And my assistant store manager, Chloe, had asked me twice if I was sick. Because I was late, she'd said. And I was *never* late. And because I looked a little feverish too, she'd added. Her observations had made me laugh. And of course, my giggles had worsened her concern. She'd actually put the back of her hand on my forehead. I'd just laughed harder. And I decided it was probably better for me do some office work rather than stick around the store itself.

But once I'd jimmied my way through my broken door, called an electrician about my lighting issue, and contacted the tech guru up the street to put in a request for a new cell phone *and* a laptop emergency, I was left a little lost. Thoughts of Ethan kept sneaking in. As I dragged out my latest design plans—done on good, old-fashioned paper, thank goodness—I couldn't stop myself from picturing his hands running over my jewelry. And that wasn't a euphemism for anything naughty. Genuinely curious as to what he might think of what I did for a living, I was literally thinking about how the delicate items might look in his hands.

My business was my heart and soul. The one thing I could lose myself in. Where I could *be* myself. Designing unique products, making them by hand, customizing items…it was all a labor of love. And I knew from experience that finding something that was both joyous and genuine was uncommon. One part passion, one part luck, and a whole lotta need to prove myself had got me to where I was. Respected in the tight-knit business. Making a profit that surpassed what I'd hoped for. I didn't brag about it. I also knew from experience that the rug could be ripped out from under me. But for some reason, I really wished I'd invited Ethan in to have a look at my life's work.

So why'd you insist on being dropped off on the corner?

The thought gave me pause. I wouldn't have consciously called it insistence. But now my mind backtracked, going over the morning to see if there was any merit to the descriptive label.

After booking another night at the Memory Motel, we'd decided to walk together back toward my shop. I was already late anyway, and the rain from the night before had eased off, and the air was cool and fresh. His fingers gripped mine like it was something we did every day, and we made plans to find an out-of-the-way place for a late dinner. When we'd reached the corner by the big oak tree—our tree, Ethan had called it—we'd paused to laugh at the fact that my shoes were just visible from below. Then we'd started to walk again. And I'd been the one to stop. My heart had fluttered with a little stab of anxiety, but I'd attributed it to a moment of self-doubt. I'd brushed it off easy enough too. It wasn't like I owed anyone an explanation. I really didn't need to excuse my desire to indulge in a physical encounter with a totally hot guy. I was single. Twenty-seven. A business owner. And fully in charge of my own future.

But that was the moment that I'd made the suggestion of separating. But it wasn't *insistence*. Ethan hadn't protested against leaving me at the corner. Just asked if I was sure.

But what if he had *argued?* I wondered.

Would I have let him follow me back to Trinkets and Treasures? I'd built the store from nothing. Against noisy objections that it was a risky move. Even my family, who were supportive of everything I did, had questioned my decision. But I'd proved them wrong. Shown that I was capable. I ran my business with cool efficiency. My staff liked me and respected me. And the woman I was when I was at work, she was nothing like the woman who'd gone to bed with Ethan last night. The former thought everything through. The latter, well, she climbed out windows and kissed strangers, didn't she? It wouldn't be good for the two worlds to crash into each other.

I pictured how it would go.

In all likelihood, I would have to introduce him to my assistant manager. She was friendly. But curious. So I would've looked for a way out. Probably by bringing him upstairs to show him my designs. And the designs would've turned out to be a pretense to get him alone. Because what I'd *really* want was for him to take my face in his hands and kiss me. To lift me to the desk. Unbutton my jeans. Slide his hand inside. Make me quake with need all over again. I could practically feel his fingers already, stroking me and making my pulse rise. Blood rushed through me, and a little gasp escaped my mouth right before the jingle of the entrance bell downstairs jerked me out of the fantasy.

I blinked and sucked in a much-needed breath. Clearly, a single night with Ethan had turned me from a reasonable woman into a slathering, sex-starved fool. So it was probably a good thing that he'd just given me a kiss, a devilish smile, and a promise to meet me back in the same spot again in eight hours. The last thing I needed was to turn my office into a sex den.

"A sex den, Mia?" I muttered aloud. "Is that even a thing?"

"Uh, Mia?" My assistant manager's voice carried through the slightly ajar door.

I cursed my imagination for blocking out her approaching footsteps. Had she heard me say "sex den"? God, I hoped not.

"Mia?" she said again.

I cleared my throat and shuffled the papers on my desk. "I'm here. Come in."

The door creaked, and Chloe stepped through. Concern filled her face immediately.

"Are you okay? Seriously."

"I'm fine. Why wouldn't I be?"

"Your face is redder than a sunset."

"It's warm up here," I lied.

"I think you might have a fever," she replied.

"I don't get sick, Chloe. You know that."

She crossed her arms and gave me another once-over. "Well. Something's not right. And as your favorite employee, I feel a need to tell you that it worries me."

I pinched the bridge of my nose. I usually valued Chloe's sharp eye and her honesty. It was one of the reasons I'd hired her, then immediately promoted her. But she generally had her scrutiny focused on customers, sales, and the store. Not on me.

Because you always make sure you're above scrutiny. Like you should be now.

I cleared my throat again. "Did you come up here just to check on me, or..."

My cool tone didn't make her back down; she just crossed her arms over her chest and said, "Partly to check on you. And partly because there's a man downstairs."

My heart skipped a beat. "A man?"

"He says he has some business to discuss with you." She frowned. "He seems...intense."

"Dark eyes? Dark hair? Looks like a brooding underwear model?" The last bit slipped out before I could stop it.

Chloe blinked. "Like a...what?"

"He's good looking?" I rephrased.

"Very. But like I said. Intense. I was actually a little worried about Magda down there with him."

I almost laughed. Magda was one of my part-time employees—a retired teacher who'd spent her last ten years at a reform school. She had a third-degree black belt, a passion for pretty things, and took no shit from anyone. Even Ethan, with all his muscles and charm, wouldn't be a match for Magda.

Chloe shook her head, reading my face in spite of my ability to rein in my amusement.

"I'm serious," she said. "The guy was rolling off sinister vibes. If it weren't for the fact that he referred to you as 'Lu', I might've called the cops."

The genuine concern in her voice gave me pause. It *had* to be Ethan. No one on the planet but my parents, my brother—and now my future sister-in-law, and her best friend—called me Lu. Had his business meeting gone badly? Was he seeking me out for solace, or to cancel our plans? I really hoped it wasn't the second one.

For the third time in five minutes, I cleared my throat. "You can send him up."

Chloe's eyebrows shot up to her hairline. "Up?"

"Please."

"You want an angry man who knows your family nickname to come *up*." It was a disbelieving statement rather than a question.

I nodded. "It's all right. I know him."

"How?" The word burst out of her like she couldn't quite contain it.

"Chloe. You're doing a really bad job of being my favorite *employee* right now," I said it with deliberate emphasis, and at last she relented.

"Okay, fine. *Boss*. But I'm putting nine-one into my phone, and I'm prepared to add the other one at lightning speed."

"I appreciate that."

She shot me yet another look that said she wasn't buying it, then turned and walked out. I ignored her. I was too busy wishing—for the first time ever—that I had a mirror in my office. I stood up, pulled my hair from its ponytail, and tried to smooth it down. I sat down and crossed my legs. Then uncrossed them. I stood and paced the room for a moment. Then sat again. Then stood.

What are you worried about? I asked myself. *He saw you at near to your literal worst, and he still couldn't keep his hands off you.*

But the reassurance did nothing. I wanted him to want me again. I wanted the desk fantasy. Badly. Quickly.

As his heavy footsteps signaled his imminent approach, my heart fluttered and my palms dampened. And when he pushed the door open and paused in the frame, it took most of my self-restraint to keep from rushing forward to drag him in by his tie.

Wait. His tie?

He'd been in the shirt and pants I'd given him when we left each other at the corner. It was enough to distract me from the idea of jumping him then and there. I eyed his fresh clothes in puzzlement. He now wore an expensive-looking pin-striped suit, a burgundy dress shirt, and a black tie. I lifted my gaze, a question on my lips. But my words died before making it out.

Ethan's face was hard, his jaw stiff, his eyes dark. And I understood why Chloe was nervous about sending him up.

Chapter 5

Ethan

As I stepped into Lu's office—*Not Lu*, I corrected silently. *Not really*—the air in my lungs expelled in a surprisingly painful way. It seemed impossible to suck it back in. Even more impossible to say the lines I'd rehearsed. Instead, I had to fight to keep from striding forward so I could kiss her. Make her as breathless as I was already. Maybe toss aside the already strewn about paperwork and take her hard and fast on the desk.

Jesus. Get a grip.

I flexed and released my hands as the silent seconds ticked by. Her honey-browns were fixed on me. Nervous. Not that I could blame her for feeling that way. I wasn't exactly giving off a friendly vibe. Just the opposite, probably.

The seething frustration had been building for an hour. It started when I decided to chase her down. Even though we'd made plans to get together later, it felt too much like a goodbye. With not enough tongue.

Impetuously, I'd hurried after her. Followed her around the corner. Called out her name just as a bus wheezed by, then watched as she disappeared into a shop three doors up. A few steps had brought me close enough to see the sign.

Trinkets and Treasures.

And I'd just fucking *known*.

She was the woman who'd been blocking my emails and screening my calls. What were the goddamned chances?

I'd cleared out fast. Found a little coffee shop to use as a spot to regain my focus. Get a bit of perspective. Unfortunately, the caffeine didn't help. Nor did the time I spent sipping it.

I'd done my due fucking diligence when making the decision to acquire the business. I was always thorough.

First, I'd racked my brain, going over every detail of the night before in something that should've hinted at what she did. At who she was. Not a single thing came to mind.

So I'd moved on, using my phone to comb through the few emails that we'd had. Went through them, again and again. If they'd been written on real paper, they would've been tattered and torn by the time I was done with them. Each look yielded the same thing. An auto-signature with the name Mia Diaz attached to it.

Mia. How the fuck does someone get Lu *from Mia?*

Knowing full well that I was bordering on stalker status, I ramped up my search and sought out everything I could find on the web about Trinkets and Treasures. It was something I'd done once already, but I tried to come at it with fresh eyes. I found nothing new. A tidy website designed to direct traffic to the shop itself. A few options for online purchases. A newspaper article about the owner, Ms. Mia Diaz, moving up from California to take advantage of the market in Vancouver. The photo in the article showed a petite blond woman wearing sunglasses and a scarf tied around her head. No chance in hell was it *Lu*. She must've hired someone. A stunt double? A stock model? Who the hell knew. Either way, the result was the same—I didn't recognize her.

I tried to rationalize. To use that one fact to tell myself that it meant it might not be her. Except my gut was rarely wrong as far as business was concerned. I trusted my instincts. Unequivocally. If they said she was the woman, then she was the woman.

After capitulating to my overwhelming feeling of knowing my suspicion was true, I'd very nearly called a cab to get my ass to the airport so I could head straight back to Toronto. God knew this would end in a headache at best, and a disaster at worse. I was far too stubborn to give up. Far too used to winning.

In the end, I'd finally decided to come into the store and confront her. To do it, I needed to regroup. To forget the wantonness and empty condom box. To not be the man who'd begged her unashamedly to move her mouth down the length of my body. No way in hell could I even try if I showed up in the outfit she'd bought me. But a nice suit was as good as armor. Formal. Unbreakable.

I just had one little problem.

The second I saw her, I wanted her again. And now that she was standing in front of me, the plan was gone to shit. I couldn't recall what I actually *had* planned. All that came to mind was the remembered feel of her lips on mine. Of her legs around my hips. Silken skin and whispered words.

It took more willpower than I wanted to admit to forcibly shove down the memory of how she'd sounded when saying my name the night before—passionate and needy instead of hesitant and worry-tinged—and drag my attention back to the moment.

What came out of my mouth, though, wasn't even close to the tidy speech I'd prepared. "What's your real name?"

She frowned, clearly thrown off. "What?"

I tried to use her moment of confusion to ground myself, but my mouth just kept going. "I know it's not Lu."

"I told you it was a nickname."

"What's it short for?"

She narrowed her eyes. "Why are you asking, Ethan?"

I wasn't immune to the abrupt coolness in her voice. It stung, and I had a hard time disguising that fact as I answered her with a deflection.

"Why aren't you answering, Lu?"

"Are we in third grade?"

"It's just a question."

"I thought we were keeping things casual."

"We are," I said.

"So what is this?" she replied.

"You tell me. Do you own Trinkets and Treasures?"

"Yes."

"So who's the blond woman on your website?"

"On my—she's one of my jewelry models. Wait. Did you *follow* me?"

I avoided the question and took a step closer. "Last night, I spent *hours* getting to know your body. Its curves. Its freckles. The way it tastes."

She lifted her face challengingly and didn't move away. "And you thought that gave you permission to look me up online?"

"Public information." I offered as casual a shrug as I could manage.

"Okay. But if you were on my website, then you already know my name."

"Mia Diaz." I expected it to come out bitterly. I'd certainly spent enough time grinding my teeth at the name for the last few weeks. Instead, it came out whipped-cream smooth. Silky. Sweet. I liked it entirely more than I wanted to. Even when she clarified.

"It's *Lu*mia Diaz, actually."

"Unusual."

"It was my great-grandmother's. And yes, it's unusual. Which is why I go by Mia ninety-nine percent of the time. Including where my business is concerned." She continued to hold my gaze. "And what do *you* go by?"

"To my face, I usually get 'sir.' Behind my back? I think it's mostly 'ruthless bastard.'"

She rolled her eyes. "Your name."

I drew in a breath. I could smell her sweet smell. Feel the heat of her body. And suddenly I didn't *want* to tell her anything. I wondered if I could get away without saying a word. Just pick up where we'd left off the night before, go home on Tuesday like I'd planned, then store away our time together. Put it at the back of my mind.

Do you really think you could abandon the acquisition? asked a little voice in my head.

I acknowledged it with a mental nod.

Maybe.

The humiliation of not closing the deal, just this once, almost seemed worth it.

Okay, I thought. *Let's say you decided to let Trinkets and Treasures go... Could you let* Mia *go too?*

The question startled me. I'd had one night with the woman. An incredible night, yes. But still just a night. There wasn't anything to lose except the smallest hint of morality. Even that was a bit gray. I knew who she was, but I wasn't using that knowledge to get anything. No seduction, no business perk at the end. So why the hell did I feel like I couldn't just let it—let *her*—go?

"Ethan..."

Her voice wrapped around my name, pulling me back to the moment. She said it the same way she had when her mouth was pressed to my ear, and it only took me a second to figure out why. I was touching her without even meaning to. My hands were on her hips. A light grip, but not excusable as an accident. I started to lift them. She stopped me. Her soft, warm fingers came down on top of mine and pressed them more firmly into place.

Reflexively, I dragged her forward to pull her body flush against me. She released my hands, looped her arms over my shoulders, and pushed up to her toes, her lips parted.

It was impossible to not want her.

Fuck the business, I thought.

I tipped my head and brushed my mouth against hers. A light kiss. A promise.

"The desk," she murmured.

"The desk?" I repeated.

"Take me there. I've been thinking about it since the second I left you this morning."

I'd never heard a sexier statement. I slid my hands over the swell of her hips, bent a little to grip her thighs, then lifted her from the ground. Her legs wrapped around me, and my cock throbbed in anticipation. I couldn't get her to the desk fast enough.

With no regard for the paperwork cluttering the wood top, I dropped her down, then reached for the hem of her shirt. She lifted her arms to let me pull it over her head. I tossed it aside and allowed myself a moment to admire her bare form. Her full breasts spilled from her lacy, royal-blue bra, rising and falling with the quickness of her breaths.

So fucking beautiful.

I started to lift my eyes to her face, but paused when she leaned back and brought her hands to the button of her jeans. My gaze hung on her slim fingers as they undid it, then slid her zipper open too. I could just see the top of her low-rise panties, the same blue as her bra.

Then her hands dropped. One to the desk beside her, the other to my wrist. I watched, mesmerized and rock hard, as she dragged my fingers to the sexy slope just below her belly button. She inched our hands lower. I hissed in a breath as we reached the lace, and I at last moved my gaze up. I wanted to stare into those captivating eyes of hers as I made her come.

Except when I looked up, guilt—unexpected and overwhelming—hit me. Almost knocked the wind out of me. I fought it for a moment before realizing I couldn't win. I stilled our hands, then leaned forward and kissed her cheek before pulling back.

"It's Burke," I said.

Lu's—Mia's—brows knit together. "What is?"

"My name. Ninety-nine percent of the time, I go by Ethan Bradley Burke."

I waited. I knew it would only take her a second. And it did.

"E. B. Burke," she whispered.

"That's me," I confirmed.

* * * *

Mia

I was suffocating. It was the only explanation for the crushed-in feeling in my chest. It was one part humiliation, and one part anger. And there was a healthy dose of shock mixed in there too.

I was aware that I was sitting in a very compromising position. Topless. Pants undone. Physical desire still coursing through me even though my pride bucked against it. But I couldn't seem to do much about any of it.

I was too busy trying to breathe. And too busy trying to slam the appropriate pieces into place too.

Ethan Burke. *E. B. Burke.* The man had been hounding me for weeks. Demanding ownership of my business. He was an arrogant bastard. An *entitled* bastard. I'd known it from the second he reached out, even when he tried to play himself off as congenial. But the niceness hadn't lasted long anyway. He'd slipped from polite-ish to bossy. From bossy to rude. It'd made me wonder how he even managed to stay in business. And his subsequent messages hadn't just rubbed me the wrong way—they'd set my teeth completely on edge.

The last one I'd read—where he'd gone so far as to suggest that I wasn't capable of taking Trinkets and Treasures as far as it could go and that I was blind to that fact—had made me lose my temper. I'd done something I hadn't done in years and actually thrown something across my bedroom.

I was near the edge again now.

The nerve of him showing up at my store. Of him—*God.*

At last the oxygen came in, giving me just enough breath to gasp, "You sonofabitch. Did you know last night?"

He sighed and stepped back, leaving me feeling even more exposed. But now pride and stubbornness reared their heads, and I *refused* to look like I was scrambling to regain some dignity.

I didn't even cross my arms as I prodded, "Well?"

Ethan's dark eyes grew darker, and he shook his head. "No."

"Am I supposed to believe that?"

"I'm not stupid enough to jeopardize my chances of closing the deal like that."

"But judging by your emails, you're unscrupulous enough to—"

"No. Believe what you want, but it's true either way. Last night, you were just a pretty redhead who fell from a tree and landed in my lap."

His dismissive tone made me bristle. Probably because it sounded so much like his egotistical emails.

"Then I guess it's just a shitty coincidence." I said.

"It didn't seem so shitty last night, did it?" he replied.

I sucked in a breath. How had he gone so quickly from being the charming, sexy man I'd taken to bed to being this cocky jerk? I almost shook my head, disgusted at myself for even wondering. The intrinsic nature of a one-night stand was not knowing someone well enough to figure out if they were *truly* sexy and charming. Not giving it the time to happen. This was a perfect example of why. Clearly, one-night-stand Ethan, and work-Ethan were two very different people.

Then it struck me. Just minutes earlier, I'd been thinking about that same thing in relation to myself. Work-me and one-night-stand me were never meant to be in the same place.

I exhaled. "It wasn't shitty last night because you weren't Ethan Burke, and I wasn't Mia Diaz."

"Lu—"

"Mia."

"Lumia."

"Stop."

He ran a tanned hand over his dark hair, then turned and stepped toward the window, not looking at me as he spoke. "If I'd known who you were, I wouldn't have—"

I cut him off because I didn't want to hear him say it. "Ditto. And just in case you were thinking it might…at all…it doesn't change my answer. I have no interest in parting with my company."

"We haven't even discussed it."

"The emails were enough."

"You ignored my emails."

"I blocked them," I corrected. "And only after you wouldn't take no for an answer."

"I'm not in the *habit* of taking no for an answer," he replied.

"No shit."

"I came all the way from Toronto. You owe me the courtesy of a discussion."

"That's where you're wrong, Ethan," I said. "I don't owe you anything. You should've taken the hint and stayed in Toronto. In fact, you don't even need to wait until Tuesday to go back again. You can take whatever it is you're offering and fly home today."

He spun to face me, his expression hard. His eyes raked over my half-bared body.

"Could you…" He trailed off and waved an arm.

"Could I what?" I asked.

"Put on a damned shirt."

"You're kidding, right?"

"No. I'm not fucking kidding."

"You took *off* my shirt," I reminded him.

"That was…" He did the arm wave again.

"Before you realized you were trying to steal my business out from under me?"

"No. I figured that out this morning."

"Oh, really?"

"Yes."

"So you knew who I was, but you came in and asked me my name anyway. Then you put me up on the desk, and—"

"You *asked* me to put you on the desk," he said, "In fact, 'asked' is a nice word."

I felt my face burn, and I pushed up from the desk in question, did up my pants, and shot him my darkest glare. "You need to leave."

He stepped toward me. "I won't walk away that easily."

"I'd prefer not to call the authorities."

"That'd be an excessive reaction to a business negotiation."

"This is *not* a business negotiation. I have zero interest in discussing a single thing with you."

"Not what you said last—"

"You need to go, Ethan," I said stiffly. "Forget last night. Forget the desk. I don't want to negotiate a deal. I *won't* negotiate one."

"I'm going to leave, *Mia*," he replied. "Not because I'm conceding, but because I think you need some time to cool off before we move forward."

I glared harder at him, irritated by the sureness of his tone. "You arrogant, self-righteous—"

"Jerk? Asshole? I've heard it all before. There's no name you can call me that's going to make me less persistent."

"Get. Out."

"I'm going."

He turned to leave. But at the door, he paused and turned back. He looked me over. Head to toe. Slowly. And as much as I wished I didn't...I felt his gaze as it moved over every inch of me. It was a slow, gasp-worthy perusal that made my pulse warm. My body clearly remembered the previous night's passion with far too much eagerness. My brain couldn't shut down the recollection, and I actually had to fight to keep from closing the gap between us.

Pheromones. Damn them all to hell.

Then he spun back toward the stairs, his dark head disappearing in an instant. And instead of being relieved—which I knew I should be—I was disappointed. I even took a step closer to the door, straining to hear him leave. Thinking I might feel better if I knew for sure that he'd exited the building completely, I waited for the telltale sound of the bell over the shop door. Instead, I heard his chuckle carry up the stairs. And his laugh was followed by a feminine giggle, and I realized he was talking to Magda. *Charming* her, probably. Maybe Chloe too.

A flicker of envy made my heart squeeze. I wasn't jealous. Magda was more than twice Ethan's age, and Chloe was happily married. But I'd enjoyed the charming side of the dark-eyed man when he'd been in my arms. I'd been looking forward to another night with him. And hearing him laugh…I kind of wished he hadn't told me who he was. It would almost have been preferable.

Are you sure it's just almost?

"Don't be an idiot," I muttered.

But it did give me pause. Because he could've done it. He could've just *not* told me about our connection and taken advantage of the situation. Why hadn't he? I was sure it wasn't because he hadn't enjoyed the night with me. The look he'd given me on the way out the door was enough to be ninety-nine-point-nine percent sure. I was also pretty sure it wasn't guilt. Or moral obligation. It wasn't like he'd come in begging for understanding. He hadn't even offered an apology.

I tapped my fingers on my thigh, frowning as his chuckle carried up again. I could only think of one other reason for him to have confessed the truth—that work was more important to him than sex. The thought made me want to shake my head. What kind of man liked work better than sex? None that I'd ever met. And it was insulting, too, since the sex was with me.

Well. I guess that's what I get for taking Liv's advice and unlocking the Fort Knox of vaginas.

The thought startled me. Mainly because I'd managed to forget that was how the whole thing started. *She* certainly wouldn't have forgotten about the dare as easily I had. And Liv being Liv, she'd probably find a way to pry it out of me. Then she'd find a way to twist Ethan and his swoon-worthy body into something more than it was. It was the last thing I needed. And it wasn't even like I could avoid her because we still had five hundred wedding things to get through before—

I blinked as surprise hit me again, this time with more force.

The wedding.

Somehow, in the midst of getting naked with Ethan, I'd also put *that* to the back of my mind. Which seemed a little impossible, since the planning had been all-consuming for the last few months. Flowers and tulle and misplaced dread that no one would understand. They'd haunted every waking moment. And more than a few sleeping ones too. But my dark-eyed stranger had made me forget.

Not your *dark-eyed stranger,* I corrected silently. *And not really a stranger anymore, either.*

With a sigh, I forced myself to stop pacing the room. I needed to get back to reality. And I could start with putting on my shirt, which was currently hanging from the curtain rod.

Determined to get a hold of myself, I stalked toward it. But as luck would have it, the move was ill-timed. Just as I reached the window, Ethan stepped into view below. He took three, purposeful strides to the sidewalk, then shoved his hands into his pockets and tilted his head up. I knew for a fact that he couldn't see in. I'd stared up enough times myself to know that the tint on the glass didn't allow any prying eyes. But it still gave me a jolt to see his eyes fixed in my direction. And I couldn't even lie and say my breath didn't catch.

His expression was…pained. Or maybe torn. Either way, there was no hint of professional dispassion. What was he thinking about? Me? Our night together? I had an overwhelming need to know. I reached up to touch the window without even realizing I was doing it until the tips of my fingers met the cool glass. I jerked back, embarrassed at the reaction.

He's probably just plotting the best way to rip you off, I thought.

But it didn't stop another stab of regret from digging at my gut as Ethan cast a final look up, then turned and walked away.

Chapter 6

Ethan

Twenty-four hours had passed since my exit from Trinkets and Treasures, and each moment had been a teeth-grinding one. The shittiest of all shitty Mondays hadn't passed quickly. Full of unexpected second guesses, when second guesses were something I didn't indulge in. Ever.

Normally, if I was meeting resistance in a purchase, I wined, dined, and reasoned. It usually worked.

But there's nothing normal about this, is there?

Even before the complete breakdown of natural order—i.e., accidentally sleeping with the target of my takeover—things hadn't been going as planned. No one had fought me quite so hard as Mia did. Some people just handed over the keys. Others quibbled about price. A few argued, but even those who did usually felt obligated to meet with me if I asked.

Not Mia.

She hadn't even considered it. Not for a second, from what I'd seen. Not even factoring in that the passion of two nights ago might be a sign that we had a connection of some kind already. She was angry. Not in the mood to be wined, dined, *or* reasoned with.

Though I couldn't blame her for being pissed off. Hell. I was pissed off too. More than pissed off. Thrown for a fucking loop. As was proved by my lack of sleep, the serious razor burn on my neck from my botched attempt to clean up, and the way my body railed against the constraints of my new clothes.

I gave my reflection in the mirror a glare and loosened my tie marginally. It fit just fine. So did the suit that it accompanied. I knew it for a fact because I'd paid a hell of a lot extra to have the tailor place my alterations above his other orders. Except knowing it didn't seem to be helping me with the feeling that every damned thing was out of place.

"One night of mind-blowing sex does *not* make you a different man," I said to my reflection.

Then I rolled my eyes as I realized I was giving myself a pep talk. Something I hadn't needed to do since the moment I first started my company, which made my statement more than a little ironic.

I turned to slide my shoes out from their spot at the edge of the bed, and I wondered for the twentieth time if moving from the Memory Motel to the Regent Inn might've helped my mood. I don't even know why the hell I hadn't done it. The tattooed, pierced kid with the gift for nonchalance had been replaced by his kindly grandmother, who I'm sure would gladly have released me from the extra night. Not that I gave a shit about the lost money, but the room at the Regent was prepaid and written off as a business expense, so it was just plain wasteful to hold on to both. The Regent also had the added bonus of not being laced with Mia Diaz's residual perfume.

But maybe that's why you did *stay?*

"Shut up," I muttered as I slipped out the door and headed down the stairs.

Tossing and turning all night had given me more than enough time to argue with myself about everything Mia-related. Ultimately, I needed to let it go. I had to grab my business sense, forget the past few days, and do what I'd come to do. That meant realigning my brain—and my overactive cock—to think of her the same way I thought of every other potential buyout owner, so that I could figure out what she wanted, then find a way to get it to her.

Which is precisely why I was going to intercept her. An early call to her shop had given me the idea. Though Mia hadn't been available, the very friendly clerk from the day before had let it slip that my favorite redhead had the better part of the day off to attend a family lunch. A few quick questions had pointed me in the direction of the right restaurant. A charm-fueled chat with the daytime hostess had confirmed that Diaz, party of five, would be in attendance at Ella's Ristorante at noon. Just five short blocks from where I was now.

And just the right amount of fresh air to clear your head between here and there, I told myself firmly.

Resolving not to think about Mia for the next few minutes, I gave the elderly woman at the front desk a wave, pushed out the door, and turned my attention to following the directions I'd memorized. I took my time making my way through the streets, glad that the rain—which had pounded against the roof and windows all night—had once again tapered off. It was an eclectic area. Older homes with evidence of families living inside, but houses converted into shops or businesses too, much like the motel. A tattoo shop shared a yard with a daycare. A few entrepreneurial spirits with sales carts set up on the corners. I even spotted a sign advertising an outlet mall somewhere close by.

Without the rain, the whole thing was actually pleasant.

I had to give Vancouver some credit for its greenery too. The constant downpour brought a long growing season. Trees and grass lined the streets, and spring flowers hung from pretty much every stoop. Back home in Toronto, we were just barely turning the corner of winter, and there'd even been a prediction of some late snow coming in.

And that, I can do without.

As I rounded the final corner to the street that led to the restaurant, a pleasant aroma filled my nose, and I paused to inhale it. Compelled to find the source, I slowed even more. It only took a few seconds for the smell to lead me to an alley. I frowned, thinking maybe I'd been mistaken. But then I spotted a small, wooden sign—*Joyful Jo's*—and I knew I'd stopped in the right spot.

Not sure what to expect, I pushed through the door, and both a cloud of scented dust and a woman's voice greeted me, stopping me in my tracks. "I sell soap!" she said.

"I...uh. What?" I replied, squinting through the scented haze.

"I can tell when someone comes in without knowing what they're here for."

"Where *are* you?" I asked.

"Behind the counter, cleaning up some gunk. Had a bit of an explosion with some supplies."

"Ah. I can leave."

"No, don't do that. Hang tight. I'll be right up."

Sure enough, a moment later, a tall, thirty-something blond woman popped up from behind the counter in question. She wiped her hands on her pants, shot a rueful look at the powdery mess, then shrugged.

"I'm Joanna," she said. "Welcome to Joyful Jo's, where it's usually much cleaner."

I couldn't help but laugh. "Nice to meet you."

"Don't get too close or you'll ruin your pretty suit," she warned.

"So. You want me to stay, but not to come close?"

"Exactly." She smiled. "You're lucky, actually. I don't normally let people buy gifts for others without a consultation."

"You don't *allow* them to?" I asked.

"That's right. But I'll still get the soap you came in for."

"I thought you said I didn't know what I was here for."

"Uh huh. But I didn't say that *I* didn't know."

"*You* know what *I* want?"

She nodded like it was the most obvious thing in the world. "Of course."

I wanted to scratch my head, but nodded back instead and repeated her words. "Of course."

"You're skeptical. I can tell. But here's a fun tidbit for you. I was about to close up shop 'cause there's no way I can do business with this mess around, and most of my cash and carry stuff'll need a cleanup too. Something stopped me. And it was you."

"Me?"

"You're still skeptical. But hang on." Joanna ducked behind the counter, bent down again, then popped up, holding out a wrapped bag in her hands. "Here."

I took it automatically. "What is it?"

"Smell it," she ordered.

I lifted the bag, expecting that the aroma in the store to overwhelm whatever was inside. Instead, a light, honey scent wafted up. It made my mouth water.

"I think she'll like it," Joanna stated.

I started to ask who she meant, but the words didn't quite make it out. Whether she meant it as a general question, or if she was being deliberately enigmatic again was irrelevant. A name had already jumped into my head.

Mia Diaz.

I could far too easily picture her lathering up with the fragranced soap. I had no trouble imagining myself bending over her, running my nose over her skin to inhale the honey. My pants immediately tightened.

Christ.

"I'll take it," I told the shop owner.

"Of course you will," she said.

I rolled my eyes at her smugness, but dragged my wallet out and slapped down my credit card.

Less than two minutes later, I was back on the street, with the bag in my hand and Mia on my mind. I was fully aware that the turn of my thoughts went against the resolve to think of her as just another target. That didn't mean I could stop them from sticking in my mind. I decided quickly that I didn't care. It didn't even matter if I ever got to give the bag of soap to her. Just the thought that I'd picked it up was enough to make me smile as I strode toward Ella's Ristorante.

* * * *
Mia

I smiled and let out a fully fake laugh at something my brother said, then immediately braced for him to call me out on it. For all present to follow suit. But instead of brotherly concern turned my way, Marcelo brought his eyes to his bride-to-be. Clearly, she was more interesting than my obviously falsified humor. Which was a good thing. Normally, my too-astute family would've noticed if I was slightly off. They would've spent the last twenty minutes poking at me with nosy inquiries as they tried to discern an explanation. But right that second, they were immersed in the fact that Aysia's dress had arrived missing a pearl from the bodice. And for once, I was thankful for the way Marc and Aysia's wedding preoccupied everyone's minds. It provided a welcome diversion from the way my inner self couldn't stop pacing and ringing her hands over Ethan B. Burke.

Why hasn't he called? I wondered for the millionth time.

The question plagued me as much for the fact that I wanted an answer as it did for its very existence. I didn't want to care that I hadn't heard from him. And if I *had* to care, then I wanted it to be because I needed to know what I was up against. Honestly, worrying about that was enough. He'd made a threat-slash-promise to not give up, and I assumed he was going to follow up on it.

But when?

Really, I'd expected to find him and his self-assured glower sitting outside my store after work the day before. I'd even half prepared an angry speech. Then felt a touch deflated when I found the street devoid of Ethan. And ever since then, I'd been battling the on-edge feeling that kept me from being able to settle. I wasn't even sure I'd be able to eat the lunch I'd planned to order. I already felt full. Stuffed and uncomfortable.

"Lu?"

At the sound of my brother's voice, I looked up and forced yet another smile. "What?"

"Did you even *taste* that wine?" he teased.

I dropped my gaze to my glass. It was clutched in my hand. And empty. "I was thirsty," I said lamely.

Thankfully, everyone at the table laughed. But not so thankfully, the attention was on me now. My mom pursed her lips, and I knew a question was coming. One likely to make me feel awkward, judging by the look on her face.

And I wasn't wrong.

"Lumia," she said, "have you a hundred percent decided that you're not bringing a date to the wedding?"

I suppressed a groan, but I was thankful that it was at least a question I could answer. "I've told you no fewer than three hundred and eighty-two times that I'm not."

"Three hundred and eighty-two times?" my future sister-in-law echoed, sounding amused.

My mom ignored both of us. "It wouldn't have to be a *boyfriend*. Just a *date*."

I turned to my dad. "Aren't you going to tell her that your baby girl doesn't need a date?"

"I'm staying out of it," he replied.

"Seriously?" I said.

He shrugged. "Sorry, sweetheart. Your mom got to me before we even left the house."

I shot my brother an accusing look. "Let me guess. You too?"

"Even Liv is bringing someone," he said. "We all just kind of assumed you'd *want* a date, so we left the plus one as is."

"God. You're *all* in on it!" I shook my head in disgust. "Can a grown woman really not go to a wedding by herself?"

"Of course she can," my mother soothed.

"Unless she's *me*," I countered.

Aysia seemed to take pity on me, cutting in to say, "Speaking of dates... did I tell you guys that my cousin called and asked if she could bring both her boyfriend *and* her husband?"

The conversation steered away from me then, and I sighed and sat back. But instead of being able to relax, all I did was notice just how conspicuous the empty chair beside me was. For an irrational moment, I was annoyed at the restaurant for not taking it away. After all, we'd made the reservations for five people. Why leave the sixth chair? All it did was draw attention to the fact that I was alone.

Alone and lonely are not *the same thing*, I reminded myself.

In fact, I usually valued my independence. I'd fought for it. I'd won it. And now, a stupid wedding, and a stupid empty chair, and stupid one-night stand had me questioning it.

Great, I thought. *Now you're back to Ethan Burke. Can you really not go a minute without thinking about him?*

But suddenly—like he'd been ripped from my mind and deposited into Ella's Ristorante—there he was. Or to be more accurate, there was his laugh. The throaty, charming sound of it lifted through the air. And my gaze couldn't help but seek out the sound. It only took a second to find him. He stood just at the front of the restaurant, and he had his back to me, but I knew it was him. His tall, wide-shouldered form and thick, dark hair were unmistakable.

I blinked, thinking it—he—had to be a mirage. But he didn't disappear with the rapid flicking of my lids and lashes. If anything, he...solidified.

He wore yet another new suit, this one pale, pale blue. On anyone else, the color might've looked washed out. But when he turned just enough that I could see his profile, I could also see that it contrasted perfectly with his ruddy skin. The hint of scruff he'd had for the last two days was gone, revealing his strong jaw, which dropped open as he let out another laugh.

My eyes darted from him to the source of his amusement—a petite hostess who was looking up at him with unashamed interest. And I couldn't blame her. Ethan exuded strength. Wealth. Power. Confidence. I watched with narrowed eyes, vague irritation nipping at me, as the hostess led him across the dining room to a two-seater table. Not once did he look my way. And that bothered me even more. But not quite as much as it bothered me when he brought up his hand and set a small, silver gift bag on the table.

I *knew* that bag. Joyful Jo's. The little shop had a reputation for sensually stimulating scents, and seeing the familiarly wrapped item made my throat squeeze for some inexplicable reason. Why had Ethan gone in? And what had he bought there? Something for himself?

You really think he bought himself soap, had it gift wrapped, then brought it here?

I swallowed against a strange thickness in my throat, then shoved my chair back harder than necessary and excused myself to use the bathroom. But I only made it two steps before I realized that he might see me and approach me. And that would lead to an awful lot of questions from my family.

Deciding it was better not to leave a meeting to chance, I took a breath, swung in his direction, and reworked my path so that it'd take me past him. The closer I got, the dryer my mouth went and the more sweat beaded along my forehead. My heart hammered so hard that I was sure every patron around me could hear it. And the worst part was that it wasn't *dread* making me light-headed.

It was anticipation. Accompanied by an embarrassing need to hurry. So I forced myself to keep my eyes on the bag from Joyful Jo's and moved at a measured pace, silently counting off the rest of the tables between us.

Four.

Three.

Two.

O—

"Hello, Mia." Ethan spoke without turning around, and his voice—low and mildly amused—sent an unwanted shiver through me.

I flicked my gaze to the gift bag once more, then unbuckled my purse and deliberately dumped the contents on the floor beside him. "Whoops! Would you mind?"

He lifted an eyebrow, but slid from his chair and bent down on one knee anyway. "Everything all right?"

"Fine. Thanks so much for helping me out." I said it loudly and cheerily as I started to scoop up my scattered items, then dropped my voice for his ears only. "What are you doing here, Ethan?"

"Lunch," he replied easily.

"At the same restaurant as me?"

"Coincidence."

"Bullshit. And I'm here with my family. So if you're planning on making a scene to get your way…don't."

"I'm hardly that uncouth," he said.

I snorted. "You admitted to being a ruthless bastard, so…"

"I'm ruthless. I'm not a total douche."

"Right."

"Do you really think I'm a total douche?" He almost sounded hurt.

I couldn't help but soften. "No."

"Good."

He picked up my lip gloss—the last item on the floor—and held it out. I slid my fingers across to the tube, and his immediately enveloped mine, pinning them in place. Fighting the rapid pace of my pulse, I brought my eyes up to meet his. For a moment, the full force of his dark gaze hit me. I forgot all about the scented soap. But I remembered how his eyes looked in the dark in the throes of passion. How they consumed me as he had entered me without breaking our shared stare. I remembered how he'd wrapped his tongue around a rough and pleasant curse of approval. I remembered *him*. And I wanted all of it again. I could swear that if he'd reached for me right then and offered to press me to the ground and take me, I would've said yes. Screamed it, maybe.

Oh, God.

I took a slightly ragged breath and forced myself to remember something else—even if he *wasn't* a total douche, he was the enemy, and I wasn't *supposed* to want him.

I cleared my throat, tugged the lip gloss free, then stood so quickly that it almost made me dizzy, then planted a too-big smile on my face. "Thanks again.

I didn't run. Not quite. But my feet definitely carried me to the bathroom far faster than was natural.

Chapter 7

Ethan

Shit.

It was the only word that came to mind as Mia tossed her newly refilled purse over her shoulder and huffed her way across the dining room. The sway of her dress—a flirty, pink-and-purple flowered deal—showcased both her ass and her irritation.

Shit.

If I'd had a plan to stay cool, calm, and collected, it'd gone out the fucking window the second she got close enough for me to smell. Her scent had mingled perfectly with the honey-tinged soap in the little bag, giving me a hopeless hard-on and—*again*—making it impossible for me drop the speech I'd mentally prepared.

She was a plan wrecker. A destroyer of logical thought. And she was getting away.

Shit. Again.

Paying no mind to the whether or not anyone noticed, I shoved to my feet, grabbed the bag from Joyful Jo's, and pushed through the restaurant to follow her. I reached the edge of the little hallway where she'd disappeared just in time to see her slip through a door.

Somewhere in the back of my mind, I knew it had to be the bathroom. I didn't care. I stepped into the hall, slammed a hand to the same door, and shoved it open.

Eyes wide, Mia jumped back. Her ass smacked against the wall of the single-stall room, and her mouth dropped open.

"You can't be in here!" she gasped.

I clicked the lock shut behind me. "But I *am* in here."

"You can't intimidate me."

"Intimidation isn't a tactic I usually employ."

"So why follow me to the bathroom, then? Why show up at the restaurant in the first place?"

My mind blanked. Why the hell *had* I thought it would be a good to come? Lord knew stalking wasn't the best business tactic.

"Having trouble coming up with a reasonable lie?" she taunted.

I refused to let her know it was damned near the truth, and I held the gift bag out on my finger. "Maybe I came to give you *this*."

Her eyes flicked from me to the soap, then back again. "Bullshit."

"Is that your word of the day?"

"Where you're concerned."

"Is it so hard to believe that I bought you a gift?"

"Yes. And I think you should leave."

"Not until we've had a proper conversation," I said.

"I told you I don't want to talk," she replied. "Let me leave, or I'll scream."

I took a small step forward, and my eyes dropped to her lips. "I'm sure I can come up with a creative means of stopping you."

A blush lifted under her freckles. "You wouldn't dare."

"Try me."

I stepped closer again, noting how her breath quickened. *Dammit.* I wanted her to do it. It'd give me the excuse I needed to eliminate the space between us.

"Scream, Mia," I said, unembarrassed by the raw desire in my voice.

Her chest rose and fell a little more rapidly, and her gaze fell to my mouth, but she still shook her head. "So you can get your way?"

"My way involves a different kind of screaming," I replied. "But you know that already, don't you?"

"You're a bastard."

"So you keep saying."

"What do you *want*?"

You.

The answer popped into my head before I could stop it, and once it was there, I couldn't dismiss it. I *did* want her. Badly. My body ached with a distinct throb. It sure as hell wasn't something I could admit, though.

I forced myself to say something else instead. "What're you going to choose?"

She blinked. "What?"

"Are you going to scream and give me my way, or are you going to accept the gift?"

"I…"

"You what?"

She swallowed, her eyes finding the gift bag again. "I'm not taking a bribe."

"A scream it is, then," I replied.

She lifted her chin in a challenge. "So you admit that it's a bribe?"

I fought a chuckle at her slightly triumphant tone. "I told you. It's a gift."

"And *I* told *you*. I don't buy it."

"It's the truth," I said.

"Why?"

"Why is it the truth?"

"Why would you buy me a gift, other than to try to convince me to listen to you?"

I set the gift bag down on the edge of the sink, shook my head, and ran a frustrated hand over my hair. "It was an impulse."

"Joanna doesn't allow impulsive gifts," she said.

"You know her?"

"Everyone who works in the neighborhood knows her."

"Good. That means you can go in and confirm that my story is true. I impulsively walked in and impulsively bought what she offered."

Her gaze sought the bag yet again, and I realized something. She wanted it. She *really* wanted it, and she didn't even know what it was.

But for some reason, I couldn't make myself use it as a game piece.

"If Joanna sold it to me, then it really must be for you," I said softly. "Take it. No strings."

"Not a single one," she warned.

"I promise."

She stepped forward, scooped up the bag, and immediately lifted it to her nose. I watched, liking the way her eyes drifted half-shut as she inhaled. Liking even more how it brought her near enough that I could feel the warmth radiating from her body. I wanted to pull her even closer. To drag out the soap from the bag and hold it against her skin and tell her how I imagined the honey scent covering her, head to toe. How I wanted to taste it on her.

Why, oh why hadn't she chosen the damned scream?

I made myself take a little step away as I asked, "Any good?"

She offered me the smallest, tiniest, barest smile. "Very. Thank you."

"You're welcome."

"You know that this doesn't change anything."

"Not for me, either," I said. "I still want what I want."

"And I'm still not giving it to you," she informed me. "How long until you leave?"

"My flight goes out tomorrow, late evening."

A hint of disappointment seemed to flicker across her features, but she covered it quickly with another smile—this one wide and self-satisfied. "So. Does that mean you want me to ask my assistant store manager to draft up a copy of my complete schedule? It would save you the trouble of manually tracking me down."

I smiled back, just as smug. "Actually. Tracking you down is a point of pride."

"Aha."

"Aha, what?"

"That's the real reason you followed me here."

"Pride?"

"To prove that you could do it."

"And what good would that do? What would it prove?" I asked.

She lifted an eyebrow. "It would show me just how powerful you are."

"And did it work?"

"No. It just proved that you're easily distracted by shiny things." She waved the gift bag at me.

"Hilarious," I said dryly.

"I thought so. Now…if there's nothing else…" She moved as if to slip by me.

I grabbed her elbow and dragged her back before she could close her fingers on the door. I expected her to yank herself away and push past. I wouldn't have blamed her for doing it. Except she didn't. What she did do was stop right where she was—no more than an inch or two between us—and lifted her eyes to meet mine. And I was lost. Drowning in that sweet stare.

Power? You have none. Not a modicum, I chastised myself silently. *You don't stand a fucking chance, Burke.*

"Mia…" My voice was raw again, and I didn't care.

She didn't pull her gaze away. "Yes?"

"Are you still going to scream if I stop you from leaving?"

"Why don't you try it and find out."

"Maybe I will."

I gave her elbow a little tug. She tugged back. The only result was that instead of having a hairsbreadth of space between us, we had none. Her full, tempting breasts pressed to my chest as her inhales and exhales quickened. And my erection thickened to the point of painful.

"No scream yet," she breathed.

"Give me a second," I countered. "Trapping women in bathrooms is a relatively new endeavor for me."

"Relatively?"

"Fine. A brand-new skill." I bent my mouth to her ear. "But I don't usually admit my virginity so easily."

I pulled away so I could slide my hand up to her bare shoulder, then lifted my other hand to the same position on the other side. I took a step forward, and she had no choice but to either back up or be bowled over. In a heartbeat, I had her pressed to the locked door.

"Gonna be tough for you get out now," I said.

She arched a brow. "And still..."

"No screaming," I filled in.

"I guess you'll have to try harder?"

"Actually...I don't know if it *gets* any harder than this."

"What do you—*oh!*"

She gasped out the last bit as I grabbed her hand and slid it to my lust-thick cock. I let her palm rest there for a long moment, enjoying the way her fingers tightened around me. I leaned in to the first little stroke, muttering a curse at the fact that my pants were in the way of a true touch.

It was the best kind of torture.

But strangely, not what I was in the mood for, so I slid my fingers over her knuckles and dragged her hand up to my shoulder.

Mia tipped her face up, a little frown creasing her forehead. "Is something wrong?"

I touched my lips to hers in a ghost of a kiss. "I said I was giving you a gift with no strings."

"Me touching you is...a string?"

"You touching me is fucking amazing. But I don't want any misunderstanding. I gave you that soap and I didn't expect anything in return."

A sweet, sexy little laugh escaped her lips. "Does that qualify as pillow talk in your books?"

I moved my hands to the knee-length hem of her dress and inched it up.

"No," I said. "But it sure as shit qualifies as shove you against a bathroom door and put my tongue between your legs talk."

I didn't wait for her to react. I just dropped to my knees and did what I'd just promised.

* * * *

Mia

For about ten seconds—the same amount of time it took for Ethan to kiss his way up one of my thighs—I questioned my sanity. Strings or bribes or no, having oral sex in a bathroom wasn't high up on my to-do list.

For about ten seconds more—the same amount of time it took Ethan to move to the other thigh—I reasoned that I *wasn't* giving in to *him*. I was giving in to my own physical needs. Which was a good thing. Far, far too good.

Another ten seconds—the same amount of time it took Ethan to flick his tongue along the lacy edge of my underwear—was all I had to think about it at all. Because honestly...how much thinking could I be expected to do when an undeniably skilled man had his mouth working over my most intimate places? And it *was* working.

"Oh, God!" I gasped as his tongue found its way *under* the lace and took its first taste of me.

At my exclamation, Ethan made a small noise—a pleased little hum that vibrated straight through me. My hips thrust forward, begging for more. And he gave it to me. For a moment. *Lick-suck-lick.* Then he paused.

Torment, I thought, my hands balling into desperate fists.

"Ethan." His named slipped out as a plea, and he brought his mouth to me again.

Lick-lick-suck. Slooooooow lick. Pause.

"You taste good," he murmured, his breath hot on my skin.

Lick-nibble-suck. Another pause.

"Wet and sweet," he added.

And I realized the torment was on purpose, fully intended to drive me insane with want.

Suck-suck-nibble-lick. Break.

"And these panties. Always thought I was into black lace. But I'm damned sure purple is my new favorite color."

Lick-circle-lick-lick. P—

My hands unfurled and whipped up to land on his head.

"Don't," I begged.

Lick. "Don't?" *Suck-suck.* "Or don't stop?" *Lick.*

"Yes," I moaned.

"Which one?" he teased.

"Please, Ethan. Don't stop."

"All right, baby."

And—blissfully—he ceased his teasing.

He swore in that reverent, under-his-breath way that he had, and his fingers came up to push away my underwear and join the sensuous dance of his tongue. Together, they circled my clit, driving my want higher. My breaths echoed off the walls, and my hands pulled so hard on his thick hair that I knew I had to be hurting him. But I couldn't stop grasping him. I needed to hold on. To anchor myself and prolong the pleasure. It was like riding along the edge of bumpy cliff, knowing full well that the rush was going to crescendo any moment. The high could only get so high before it crashed. Before *I* crashed. And I was getting closer by the ragged-breath second.

And when his finger plunged into me, I knew I was done. As he stroked me—in-out, in-out—and circled his tongue over my clit—around-and-down, around-and-up—my body exploded in heat. Wave after dizzying wave of climactic throbs rolled through me as Ethan clamped his mouth and hand down on me.

Dear God.

It was the orgasm by which to measure every other orgasm from here on out.

I said his name again. Or tried to. What actually came out of my mouth was a mushy, garbled mess that made him chuckle against my still-pulsing sex. It should've been embarrassing. The laugh. My quickness. Our location. Instead, it was just hot. And as Ethan released me and slid up my body, I felt an incredible need to make sure he felt the same way. No strings be damned. I was happy to reciprocate. But before I could even get my hands as far as his belt, a knock on the door froze me in place.

"Lu? Are you in there?" My brother's voice carried in, his tone just shy of deeply concerned.

"Crap," I muttered.

"Lu?" Marc called again.

Ignoring the slightly amused look on Ethan's face, I pushed him away and stepped back from the door so as to answer from a more reasonable space in the bathroom.

"I'm here," I called back, turning on the tap for emphasis. "Just washing my hands."

"Are you okay? You've been in there a while."

"What are you? My personal bathroom clock?"

His sigh was audible through the door. "Hardly. Mom sent me."

"She sent *you* to the ladies' bathroom?"

"She said you'd be annoyed if *she* came and embarrassed if *Aysia* did."

"And you're *less* annoying and embarrassing?" I countered.

He sighed again, even more noisily. "I basically drew the short straw. Just tell me you're not dying, give me an excuse, then offer an ETA for me to take back to Mom."

"Fine," I said. "My ETA is two minutes. I'm not dying."

"And the excuse? 'Cause you know Mom'll want one."

"I don't *need* an excuse. I wasn't in here the whole time. I got...distracted on the way. By a...business associate."

If Marc noted my hesitant and seemingly obvious lie, he didn't say. "Okay. So long as you're sure you're all right."

"Better than all right."

Ethan let out a muffled laugh, and I shot him a warning look. But thankfully, Marc didn't appear to have heard him.

"You want me to wait?" Marc asked through the door.

"That would be exceedingly weird," I replied.

"Yeah. I suppose. See you back at the table."

I waited until the thud of my brother's shoes signaled that he'd disappeared up the hall and into the restaurant, then opened my attention to Ethan.

He wore a devilish grin, and he spoke before I could. "Distracted?"

I blew out a breath. "What would you have said?"

"I dunno. 'Sorry. I was on the receiving end of my business associate's tongue'?" he suggested.

"Right. And then, *you* would've been on the receiving end of my brother's fist. Which I suspect wouldn't be quite as pleasant."

"But the rest of it *was* pleasant?"

"Yes."

"*Only* pleasant?" he teased.

I rolled my eyes. "Don't pretend to be less arrogant than you are."

"Arrogance implies an inflated sense of self-worth," he said good-naturedly. "I'm just confident."

"You know that there's a line between confident and cocky, right?"

His eyes glinted lasciviously. "Cocky, hmm?"

I snorted. "Subtle."

"That's one thing I never am." His eyes traveled the length of my body, then came to rest on my face, a surprising hint of softness making its way into his gaze as he added, "But I *was* aiming to please."

Warmth tingled through me far more easily than I wanted it to. "You did."

"But nothing's changed."

"No."

"And you need to get back to your family lunch."

"I do."

"You sure that's what you want?"

"Yes."

Except it was a lie. What I wanted to do was back *him* to the door. Unbuckle that belt of his. Drop to *my* knees, and—

"I have to go," I said abruptly.

He gestured toward the door. "Go ahead. I promise not to scream."

"Funny."

"Mia."

I'd started to reach for the door, but my name on his lips stopped me. As much as I wished I could ignore him, I couldn't. "Yes?"

"See me again tonight," he said.

"I think that would be a very bad idea."

"Don't trust yourself to be alone with me?"

I shook my head. "I don't trust myself with you in a roomful of people."

His mouth twitched. "A compliment that feels like an insult."

"Sorry."

I reached for the door a second time, and for a second time his voice stopped me. "What if I dare you to do it?"

I frowned. "What?"

"What if I dare you to go out with me...like your friend dared you to kiss me?"

"It wasn't *you* she dared me to kiss," I reminded him. "It was the next attractive man I saw."

"Who turned out to be me," he stated.

"Not the point."

"So you won't take my dare?"

"It doesn't work like that."

"Why not? Have you got a one dare per week limit?"

"One per decade." The words were out before I could stop them.

Both his eyebrows went up. "Sounds like there's a story there."

If I could've kicked myself for piquing his curiosity, I would have. "Maybe there is. But it's not one I'm inclined to share with men in bathrooms."

"Are there a lot of us?"

"One too many. I really have to go, Ethan."

This time, I *did* manage to reach past him then unlocked the door. But I only made it two steps into the hall before he caught up and stopped me yet again, this time with his hand on my arm.

"What if I promise that it's not about business," he said.

I met his eyes. "Are you saying you don't want Trinkets and Treasures anymore?"

"No. I'm not saying that."

"Then it would still be about business. The fact that you want to steal my company out from under me would be hanging over us."

"I don't want to *steal it*," he said.

"You want to buy it, and I don't want to sell it. It boils down the same thing," I argued.

"That's not an accurate—"

A throat clearing cut him off, and I fought a groan as my future sister-in-law issued a greeting. "Hey, Lu. Everything all right?"

"Fine!" I nearly snapped. "Did my mom send you too?"

Aysia's gaze dropped to Ethan's hand on my elbow. "*Should* she have sent me?"

I swallowed and shook off his grip with all the subtlety of a walrus jumping from a diving board into a wading pool. "I'm perfectly capable of coming and going on my own."

"And of being accosted by handsome strangers," Aysia said, eyeing Ethan with interest.

He smiled his charmingly crooked half-smile. "I'm neither accosting nor a stranger. E. B. Burke. A potential business associate of Mia's."

"Notice that he didn't say he wasn't *handsome*," I muttered.

They both ignored me.

"I'm Aysia," said my future sister-in-law. "Did you say business? Are you into jewelry too?"

Ethan's smile widened. "Shiny things in general, actually."

I fought a groan. And it only got worse.

"Are you in a business meeting here at Ella's?" Aysia asked.

"Nope." Ethan's mouth twitched even more. "Just in for a pure pleasure lunch. I was just getting ready to order."

"Were you eating alone?"

"I was."

"Not anymore," Aysia told him firmly. "We have an extra seat. Join us."

And before I could muster up a logical protest, the man who'd just spent several very long, whole-body-shuddering minutes with his mouth sliding along underneath my still-wet panties was on his way to meeting my whole damned family.

Chapter 8

Ethan

If someone had handed me a Tuesday itinerary that looked like this, I would've read it over and laughed. Hard and long. No innuendo intended. First, I would've chortled at the suggestion that I might start a Tuesday by buying soap for a woman. Then I would've really let it rip at the idea that the same woman might be coming against my mouth one minute, then eating lunch with me and her family the next. In fact, after laughing my ass off, I'm sure I would've simply told the person holding the itinerary to get the fuck out. Because it was ridiculous.

Yet it was all true, and here I was.

Soap? Check.

Taste of Mia on my lips? Check, check.

Diaz family introducing themselves, one by one? Check, check. Check.

It all seemed a little surreal.

Because apparently it's easier to accept that you went down on Mia in the bathroom than it is to accept having a meal with her family?

I scoffed at the self-directed question, but as we ordered our lunch and the conversation turned to what I did for work, I had to admit that it was true. Maybe a *little* because discussing the inner workings of my business with strangers wasn't something I did. Maybe a *lot* because explaining it to the family of a woman whose leg kept brushing mine under the table—unintentional but distracting as hell—should've been out of the question. Yet somehow, I found myself doing it with Mia's father anyway. Enjoying it, even.

Of course, enjoying it didn't change the fact that the whole time we spoke, I had what was starting to feel like a permanent, half-mast erection. Each accidental tap of Mia's knee against mine drew attention to it, reminding me of how badly I wanted her and driving me a little crazier each second.

He'd ask an innocuous question like, "So you and your assistant in the office, and everyone else working virtually? Must save a lot on overhead."

Then Mia's knee would bump mine, her warmth seeping through for a heartbeat.

I'd try to answer in a calm voice. "Saves a lot of headache, and I care more about that than about overhead, but yes. I offer full-time and part-time packages, decent benefits, and a flexible schedule. My people can set their own hours, and all that matters to me is that their tasks are done right, and that they're done on time."

Then Mia would exhale, her breath making my skin tingle.

It went on like that for the whole damned meal, leaving me in an incomprehensibly contradictory position.

On the one hand, I genuinely wanted to carry on the dialogue. I couldn't remember the last time I'd just sat down and told someone about how I did things at Burke Holdings. At least, not without assuming the person on the other end had some agenda for wanting to know. Mr. Diaz—and the rest of Mia's family, actually—seemed genuinely interested.

On the other hand, the ache in my cock battled with the simple pleasure of conversation. I kind of wanted to tell them all to shut the hell up so I could do something about it. A quick, hard fuck in the already christened bathroom. Though judging from the murderous looks I was receiving periodically from Mia, I knew it was far more likely that I'd be heading back to my hotel room solo. Left to find my own release as I fantasized about the way I knew she felt underneath me.

Except it didn't play out like that at all.

At some point during the meal—maybe when Mia got her stir fry bowl, and her mother stopped the server to check if there were bean sprouts in it, because Mia was allergic, or maybe when her brother asked her about a car repair that was taking a little too long, and offered to "chat" with the mechanic—I became aware of a dynamic in the family that struck me as odd.

Not that it was any of my damned business. Or that I had anything more than two days of experience with Mia to give me reason to comment on it.

But every one of them—Mr. and Mrs. Diaz, meat-fisted Marcelo Diaz, and even Aysia Not-Quite-Diaz—seemed to see Mia as someone they had to protect. When another patron knocked her chair as he passed, and Mia spilled her wine, I thought the whole table might have an apoplexy trying to get her a napkin.

They definitely weren't condescending about it, or even visibly conscious. I didn't like them any less because of it, either. If anything, the behavior was almost endearing. In fact, it might've been *completely* endearing if it wasn't strange as hell. Their view of her was totally at odds with the woman who'd kissed me under a tree without having a clue who I was. Even though I'd only met her two days ago, I already knew just how tough she was. How in charge and in control, even when she was surrendering.

The weirdest part about it all came when I realized her father had no clue just how successful Trinkets and Treasures was. Mia made an offhand remark about the cost of some pair of shoes, and Mr. Diaz actually reached for his wallet. She had to talk him out of giving her a stack of cash.

As the little argument unfolded, my mouth dropped open, a question on my lips. The only thing that stopped it from slipping out was the way Mia's hand very abruptly landed on my knee. In fact, I just about *choked* on the words, and my eyes automatically tipped her way. She gave me the smallest headshake. A warning. And the look in her eyes was a plea for silence.

Which made me realize that she knew—at the very least—how her father perceived her. Likely how the others did too. And Mia didn't want to draw attention to it.

A dozen questions flitted to mind, and I couldn't ask a single one. Not just because she was clearly asking me not to, but also because of the way her hand *stayed* on my knee. Warm. Beyond distracting. Moving back and forth in just the right way to make me crazy.

My eyes flicked around the group, trying to discern if anyone had noticed the intimate contact.

I had zero problem imagining her big, dark-haired brother diving across the table to knock my teeth out. Or her dad for that matter. Maybe her mom or Aysia might like to stab me with a fork. For all I knew, the two women were more protective than the men. At that moment, though, I didn't have to worry about their murderous ways. They were too immersed in their own conversation—back to the all-consuming wedding—to pay attention to me. To Mia and her erection-inducing touch. So I just lifted my glass and took a sip, trying to cool the flow of blood to my crotch with the chilled liquid on my tongue.

Of course, the cooling didn't happen. If anything, my need for her only spiraled higher. Hotter. That wasn't surprising. What did catch me off guard, though, was the secondary warmth. It started in the middle of my chest and quickly bloomed out, not quite overshadowing my lust, but giving it a run for its money. The feeling prodded me to slide my own hand under the table to grasp hers and give it a reassuring squeeze. If she didn't want her family to know she saw how they were babying her, then I wouldn't be the one to give it away.

Reading my gesture perfectly, Mia shot me another look, this one grateful. Then she released my hand and resumed her part in the discussion at the table. As her family argued good-naturedly over seating arrangements for Marc and Aysia's fast-approaching wedding—even laughingly asking me if *I* thought someone named Aunt Wanda would throw a fit if she had to sit beside cousin Freddy—my desire for Mia tapered off to a dull roar. There and ready, but in the background now. I couldn't say the same for the other warmth. It was still thumping in time with my heart. Still making my smile hang on my lips, even when there was no good reason for it to be there. It was all well and good until I figured out *why*. Which took me a stupidly long time, actually.

I made it through the end of lunch. Through what was apparently a Diaz family tradition of each person choosing a dessert, then the whole table sharing bite-sized pieces. Even through a slow round of coffees.

It wasn't until I sat back with my mug in hand, that it hit me.

I liked every damned thing about my insane Tuesday itinerary. Buying the soap with Mia in mind. Following Mia to the bathroom and using that small space to my advantage. Sitting with Mia and her family, and knowing I was carrying a secret for her, however small.

Then, as I took a satisfying slurp of my coffee, Mia's honeyed gaze came my way. She was laughing at something her brother had said, but the muted heat in her eyes was all for me. The same heat *I* had banked. I wondered if she felt the other warmth too. I hoped she did. And it *really* hit me.

It's not the crazy Tuesday you like, you idiot. *What you like is* her. *Mia Diaz.*

And like a giant chickenshit, I panicked. I excused myself to use the bathroom, then hid in the hall beside it instead.

Logically, I knew I was being ridiculous. Of course I liked Mia. If I hadn't, I sure as hell wouldn't have spent the night with her. It had to be all the other family shit that got to me. The laughs and private jokes. The genuine enjoyment of each other's company, and worse…how they made me feel like a part of it without knowing a damned thing about me. The last bit made my palms sweaty.

How the fuck could I possibly conduct a normal business transaction with her?

For the first time in the ten years since I'd first come up with the idea for Burke Holdings, I questioned whether I was making the right decision. The self-doubt made the chickenshit-ness spread like a rash.

Slowly—knowing completely what a jackass I was being—I took a cautious step back into the dining area. Mia and her family were engrossed in one another, so I made a stealthy move toward our server, quickly picked up the whole tab, then took a breath and yanked my phone from my pocket and stuck it to my ear. Feigning a work call, I moved toward the Diazes. I mouthed what I hoped was a sincere apology, then cut out of the restaurant so fast that a cartoon blur probably followed in my wake.

* * * *

Mia

I was mad. Punch something mad. Insides coiled up and ready to explode mad. And it made no sense. Ethan had been nothing but nice to my family. He'd been nothing but nice to *me*. And paying for the entire lunch? It was unexpected and generous. And it annoyed me to no end. In fact, it made my insides pucker with sour irritation that hung on. Long after the meal was done. Long after I'd gone by my store to finish off the day, and even long after I'd taken what was supposed to be a relaxing bath.

Even now, as I flopped down on my couch in my pj's, I couldn't help but give the clock below the TV a glare. It was near eight o'clock, and I knew Ethan had to be boarding his plane about now. Likely in first class. Maybe with one of those little eye covers over his face. I could picture him being the do-not-disturb type on a plane.

"Right," I muttered, viciously driving my finger into the remote control to change the channels. "And if I were sitting next to him, I'd snap the elastic on the side of his mask just to spite him."

After a few more seconds of searching in vain for something to watch, I gave up on the TV and decided just to sit and stew.

My parents had liked Ethan. Aysia had too. Even Marcelo had grunted a grudging acknowledgement that they'd had a good time talking about their shared interest in sustainable resources.

And truthfully, I'd enjoyed having him in the otherwise empty seat at our table. He fit.

Even when he was talking in earnest about his company, and how it all worked, I felt comfortable. I'd been surprised at how forthcoming he was, actually, and found myself listening intently, curious about the process. In my head, he was a ruthless product hunter. A destroyer of small businesses.

I hated that I was impressed, and I hated that I could see how he'd become as successful as he was.

The Ethan who laughed when my dad told him about how, as a toddler, I'd plugged one of our toilets with a rubber duck? That guy was a long way off from the man who'd sent me the demanding emails. The one who'd refused to take no for an answer. That guy hadn't made me smile. He *wouldn't* have made me smile. Or made me warm from the inside out as he caught on to the way my family tiptoed around me and kept his mouth shut about it.

I pinched the bridge of my nose between my fingers and tried to steer my mind in another direction. It was impossible. My brain wanted to analyze every detail. To write a compare and contrast essay. Or to jot down a list. Email Ethan versus In-person Ethan.

"Who wore it better?" I murmured with a self-directed eye roll.

But then I paused. Why *not* make a list? I mean, sure. It might not serve any real purpose. After all, Ethan was already on his way back to Toronto. And that kind of meant I won already. But the frothy anger didn't show any sign of dissipating, and the thought of putting my feelings down somewhere had an undeniable appeal. It was organized and logical. Just how I liked things.

And it might even be therapeutic, I decided as I reached for my laptop.

But when I punched in my password and saw my email open and waiting, I couldn't quite stop myself from doing something else instead. I clicked through to the blocked senders list and found Ethan's name. I highlighted it. Then clicked again. Right away, every deleted email came up in their own little window. I bit my lip a little guiltily and tapped one at random.

To: mdiaz@trinketsandtreasures.com
From: ebburke@burkeholdings.com
Subject: Meeting

Dear Ms. Diaz,

It appears that we've somehow got off on the wrong foot. I truly think you're making a mistake in not hearing me out. Could we schedule something on the phone?

E. B. Burke.

I read it. Then reread it. The words didn't change, obviously. But they didn't sting the way they had when I first read them, either. I narrowed my eyes and looked for something more.

More what? But I answered my own silent question as quickly as I asked it. *More likely to have made you throw a mug?*

I distinctly recalled it was the *third* time he'd told me I'd made a mistake. It was one of the last ones to come through before I set his address to bounce, and it was also one that'd tipped my temper over the edge. And it was only three lines long.

Feeling a need to justify my reaction—both then and now—I flipped back to the list of emails. I clicked another, this one farther up. I scanned it quickly, pleased to find that it was longer winded, and far easier to see as an insult. It talked about my lack of experience and lack of reach. About how much more Burke Holdings could do for me than I could do for myself. High-handed. That's what it was. And it made me feel a little better about my current, riled-up state.

But that's not really why you're mad, are you?

I admitted to myself that it was true. While I still had zero interest in selling my business to Ethan, the emails and the demands weren't responsible for my agitation now. This was something else entirely.

Frustrated, I started to shove the laptop closed. But my elbow bumped the arm of the couch, and instead of shutting the computer, I accidentally opened up a reply window. I only stared at it for a second before my fingers started flying over the keyboard, drafting a letter that I had no intention of ever sending.

It took me a good twenty minutes, but I outlined everything that made me seethe. The bitterness at being assumed to be a bad businesswoman. The way sleeping with him felt like a deception, even though I was a hundred percent sure it wasn't purposeful. How annoyed I was at myself for being glad he followed me into the bathroom. The fact that he'd charmed my family, and pulled me under the same spell. And how he'd more or less walked out without a word, paying for the meal like some kind of consolation prize.

The jerk.

When I was done writing, I actually *did* feel a little better. Not perfect, but at least like a small weight had been lifted. But as I sat back to read over what I'd written, my heart sank. Because I knew the truth. While everything in the letter was honest, it was really the very last thing that upset me the most.

Why did he leave like that?

I didn't buy the whole emergency-at-work excuse. Sure, he could've had one. But I couldn't believe that—even *with* an emergency in play—E. B. Burke would just walk away from a deal he wanted so badly. A deal he'd been willing to travel across the country to get. At the very least, it seemed like he should've threatened to follow up. Maybe stalked me to my two-bedroom rancher and sat outside my house sending in hostile takeover vibes.

I sneaked a glance out the window. My street was devoid of vibes. Almost disappointingly so.

Fighting an uncomfortable, itchy ache in my throat, I turned my attention back to the letter. I highlighted everything except the last bit, then made myself type again. This time, it only took two minutes. And while every word in the other letter was true, the new shorter one felt far more authentic.

To: ebburke@burkeholdings.com
From: mdiaz@trinketsandtreasures.com
Subject: re: Meeting

Ethan,

I just wrote you a two-page email full of the reasons I resent you. Why I can't stand you. Why you made me throw a mug. Then I deleted it all. Because I don't hate you. I barely know you. But I'm still sure that if I were being really honest, I'd have admit that what I do know...it makes me like you quite a bit. And I'm sad that you left, because I wouldn't have minded getting to like you even more.

Lu.

It was a simple email. To the point. Maybe a little embarrassing in that it was a grown woman's crush confession. But it did the job. My anger was gone. Morphed into disappointment and intensifying the ache in my throat.

I swallowed, trying to rid myself of the feeling, and reached across the keyboard to hit delete. But just as my finger hit the right spot, a faraway siren wailed to life, startling me. My hand jerked, and the keyboard clicked where the soft part of my palm hit it. And all I could do was stare down in horror as the email flew off to Ethan's inbox.

Chapter 9

Ethan

Normally, the mid-conversation ping of an incoming notification on my cell phone would've annoyed me. Right then, I welcomed it as an excuse to hurry along the argument with my assistant—who clearly thought I'd been abducted by aliens and replaced with a pod person—so I could get my way and hang up. My headache was bad enough without adding something else to the mix.

"Julie, I need to move this along," I said. "I've got a message coming in, and at this time of night, it could be urgent. So if you could just take care of the rebooking, I'd appreciate it."

"I'm still confused, Mr. Burke," she replied, her tone agreeing heartily with her statement.

"I can tell," I replied dryly.

"Did you really miss your flight?"

"You already asked me that, and I already answered you."

"I know. But…"

"But what?"

"You missed your flight!" The words burst into my ear, and I gritted my teeth.

I didn't need the reminder. I'd been stunned enough by the fact when I woke up an hour *after* I should've boarded.

Though maybe I should've expected it.

After I'd run out of the restaurant—far more embarrassing than missing my flight—things had gone steadily downhill for me. As much as I'd worked at ridding my thoughts of Mia Diaz, it seemed to be an impossible task.

The simple acknowledgement of *liking* her had been enough to throw me for a huge goddamned loop, apparently.

I'd actually had to physically remove myself from her little corner of Vancouver just to stop myself from sitting outside her shop. I'd paid a town car driver an insane amount of money to drive me to Stanley Park, where I'd wallowed in the soggy trees for a few hours. The rain had suited my miserable mood well anyway. What it hadn't done, though, was help me sort through any of my contradictory thoughts.

When I was sure Mia had to have gone home for the day, I had the car take me to Trinkets and Treasures. I sat outside, staring at the building for a good twenty minutes before coming to my senses. If heading back to the Memory Motel could be called coming to my senses. There, I'd used my phone to search out her home address. Good stalker that I was. I'd stopped just shy of calling the town car back so I could do a creepy drive-by.

Finally, I reached a decision. I'd fly home. Regroup. Get my shit together. Going home, spending some time in the comfort of my own office…it would get Mia Diaz out of my system and give me the recharge I needed. In a few days, I'd come back to Vancouver and pursue Trinkets and Treasures with as much zeal as I pursued everything else. After all, I'd only known Mia for two days. That wasn't long enough for someone to occupy so much space in my head.

When I got back to the Memory Motel, though, she'd plagued me again. Her head on the pillow. Her speckled skin wrapped in the sheets. Her body beneath me.

Every time I closed my eyes—even for a goddamned blink—she seemed to be there. In fact, when I'd lay back on the bed to take a breather, her full lips and tempting freckles were the last thing I saw before jolting awake—erection back in full force—and realizing the time.

I'd cursed my cock for having a mind of its own. Cursed my dreams for being full of red hair. Then cursed myself for being so weak.

What made you think it'd be that easy to block her out? I chided. *Nothing else about this particular venture has been simple.*

"Mr. Burke, are you still there?"

Julie's voice in my ear made my eyes fly open, and I forced my attention back to the phone.

"It can happen," I replied through gritted teeth.

"What?"

"Missing a flight. It can happen."

"Not to you."

I refused to admit that I'd been thinking the same thing for the last two hours. "Except it did."

"Mr. Burke…"

"Yes, Julie?"

"Is something else wrong?" she asked.

"What could possibly be wrong?" I said back.

Her voice dropped low. "Did you get arrested or something? Because I can call your lawyer."

I let out an exasperated sigh. "I didn't get arrested, Julie, and I don't want my lawyer. I just need a new flight for tomorrow."

"But you *never* need a flight rebooked," she persisted.

I almost laughed. Apparently, it was easier to accept I might be out committing crimes than it was to accept that I'd screwed up.

I made myself keep the chuckle in. "I never rebook flights. I never miss them. I never call you at home, or wake you up in the middle of the night. Not once in six years have I done these things. But I'm doing them now."

"Mr. Burke—"

"Do I need to call the goddamned airline myself?" I snapped, then immediately felt guilty, and took a breath. "Sorry. I'm not trying to be a complete ass here. And if it's really inconvenient for you, I *will* do it myself. Just tell me one way or the other. Please."

There was utter silence on the other end.

"Julie?" I prodded after a second.

"You never apologize." She sounded genuinely concerned now.

Add that to the fucking list, I thought, while aloud I said, "Maybe all the rain here in Vancouver's washed away some of the misery."

"You're not miserable."

"No need for sugarcoating. I know what people think of me."

"People?" she repeated.

I sighed, wondering if maybe *Julie* had been replaced by a pod person. While she usually didn't mind sharing her opinion if asked, she never fought with me. She was hardworking and discreet. Unflappable in the face of my tendency to be a bossy asshole of a boss. She didn't question my decisions, or call me out on the rare occasion that one of them went awry. She was the perfect assistant. Normally.

"Mr. Burke? Are you—"

"I'm fine, Julie. I'm just not infallible. I was distracted today by a… business matter."

Do you even believe that yourself?

I ground my teeth together, and added, "Things are back on track. Or they will be. Once I have my flight rebooked."

At last, she seemed to snap out of her astonishment at my mistake, and her normal efficiency took over. "Right. I'll do it now. Do you want to stick with the next red-eye?"

I fought an urge to tell her to get me the hell out as soon as possible, and instead said, "I think my preferences are on hold. Whatever direct flight is available. Business class."

"Of course."

"Just give me enough time to get some sleep tonight."

"I will. Do you need me to speak with the hotel?"

"No," I said quickly. "It's fine."

"You're sure?" she replied.

I cast a glance around my room at the Memory Motel. I could swear that Mia's lightly perfumed scent still clung to the air. I liked it. Even if switching to the Regent *was* an option, I wouldn't take it. I sure as hell wasn't going to confess any of that to Julie, though. And I didn't need her finding out on her own by mistakenly trying to extend my stay at the Regent.

"I'm here already," I told her. "I'll take care of it."

"All right," she said. "Not too early, then. I'll email you the details in a few minutes."

"Thank you."

There was a pause on the other end, and then she hesitantly said, "Mr. Burke?"

"Yes?" I braced myself for a query on whether or not I'd recently suffered a head injury.

Instead, she spoke in a rush. "I don't know what you believe people think of you, but I've never heard anyone call you miserable. Tough, yes. Unapologetic and driven, yes. But you're a fair boss, and everyone down the chain thinks so. I'll see you when you get back."

There was a click on the end, and I was left frowning at my phone. I knew my employees bowed to my will, but I'd always assumed it was out of fear rather than respect. A ruthless bastard. Wasn't that how they saw me? It was sure as hell how I saw myself. How I aimed to be, even.

"Seriously, Burke," I said aloud to the room. "One damned night, one damned bathroom quickie, and you're questioning who you are? Julie probably just wants a raise."

Maybe I'll even give her one. Once I've acquired Trinkets and Treasures, profits should increase more than enough to give her a bump.

I moved to toss the phone onto the nightstand before remembering about the notification. I debated for the briefest second ignoring whoever it was, then decided I might as well deal with it now instead of waiting for the morning. It wasn't as though I was just going to drift off to sleep easily.

I tapped the screen. Immediately, the email app came to life. Mia's name was highlighted across the top, and I couldn't deny that more than a tickle of pleasure slipped in at seeing it. I couldn't tamp it down, either. Not even when I reminded myself that I was trying *not* to think of her in any way but professional. She'd gone out of her way to block my emails. Which meant she'd now made an effort to *un*block them.

Curious—and admittedly also a little eager—I clicked on the message. My brows clenched together as I read her words. They had a confessional tone. A grudging one too. She *liked* me. But she wasn't happy about it.

So why tell me at all? I wondered. *Especially since she thinks I'm on my way home?*

I tapped the phone against my thigh, trying to come up with a reasonable explanation for it. I read the note again. She'd called herself Lu, as well, when she'd made it damned clear I shouldn't refer to her by her nickname.

"What would make *me* send someone a message like that?" I mused aloud.

Then an excuse for it occurred to me, and I typed up a quick reply.

To: mdiaz@trinketsandtreasures.com
From: ebburke@burkeholdings.com
Subject: re: re: Meeting

Hello LU.

One question before I address your concerns. Have you been drinking?

Ethan.

I didn't have to wait long for her answer. In fact, it came so soon that I almost wondered if she'd been sitting there, waiting for me to reply.

To: ebbburke@burkeholdings.com
From: mdiaz@trinketsandtreasures.com
Subject: re: re: re: Meeting

No!
And I don't have any concerns. Seriously. Just forget it.

M.

I smiled, then started a new email thread, just for the sake of being self-indulgently funny.

To: mdiaz@trinketsandtreasures.com
From: ebburke@burkeholdings.com
Subject: Methinks...

L.

Thou doth protest a LITTLE too much.

E.

Again, the reply came fast.

To: ebbburke@burkeholdings.com
From: mdiaz@trinketsandtreasures.com
Subject: re: Methinks

Very funny. I sent you that email by accident. So you can ignore it. And stop calling me Lu. That was a typo.

MIA.

I whipped up another message.

To: mdiaz@trinketsandtreasures.com
From: ebburke@burkeholdings.com
Subject: Who spells her own name wrong?

L.

Not anyone I know. Oh. Wait.

E.

This time, I didn't wait for her to answer. Instead, I went back to her
first message. I hit reply, then addressed it line by line, smiling widely
as I typed.

To: mdiaz@trinketsandtreasures.com
From: ebburke@burkeholdings.com
Subject: re: re: Meeting

Lu,

*I'm both flattered and concerned that you had two pages' worth
of material to use in your resentment of me. I'm also worried
that you can't stand me so much that you're breaking your own
dishes. Maybe try staying away from all fragile objects for the
time being?*

*I'm kind of glad you didn't "accidentally" send me the deleted
material, though. You know how fragile my ego is.*

*I don't hate you either. As weird as it might sound, I feel a bit
like I DO know you. You're smart and beautiful. You love your
family enough that you're willing to let them treat you like
one of those fragile dishes you so carelessly toss around. (I'm
genuinely interested in hearing the story behind that, by the
way. So I guess you could say I agree. I'd like to know you a
little better too.)*

Ethan.

*P.S. Try not to be too sad. The Memory Motel isn't all that far
away.*

I knew the email was bordering on cheesy, but I didn't care. It was
sincere. And truthfully, it just felt good to talk to her. Even virtually.
    Her next response almost made me laugh. I could hear her voice—a
little frustrated, a little flustered—in the single written word. I could
picture her face too—nose scrunched up, a light flush under her freckles,
and her honey-browns flashing.

To: ebburke@burkeholdings.com
From: mdiaz@trinketsandtreasures.com
Subject: re: re: re: Meeting

Ugh.

Grinning, I waited. I knew she'd have more to say, and I wasn't disappointed. My phone pinged less than two minutes later.

To: mdiaz@trinketsandtreasures.com
From: ebburke@burkeholdings.com
Subject: re: re: re: Meeting

By the way. You should be neither flattered nor concerned about the amount of time I spent writing down your annoying quirks. It's a well-known fact that my high school English teachers referred to me as "verbose."

And as it so happens, I was trying to work through some things in my head, and it helps if I write them down. (See what I did there? Now you know something else, AND I got to explain myself.)

P.S. It's nice to hear that you don't hate me. I think...

Before I even finished reading, my phone sounded again, and I knew she'd just realized what my own postscript said. Sure enough her next email contained the incredulity—though none of the verboseness—I was expecting.

To: ebburke@burkeholdings.com
From: mdiaz@trinketsandtreasures.com
Subject: Wait.

Did you say MEMORY MOTEL, Ethan?

L.

I couldn't help but chuckle. I could picture her face again. Embarrassed that she'd taken so long to really clue in. Complete crimson across her face. Down her chest.

My laughter faded, replaced by a renewed rush of blood.

Imagining a woman's blush shouldn't be the prerequisite for a hard-on, I thought.

It didn't lessen the truth of it in the slightest.

I stared down at the screen, and fought an urge to tell her as much.

Dear Lumia. The slightest thought— No. The slightest hint of a thought of your barely exposed skin is enough to make me want you a thousand times over. Ethan.

"Very fucking poetic," I muttered.

I started to type something else. Then stopped. Then started again. Before I could actually get a word finished, though, the old-fashioned phone on the nightstand came to life. I knew before I even picked it up that it would be her.

"Hello, Lu," I greeted teasingly. "Your place or mine?"

Her breathless reply came right away. "Mine."

She hung up the moment after she'd said it, and I was suddenly very glad I'd been such an efficient stalker earlier in the evening.

* * * *

Mia

I froze, staring at the dead phone in my hands, my throat going dry.

Mine? Seriously? What were you thinking?

If I'd been able to move, I would've shaken my head. The problem was that I *wasn't* thinking. I hadn't expected his greeting. I hadn't expected to hear my nickname straight off the bat. And of course, in the few hours since I'd seen Ethan, my memory had dimmed the effect his voice had on me. I'd blocked out the way it felt to have him rumble the sexiest of things against my skin. And having him speak right into my ear had brought it all back in a mad rush. Want had slid through me, skidded along my breasts and brought my nipples to attention. It had pooled between my thighs and dampened my underwear. And it had made my brain turn to a pile of mush. So the word "mine" had just slipped out.

And before I could retract it, my cell phone's battery had decided to just give up. Completely. Ethan was probably sitting on the other end, trying to figure out what kind of game I was playing.

I breathed out, trying to calm myself.

Okay, I reasoned. *He doesn't actually know where you live. Nor does he have this number. So he can't come here, and he can't just call back and ask for the address.*

But I no sooner thought it than I decided he would find a way. After all, he'd come from Toronto to Vancouver to find me. What were the chances that he wouldn't be able to search out my home address? Pretty much zero.

And speaking of Toronto...

Why, in God's name, wasn't he *there*? Why hadn't I asked him *that* rather than inviting him to my house? I'd used my solitary breath of talk-time to issue something that probably sounded more or less like a booty call.

I blew out a nervous breath and forced myself to think. I had options. All I had to do was review the simplest ones.

I didn't have a landline, but I could plug in my phone and wait a few minutes for it to charge, then call the Memory Motel again.

Or I could open up the laptop—which I'd impulsively slammed shut when I finally clued in that Ethan was still in town—and type up an email retracting my spontaneous, one-word reply.

I decided to double up. I'd plug in the phone, and while it charged, I'd send the email. But when I flipped open my laptop, the screen flickered, then went black.

"You've got to be kidding me!"

I grabbed my cell, and saw that it wasn't charging, either.

"You've *really* got to be kidding me!"

Then I groaned as an explanation occurred to me. And sure enough, as I leaned over the couch and followed the length of the extension cord both devices were regularly plugged into, I found the other end dislodged from the wall. I belatedly plugged it back in.

A glance at the TV clock told me that nine full minutes had passed since I uttered the treacherous word. Most of which I'd wasted by sitting in silent horror. And nine minutes was plenty of time for Ethan to call a cab. A Tuesday night at ten o'clock wouldn't mean much of a wait. Fifteen minutes at most. There'd be no traffic. Fifteen minutes more to my house.

I did a quick, mental calculation.

Fifteen minus nine plus fifteen. That gives you twenty-one minutes—at most—to do...something. Anything.

The TV clock flicked.

Okay. Twenty minutes now.

My phone was only just starting to boot up. My laptop showed no sign of life yet. I jumped up, wondering if it was reasonable to just walk out. After all, wasn't that what Ethan had done at the restaurant?

Yeah, sure, I said to myself. *Except he wasn't running away from his own house.*

"Right," I muttered. "I can't let him drive me out of my home as he tries to steal my business."

The last bit was enough to make me square my shoulders and narrow my eyes. No way was I going to let either of those things happen.

All you have to do is tell him to go. Preferably while dressed in something other than skimpy pajamas and a satin robe.

I glanced back at the clock. Seventeen minutes now.

I jumped up and hurried to my bedroom to paw through my clothes. I didn't want to give the impression that I'd changed into something else just because he was coming. I needed to be casual. Unsexy. But time and place appropriate.

"Because I have so many outfits that scream, 'I'm in charge, but also at home for the night,'" I grumbled.

Then my fingers brushed over a piece of flannel, and I knew I had the perfect thing. Men's pajama pants and a big, matching T-shirt. They'd been sent to me by mistake. An online ordering error that I'd never bothered to fix. But Ethan wouldn't know that. He'd probably assume they belonged to an ex, which would definitely shut down the booty-call factor.

Feeling triumphant, I yanked the items free, stripped down, and got changed. I surveyed myself in the mirror. My cheeks were still a little too flushed, and my hair a little too wild.

I tossed a look at my bedside clock. I was down to a nine-minute window of time.

Quickly, I dragged my hair into a bun, then moved to the bathroom to splash some water onto my face. I finished just in time. A sharp rap on the door—one that screamed of Ethan's confident nature, and was a full five minutes sooner that I'd calculated—carried all the way from the front entryway to where I stood in front of the sink.

"All right," I said to my reflection. "Let's go get rid of him."

I nodded, then marched up the hall and flung open the door, fully prepared to tell him to just turn around and leave. But his appearance—the broad shoulders and dark eyes and mussed-up, slept-in clothes—slowed my tongue. His musky, masculine scent wafted in too, not helping me at all. Even the forlorn-looking plastic bag in his hands slowed me down. So his words came quicker than mine.

"This is never going to work," he stated.

Annoyed that he'd beat me to it, I crossed my arms over my chest. "You stole my line."

"Should I apologize?" he asked.

"I doubt it would help."

"Would it help to know that I missed my plane because I was dreaming about you? Literally."

I echoed his own question back to him. "Should *I* apologize?"

"Hell, no," he replied. "I'm not complaining."

"Could've fooled me."

"Then let me rephrase." His eyes burned brightly, never leaving mine as he spoke. "Being inside you. Lying next to you. Tasting every inch of you. That's what kept me in bed while I should've been boarding my plane."

I drew in a breath that burned hot in my lungs. "But it's not going to work."

He took a step forward and lifted a hand as if to touch my face, but dropped it to his side again without making contact. "My line."

"Maybe. But I thought it first."

"If that *was* your line, why did you invite me here in the first place?"

"If it was yours, then why did you come?" I countered.

"I thought about that the whole way here, actually," he replied. "Just about asked the driver to turn around three times. But that dream, Lu..."

The heat in his tone distracted me from correcting him on the nickname, and my own voice was a little shaky as I made myself answer. "Was just a dream."

"More of a memory, really." His gaze slipped away from my face and slid down my body, and if the fact that I wore men's pajama bothered him as I thought it might, then he didn't show it at all. "I want to make you a proposition."

The way he said the last word made my toes want to curl, but I kept my voice neutral. "What is it?"

"Before I explain...tell me something, and be honest. Do you want me to leave?"

"I don't want you to. But I know that you should."

His mouth tipped up on one side. "Then we're on the same page. My business is everything to me. I fought for it tooth and fucking nail."

"Ditto," I said.

"And we've established that you won't budge, and that I won't back down."

"Yes."

"But you're in my head. Taking up so much damned space that I don't know how there's room for anything else." His smiled widened. "And that's a compliment, in case you couldn't tell."

"Thanks?" I posed it as a question, and Ethan laughed.

"You're welcome," he said.

"So. Do you want to come and tell me about the, uh, proposition?"

"No."

"No?"

"I'm only coming in if you accept."

My heart flip-flopped nervously in my chest. "Okay. But if you pull an engagement ring out of your pocket, I'm slamming the door."

He laughed again, low and sexy, his eyes dropping to my ring finger for the briefest second. "I think they call that a *proposal*, not a proposition."

"Funny. But it doesn't change my door-slamming plan."

"Then I guess I'd better tell you."

"Guess you'd better."

His smile dipped for a second, and I realized he might be nervous too. It made me feel the slightest bit better.

He took a visible breath before saying, "Give me tonight. Let me stay with you. I'll make it worth your while."

"It's not that it's not worth my while, Ethan."

"I know. Or I hope, anyway. And that's why my proposition has a second part."

The nervous thud came back. "Which is?"

"We forget everything else. My business, your business." He shook his head like he knew I was going to argue. "I know it won't change reality. I'm still going to wake up in the morning and catch my plane. When I get home, I'll be doing my damnedest to come up with a way to get you to work with me. You'll still be doing your damnedest to see that I go straight to hell."

"That's the worst sales pitch I've ever heard."

"I don't fuck around, Lu. I want to pretend we never found out that we're supposed to be enemies. I don't want to think or talk about work. I want *you*. Twelve hours. We go in with eyes open, knowing that it ends tomorrow morning."

"And if I tell you no?" I asked.

"Then me"—he shook the bag in his hands—"and my worldly possessions will spend the night at the airport."

"You checked out of the Memory Motel?"

"You can't win big if you don't take a risk, Lu."

"Ethan..."

"Yes?"

"Have you ever *lost*?" I asked.

Surprisingly, his features hardened for a second. "Once. Six years ago."

"And what happened?"

"A business burned to the ground."

My heart skipped a worried beat. Not because his words weren't ominous or intimidating, but because there was a glimpse of pain in his eyes. So instead of scaring me away, his statement made me curious. And even though the no-strings offer was similar to the one he'd made in the bathroom earlier, that hint of hurt pushed me into acceptance.

"Tonight," I said.

I stepped back to let him in. He eyed the opening between me and the doorframe. Then he reached for me, his strong hands lifting me from the ground while his warm lips drove into mine.

Chapter 10

Ethan

The anticipation of touching her had been killing me. The relief of doing it was a tidal wave.

I slammed the door with a kick, then pushed Mia to the wall. Her curves molded to me while her thighs pressed tight against my hips. I thrust forward, cursing the barrier of material between us.

"Too much fucking fabric," I muttered.

"Agreed," she breathed.

My hands slid to the hem of the ridiculously large T-shirt she wore, then yanked it unceremoniously over her head. For a second, I was caught off guard. In a damned good way. She wore nothing under the shirt, and her full, luscious breasts were on immediate display. Her nipples were erect, their full pinkness drawing my gaze. Making me stop and simply stare.

Then she spoke, her voice an ache. "Ethan."

I answered with my mouth, tipping my head down to give each little rosebud a suck and a roll of my tongue.

"Ethan," she said again, this time plucking at the lapels of my suit jacket.

Obediently, I shrugged out of the constricting material. The second the jacket hit the ground, Mia's fingers landed on the buttons of my shirt, tugging them free. I groaned as her hands skidded over my chest. Each touch sent another shot of need through me. My cock was so hard that I thought it might burst through the zipper on its own. And when I dragged a hand from her back to the waistband of her pajama pants and slid it inside—panty-free too, I noted through my lust-filled haze—I found her slick with a need that matched my own.

I slipped my finger into her once. Twice. Then circled her clit with my thumb. She was already quivering. I freed my hand to fumble for the bag I still had slung across the inside of my elbow. By some miracle, I managed to get the box of condoms out, open it, and slide one of the foil packages free.

Mia's fingers dropped to my pants. They pulled the button from its hole and dragged the zipper down.

I couldn't contain a throaty growl. "Fuck."

Her response was accompanied light, sexy laugh. "Yes. Please."

I didn't want to rush, but I couldn't help it. Her words. Her laugh. The feel of her. I had to have it all, right that second.

I tore unceremoniously into the condom wrapper, then lowered the latex toward my waiting, eager cock. I rolled it down, groaning as my own hand slid down my hard self. I'd never been so primed.

I leaned back just enough that I could tug down her pajama pants—down her hips, over her knees, and left hanging from one ankle—then grasped her knee and eased forward again. I tried to hold back. To drag it out. But the second I entered her, I was done for.

Her cries and gasps, and breathy whispers of my name only made me more rabid. I plunged into her again and again, trying to bury myself completely.

I was going to come, fast and hard, and there wasn't a damned thing I could do to stop it. I'd been craving her since the morning—*how the hell was it only that long ago?*—and now that I had her in my arms, it was too good.

Thankfully, just before I lost complete control, I felt her tighten around me. Her head tilted back, and she cried out a final time, finding her release just as I found mine.

I held her tightly for several moments after, reveling in the shared pulse of our bodies.

Too quick, but still fucking amazing.

I didn't realize I'd said it aloud until she laughed again, this time throatily. "We've got twelve hours. I'm sure we can do it again more slowly at least once. And yes. Amazing."

Smiling a stupidly sloppy smile, I pulled back and pressed my forehead to hers. "Once? I'm aiming for three or four times. Maybe even in the bed."

She tipped her mouth to mine for a light kiss. "What? The hallway wall isn't good enough for you?"

"Don't get me wrong. It has a certain appeal. But I wouldn't mind a tour of the rest of the house. And a coffee."

"Seriously? A post-sex coffee?"

"I'm planning on being up all night."

She laughed yet again, and I marveled at the fact that she could express so many different levels of pleasure with that tinkling sound.

"Okay," she said. "How about I show you the kitchen while I put on a pot? I'll show you the rest of my very tiny house as it brews."

"I accept your offer," I replied.

"You should probably put me down first."

"Right." I didn't let her go yet.

"And maybe dispose of the condom," she added.

"Not a bad idea. You can show me the bathroom before the kitchen."

I kissed her once more, softly this time, then pulled back and let her slide to the floor. She smiled up at me in a way that made my heart compress unexpectedly. Warmth—the same kind that had seeped in at the restaurant earlier when we'd exchange the silent understanding about her family—crept into my chest and hung there. Pleasant and unnerving at the same time. It grew even stronger when she slipped her hand into mine and pulled me up the hall.

When she pointed me through the bathroom door, I was hit by an even stranger feeling. Regret mixed with relief. I didn't want to untangle my fingers from hers, but I needed a minute to regroup.

But as I cleaned up, splashed some water on to my face, and stared into the mirror, I couldn't quite get myself centered. The heat in my chest stayed. Maybe even surged a little again when I let myself take a look around the bathroom and saw the eclectic but stylish décor.

Seashell bath soap and a claw-foot tub.

Black-and-white-tiled floor and vintage pinup girl in a frame over the toilet.

Polka-dot curtain on the tiny window.

Though I didn't know her well, I got the distinct impression that it was all very, very Mia Diaz. Classic yet quirky. I definitely liked it. But it did nothing to ease the feeling between my ribs.

Absently, I lifted my hand and pressed at the spot where the heat started, then turned back to the mirror. I searched my own face for an explanation, but all I could see was sex-mussed hair and puzzlement. Before I could analyze it much more, Mia's voice carried through the door.

"You staying in there all night?" she asked.

I forced a light tone as I called back, "Hell, no. I've got plans for you."

"I thought you wanted coffee and house tour."

"I do. But I don't see why we can't start with a tour of the bedroom."

I flung open the door, prepared to drag a deliberately lascivious look up and down her body. Instead, I stopped short. In the few minutes since she'd left me alone in the bathroom, she'd changed out of the shapeless pajamas and into a baby doll nightie. She'd also freed her hair from its pile on top of her head, and it hung loose and wild in a cascade of red past her shoulders. The exaggerated, lustful look I'd been about to give became a genuine one. If she hadn't had been holding two mugs, I would've scooped her up and given the wall another run for its money.

Clearly reading my mind, Mia shook her head. "Oh, no you don't."

I took a step closer. "Oh, I think I *do*."

She inched back. "The coffee."

"Better put it down," I warned.

Her eyes widened, then flicked back and forth. "There's nowhere to put it down."

"The floor." I took another step.

"I don't think that's a good—eep!" The steaming liquid sloshed over the side as she stumbled a little.

"Told you to put it down."

"I could've gotten burned!"

"If you had, I would've kissed it better." I put my arms out and crouched like I was about to pounce.

She bumped into the doorframe at the end of the hall. "Stop. I'm warning you, Ethan!"

"You gonna throw the coffee at me?"

"Possibly."

"Go for it," I said. "But I've gotta warn you, I'm pretty quick on my feet."

"What if I'm faster?" she countered, tipping her chin up with a defiance that made me smile.

"Guess we'll find out."

I lunged forward, and she lifted the mugs, and for a second, I thought she might actually follow through with her threat. Which was clearly her plan. As I cut short my teasing attack and lifted my arms in an automatic attempt to protect myself, she quickly bent and set down the coffee, then turned and ran.

Laughing and cursing at the same time, I gave chase. Lucky for me, her house really *was* as tiny as she'd said it was. There was only one direction she could head. And my legs were longer than hers.

She made it around the corner then to the square living room, where I easily caught up. She attempted to face off with me from behind her reclaimed-wood coffee table.

"Come on now," I said. "All I have to do it step over that thing and I've got you. You could at least make it challenging."

Her nose wrinkled. "Bite me."

"Get closer, and I just might."

I moved to make good on my promise of clambering over the table, and she jumped. Literally. Up onto the retro yellow couch, then over it. The flash of leg and ass temporarily rendered me motionless.

You're going to let yourself lose this little game because of your overactive libido?

The self-directed chiding didn't stop me from salivating like hungry, cartoon dog. It did, however, spur me to action. After all, it was *because* of my overactive libido that I had to win.

I launched myself past the couch then through the arched opening where Mia had disappeared. There was a single door on the other side, and it flapped back and forth lightly, making me sure she'd gone inside. I crept across the floor, reached out to grasp the doorknob, then flung the door open, shouting triumphantly at the last second.

"Aha!"

But the room—her bedroom—appeared to be empty. I glanced around, searching for her hiding place. A four-poster bed dominated the center of one wall, a tallboy dresser stood against another, and a freestanding clothes rack blocked the view of a third. Though there was a closet on the fourth wall, it had no doors at all, and instead of housing the usual assortment of pants and shirts, it held a desk, which was covered in jewelry design layouts. Under normal circumstances, I would've felt compelled to explore it.

But these aren't normal circumstances. This is war.

Then, as if to punctuate my thought, something small and hard pinged against my calf. Startled, I glanced down. A foam dart sat in the middle of the Mandala-themed area rug.

"Seriously?" I said.

I narrowed my eyes in search of the weapon's trajectory.

It'd hit my lower leg. So probably firing from below. My gaze sought the only low point in the room—the space under the bed.

I dropped down, fully expecting to find Mia's beautiful brown gaze peering out. Instead, I was confronted by a row of boxes. And I no sooner hit the floor than another ping hit me, this time straight in the ass.

"Ouch!"

Her muffled giggle gave away her position. I flopped over and turned my attention toward the clothes rack. Sure enough, her bare feet peeked out from beneath the row of dresses.

I didn't waste any time. I crawled over the rug, then snaked out a hand and grabbed a hold of her ankle. I gave it a yank, and with a banshee-worthy shriek, she came flying out of the clothes. The plastic dart gun fell from her hands and clattered to the floor. She tried to dive for it, but I still had my fingers clasped around her ankle. Her arms windmilled. Her legs wobbled. And backward she went, her ass landing right on my chest.

For a moment, the room was silent. Then a laugh burst from Mia, forceful enough that her rear bounced temptingly closer.

"Oh, God, that was funny," she exclaimed.

"You think so?" I replied dryly.

"Yes!"

"You might not think it was so funny if you were aware of my current view."

"What?"

"I'm conversing with your ass."

"Oh. Oh!" She scrambled around so that she was straddling me instead.

"Not sure that improved things," I said.

"Never satisfied, are you?"

"Actually. I was *very* satisfied just a short bit ago. And I'd like to be satisfied again."

"Already?" She sounded genuinely surprised.

"I can't believe you'd doubt my sex drive so easily." I grinned. "Besides that. Guerilla warfare with a hot redhead is a major turn-on."

"Pervert."

"Absolutely. Now come here and kiss me."

But as she leaned down and pushed her lips to mine, lust wasn't the dominant feeling. Instead, it was that damned heat in my chest, rolling through me like a summer storm.

* * * *

Mia

The hallway.

My bedroom floor.

The bed itself.

My little bungalow had never been so thoroughly used. The walls had never echoed so loudly. And I'd never been so sex-sore in my life. Clearly, I was out of practice.

I groaned a little and adjusted my body, wriggling closer to Ethan. His hand tightened on my hip.

"Uh-uh, buddy. Back off," I said. "I'm just using you as a heating pad to ease my aching muscles."

He chuckled a self-satisfied laugh. "Wore you out, huh?"

"I don't usually moonlight as a contortionist."

"Well, shit. There goes my business plan."

My heart dipped a little at the mention of work, and I had to force myself to answer lightly. "Shhhh. No shop talk. You promised."

He kissed the top of my head. "Sorry. Habit. I don't usually have anything else to talk about."

"Nothing?"

"Certified workaholic."

I was far more curious than I wanted to be. I knew how dedicated he was to his job. And even though he was planning to use that dedication *against* me, that didn't stop it from being an admirable quality.

But now I wondered where it came from. Was it a characteristic he saw modeled in his parents, or was he just born with that inherent drive? Did something else in his life shape him that way? I had to bite my lip to stop myself from asking.

"Politics?" I suggested instead.

"In the bedroom?" Ethan sounded so appalled that I laughed.

"Okay, then. No politics in the bedroom."

"Definitely not."

"Do you have a usual post—"

He cut me off. "Don't."

"Don't what?" I replied.

"Don't say what you were about to say."

"Postcoital?"

He groaned. "You said it!"

"For a once-an-hour sex guy, that's awfully prudish," I pointed out.

"It's the opposite of prudish. The term *postcoital* is prudish. If you'd said post-fu—"

"Okay, I get it." Then a question popped out before I could stop it. "What about the other part?"

"What part?"

"The *usual* part. What's normal bedroom talk for you?"

He twirled a finger through my hair. "Are you asking about my other lovers, Mia? That's very non-one-night-stand-ish."

I swatted playfully at his chest. "This is a two-night stand now. And no work or politics or ex-lovers? What's left? Childhood stories and lifelong dreams?"

"All right," he conceded. "I'll give you the rundown."

"A whole rundown? Aren't there too many to name?"

"Ah. An insult wrapped in a compliment. My favorite kind." His hand slid to the small of my back and circled pleasantly.

I closed my eyes, enjoying the way his fingers worked out some of my kinked muscles. "Are you saying you *aren't* a slutty Casanova?"

He laughed. "Is that the impression I give?"

"I don't know how to answer that without inflating your ego."

"Are you referring to my impressive *skills*? Because if so, then I feel like that begs the question of whether or not you're a slutty Casanova too."

My face warmed. "Shut up."

"What? It was a compliment. And also an answer to your accusation," he said. "No, I'm neither slutty, nor a Casanova. I don't have the time."

Another question popped out before I could stop it. "Wouldn't it be easier to have time for being slutty than it would to have relationships?"

"Maybe. But I don't do those, either, so I'm not sure."

I went quiet for a moment, bothered by the revelation. Not that his stance on relationships should be affecting me in any way, but I still felt a tickle of unease.

Relax, said a voice it my head. *He also said he* doesn't *sleep around.*

That shouldn't have mattered, either. But for some reason, it did.

I inhaled, trying to shake off the sudden light-headed sensation that threatened to take over. As I drew in some much-needed oxygen, I realized that Ethan had already picked up the thread of conversation again.

"...but I'm only going back six years," he was saying. "Because everything before my twenty-fourth birthday is just plain embarrassing."

I blinked. "Wait."

"What?" he asked.

"You're *thirty*?"

"Yes. Why?" He shifted on the bed, sliding up a little so he could look down at me. "How old are you?"

"Twenty-seven," I told him, feeling a little embarrassed by the surprise on his face. "Do I look older?"

"Look? No. Seem? Yep, definitely."

"How?"

He shook his head. "Suffice it to say that I suspect you're an incredibly shrewd businesswoman. If I add anything else, it'll be shop talk."

I made a face. "Fine. Back to your ex-lovers then."

He laughed, then settled his head back on the pillow. "Okay. On my twenty-fourth birthday, I went out for drinks alone."

Curiosity hit me again. "Alone?"

"Yep. But that's another shop talk story."

"I feel like I'm getting the redacted version of your love life."

"Workaholic," he reminded me. "Bound to be a bit of redaction here and there. Want me to stop?"

I shook my head. "No."

"So. Me. Three beers. Really shitty bar, even shittier mood. Then in walks a woman in a wedding dress, bawling her eyes out, and I think to myself, 'Damn. At least *someone* has it worse than I do.'"

I swallowed, my palms abruptly sweaty. "You picked up a jilted bride?"

"She picked me up," he corrected.

A vision of the scenario filled my mind. Dark lighting, the scent of stale beer, and grainy TV screens playing a sporting event overhead. Ethan, casually dressed, younger than he was now, shoveling bar peanuts into his mouth with zestful misery. And the woman in white, walking in. But in place of her face...was mine.

Nausea made me draw in a shallow breath and I managed to get out a response. "Oh."

Ethan's fingers found my face. "Hey. You all right?"

I swallowed again, and made sure my voice came out with as much lightness as possible. "I'm fine. I just don't know whether to be horrified or impressed."

"Little of both?" he suggested. "Anyway, that was Kelly. She was a train wreck."

"So that's what you're attracted to?" I replied.

He let out a chuckle. "No. But Kelly came into my life at a low point. I'm not ashamed to say that she made me feel better about myself and my situation. Which worked well until I picked myself up out of my slump."

"So then...you just left her?"

"Of course not. I'm not a bad person."

"I know."

"Do you?"

He said it almost absently—so softly too, that I wondered if he meant for me to hear it. But he also sounded so serious that I couldn't help but lift my head in surprise. I stared up at him, studying his expression. His brows were scrunched up, his jaw a little stiff. Did he really care if I thought he was a bad person? Because all the sexy, flirty pillow talk aside, he was the man trying to take over my business. It seemed like a contradiction.

Kind of like how you let him into your house and your bed in the first place? That kind of contradiction?

I shoved the thought aside and said, "So if you didn't leave, what happened?"

"We'd been together for about three months when I started to worry that her problems were more complicated. So I tried to get her some help. Offered to go to couples' therapy," he told me, shaking his head. "Three months in. I didn't ever see things progressing, yet that's where we were. Anyway. She refused. And a few weeks later, she up and left me. No explanation."

I winced. "Ouch."

"It stung," he said with a nod. "But a few very solitary, work-heavy months later, a weird thing happened. I was at a lunch thing, and got to talking with this guy. I can't even remember how we got on the subject, but the dude turned out to be Kelly's ex-fiancé. Also turned out that *she* left *him* at the altar. He said he thought she couldn't stand how happy he'd become."

"That's sad." I really meant it. My heart went out to the unhappy woman I'd never met.

And when Ethan sighed heavily, I was sure his feelings on the subject were equally genuine. "No shit. I've wondered lots of times if she ever found someone that *did* make her feel like it was okay to be happy."

"I hope so," I said sincerely.

"Me too."

We both went quiet then, his hands kneading over my shoulders, down my back, then up again. I started to drift off, lulled by the silence and the enjoyable feeling. But after a few minutes, Ethan spoke up again.

"What about you?" he asked.

"What about me, what?" I replied.

"What's your list of exes look like?" he asked teasingly. "Bikers? Playboys? Nerdy tech types?"

"No!" The word came out more forcefully than I meant it to, and I tried to cover it. "Your list can't end with Kelly."

"I did tell you that I wasn't some kind of Casanova."

"Yes. But that was six years ago. And you promised a complete rundown."

He laughed. "All right. I'm a man of my word. A year after Kelly, there was Portia. She was a forty-something divorcee with a couple of grown kids. She used me as a willing booty call for two years."

"Seriously?" I said.

"Seriously," he confirmed. "It was ideal, really. Zero commitment, zero complications."

"Zero complications?" I echoed. "It sounds like the very definition of complicated."

Ethan shrugged. "Portia got pregnant at seventeen. Married at eighteen. Second kid before her twentieth birthday. After she left her husband, she had no desire to go back to anything that resembled that life."

"But...ew."

"What's gross?"

"You were the same age as her kids!"

"Younger than one of them, actually. And accidentally meeting them is what made me cut things off. Because while there's nothing wrong with a mutually enjoyable age gap, I couldn't stop picturing *my* mother after the accidental meeting."

I laughed. "Yeah, that would be a turn-off."

"You have no idea," he said. "And that's pretty much it, by the way. Kelly, then Portia."

"You want me to believe that you've been celibate for...what? Two years?"

"Believe what you like. The truth is, you're the first woman I've been with in that long."

"I guess that explains your enthusiasm," I blurted, then immediately felt my entire body break out in a blush.

But Ethan didn't laugh at my expense. Instead, he gave my shoulder a tight squeeze and said, "Nah, honey. My enthusiasm isn't about my sadly lacking sex life."

"It isn't?"

"No. It's definitely about you."

His words made the blush change. It morphed from embarrassment to pleasure. The feeling only intensified when he adjusted his position so he could give me a long, firm kiss. And I had to admit a few things to myself.

I *did* like that he wasn't a big, giant man-slut.

I *did* care that relationships weren't an option for him.

And I was completely mad at myself for all of it.

Chapter 11

Ethan

I stood at the end of Mia's bed wondering just how the hell I was going to leave. If I *should* leave. If I should wake her before I went.

Twelve hours, I said to myself. *That's all you promised her.*

My watch told me it hadn't been quite that long. Ten and a quarter, if I was getting technical. But an urgent call had come through from Julie, informing me that my flight had been moved up by two hours, and if I didn't want to miss it a second time, I needed to be out the door quickly.

I was loath to wake Mia up. She'd slept through Julie's call. Barely stirred when I extricated myself from her sweet curves. Hadn't even noticed when I got dressed and put on a pot of coffee. It might've been insulting if I wasn't so sure that her exhaustion extended from me keeping her up all night.

Plus, she was downright stunning at that moment. Thick, gorgeous thighs poking out from under her blanket. The curve of one breast and the barest hint of pink nipple visible along the curve of the pillow she held in her arms.

Staring at her like that made desire leap to life again, and I knew if I *didn't* leave some time very soon, I'd give in to the need to wake her up. Probably with my mouth between her thighs. I took a step closer. I couldn't help it.

Seriously, Burke, the plane.

I forced myself to spin on my heel and walk out without looking back. I barely made it to the front door before pausing again. It didn't feel right to go without saying a word. It felt…dishonest. Like leaving to buy a jug of milk and never coming back. Only worse. Because I *was* coming back.

Only it wouldn't be with the milk. It would be with mental armor and an arsenal of business tactics.

Melodramatic much?

"Shut up," I muttered to myself.

But my feet wouldn't move. My hand was extended to the doorknob. Poised. Ready to go. Except I completely couldn't do it.

Would it be so bad, to turn back? To crawl into the bed beside her and murmur that I'd missed my flight again, and that I wanted another few hours? Maybe even a few days. It'd raise eyebrows back at the office. Possibly give my assistant a heart attack.

And be worth it.

I dropped the handle and almost turned to follow through on the urge, but before I could take a step, a horn sounded from outside. A glance through the window told me my cab was already there.

"Shit."

I looked from the hall that led to Mia, then back to the waiting car. The honk sounded again, bringing me to my senses. A few more hours…a few more days. It would just hamper my ability to be objective. Already, I could sense the doubt. But I sure as shit wasn't going to give up going after Trinkets and Treasures. I knew too well how being soft on a deal turned out. How things went when I lost.

Burned to the ground.

Hadn't I said that exact thing to Mia? I shook my head, wondering why I'd shown her that bit of weakness. My failings weren't something I talked about. Ever. I'd said it before I even stepped through her door too, so it wasn't like I could blame the slip on a sex-addled mind. Not that I could imagine Mia trying to use it against me. In fact, she hadn't even pressed me for more information. Just stepped aside and let me in.

I frowned. *Why* didn't *she press for information?*

It was the kind of thing that should have prompted some curiosity. Or maybe scared her the hell off.

The horn honked a third time, and I jerked my attention back to the window just in time to see the driver's-side door open.

"Shit," I said again.

The last thing I needed was to be caught in the act of sneaking off.

And if nothing else, that worry should tell you just how wrong it is to do this.

I forced the thought aside, then turned the handle. I stepped outside and signaled to the driver that he didn't need to come up. But as I made my way down the little walkway, I heard a light creak, and I knew without turning around that Mia stood in the door. I was also sure that so long as I kept moving, she would just watch me go. I almost let it happen. Maybe I *would* have, if my gaze hadn't landed on the driver right then.

I could see that his eyes were fixed behind me, and there was no mistaking the appreciation on his face. The little smile. The way both eyebrows kind of lifted. It immediately pissed me off.

I shot him my dirtiest look—wasted, because he didn't look my way—then turned back up the walk. Admittedly, I could see why his expression held so much admiration.

Mia wore nothing but the blanket I'd left her in a minute earlier. She gripped it tightly, but it still slipped off one freckled shoulder. Her exposed feet added coy sex appeal, and her hair was a wild, just-fucked mess.

So, yeah. I understood why the other man was staring at her. That didn't mean I liked it. In fact, I hated it.

"I'll give you something to look at, asshole," I muttered.

I stalked toward Mia, knowing I was being unreasonable. I had no claim on her. No excuse for not wanting the cab driver to check her out. *Less* than no excuse, really.

I didn't care.

In a few quick steps I had her in my arms, one hand on her hip, the other on her cheek. I drew her in and pulled her lips to mine. I kissed her hard. Possessive. Like she was mine to keep, and I didn't let her go until I was sure that the cab driver had got a good eyeful.

"Got something to prove?" Mia breathed when I finally pulled away.

"Maybe I do," I replied.

"And is that 'something' that you're not a total asshole for running out on me without saying goodbye, or is it to show off to that cab driver down there?"

Unexpectedly, the heat of embarrassment made me warm under my collar, and I answered gruffly, "Could be the second thing."

She laughed, clearly entertained by my discomfort. "Then what're you going to do about the first 'something,' hmm?"

"This."

I dragged her in for another long kiss, exploring the corners of her mouth with my tongue while my hands hugged her curves and dips. I would've kept going, but her blanket slipped, and suddenly we were both scrambling to keep it from completely dropping to the ground. When Mia had the fabric back in place, she took a shaky breath and stepped back. I felt the space between us acutely.

Her next question had an undeniable undercurrent of hurt. "Let me guess. You think that makes up for the two hours that you robbed from me too?"

I shook my head. "No. For that, I'll give you an apology. I'm sorry, Mia. My flight got changed, and I didn't want to wake you and offer an imperfect goodbye after such a perfect night."

As soon as the words were out, I realized they were true. There wasn't a good way to follow a night like that. Not while knowing that it was done.

Done. Christ.

The usual, Mia-induced warmth in my chest turned cold. Icy. The next time I saw her, it would be all business.

I met her eyes, and saw that she knew it too.

"I accept your apology." She said it like it was meant to be a joke, but her tone was too flat for the punch line.

My response was equally lacking in humor. "Then I guess that's my cue to go."

She shifted from foot to foot. "Thanks for coming by."

"Thanks for inviting me." I heard the lameness in our exchange, and I sighed. "And this is why I didn't wake you."

Her mouth tipped up. "We should probably end this in a fight."

My lips twitched. "You think?"

She nodded. "Yes."

"Okay," I said. "Hurl an insult at me."

"Like...yellow-bellied landlubber?"

"Maybe go with something less pirate-y?" I suggested.

Her face scrunched up like she was really thinking about it, and I braced myself for the mother of all insults. When she spoke, though, it was to say something unexpected.

"It was an accident," she told me.

"What was?" I asked.

"Inviting you here."

"What do you mean?"

"When you said, 'Your place or mine,' and I said, 'Mine'...I didn't mean to."

"So...the verbal version of a typo?"

Her blush came out in full force. "Something like that."

I frowned. "Something like that. But not quite like that."

"Maybe I should rephrase. Not I didn't mean *to*. I didn't mean *it*."

"You didn't want me to come over?"

Mia shook her head. "No, I didn't. Saying 'mine' was a reflex. Like when the doctor taps your knee with the little hammer."

In spite of the way I tried to keep it down, irritation bubbled up. "What *did* you mean to say?"

"I don't know. I didn't get a chance to figure that out. Which brings me to the second thing I should probably tell you."

"I'm all ears," I said sarcastically.

She didn't flinch at my caustic tone. "I didn't hang up on you. My phone died. So there was no invitation, and no big, mysterious lead-up."

"Good to know."

"And if I'd been able to, I would've called back and retracted it."

"Right." My heart was twisting bitterly in my chest. "I guess that's *really* my cue to go. Or maybe the hint that I shouldn't have come at all."

Her face was utterly expressionless. "Goodbye, Ethan."

"See you soon, Mia," I corrected, then turned and walked away—this time, without looking back.

* * * *

Mia

I didn't stand on the stoop and watch Ethan get into the cab. I didn't look as the yellow car pulled into the street, then wait for it to get smaller and smaller as it drove away.

But I *wanted* to.

Just like I wanted to call after him and tell him that even though I really hadn't meant to invite him over, I was glad for the knee-jerk reaction. I was thankful that I hadn't been able to call him back, and that I hadn't been able to gather my wits quickly enough to send him a retraction via email.

What I wasn't thankful for, and what I didn't want, was the solid ache in my chest, and the moments that had led to it.

I hated the fact that I'd reached for him when I woke up. That my heart had dropped when I found the bed empty, and that it lifted when I realized he was just outside, still close enough to catch.

I despised how my voice had dried up in my throat, not quite strong enough to call out to him.

I resented the relief at seeing him turn and come back on his own. The satisfaction at folding myself into his arms like I belonged there.

Most of all, I couldn't stand that the second I'd closed the door, tears filled my eyes. I couldn't stop them. As though his leaving was the end of something that hadn't even had a chance to get started.

It was your *idea to end it in a fight*, I reminded myself as I sank against the door and closed my eyes.

I'd been half joking when I said it. But when the admission over my not-so-inviting invitation came out, I realized I could use it to drive the necessary wedge into place. Because without that wedge, I'd be weak.

In fact, I'd already softened a little, hadn't I? Unblocking his email. Keeping his true motivation a secret from my parents and Marcelo and Aysia. Even following him outside a few minutes earlier when I could've just let him go.

But are you really so weak that you'd think about selling him your business?

I answered my own, silent question aloud. "Hell, no."

That wasn't the issue. I'd never, ever turn Trinket and Treasures over to someone else. Especially a man who thought he could handle the job better than I could myself. I'd been duped once in the past. Taken advantage of. It had torn me apart and made me question my self-worth. And it hadn't just affected *me*, either. It had hurt my family.

I wouldn't let it happen again.

And the only way to guarantee that it didn't was to stay away from temptation. God knew Ethan was more than tempting.

Speaking of which...

I opened my eyes and pushed off the wall. I'd already decided when I'd woken up alone that the first thing I'd do was a mini-purge. It wasn't the same as a real breakup, and it was a little juvenile, but I figured the premise would do. The two-night-stand equivalent of piling mementoes into a box and burning them. At the very least, I'd feel better about tackling the issue head on. It was also my day off—Wednesday and Thursday was my version of a weekend—so it gave me something with which to fill the hours too.

"All right," I murmured with a quick look around. "First things first. Clothes."

After I slipped into a pair of yoga pants and a tank top, I started the Ethan-themed cleanse. Slowly to begin with, then with increasing vigor.

I swept up the little vase we'd broken in our enthusiasm, then changed every garbage can in the house and tossed it all into the bin outside.

I shoved everything that *could* go into the washing machine straight onto the hot cycle. Blankets and sheets. My sexy nightie and my men's pajamas. I stuck in my underwear too, vowing to run them through twice even though I'd worn them hardly at all.

Once I had that going, I opened all the windows, grabbed a cloth and spray cleaner, and scrubbed down every surface he might've touched. The wall where we'd had the quickie. The bathroom where we showered together—sensual but not outright sexual. The dishes we'd used to share a slice of pie, and the mugs that had held our cold coffee. I even made sure to give the door handles a wipe.

When I finished with the hard surfaces, I transferred the laundry to the dryer, then moved on to the soft surfaces. Fabric refresher on the couch and on my mandala rug. A special spray that was designed for the mattress. For the finishing touch, I performed a thorough vacuuming job.

I surveyed my handiwork. The house was spotless. No sign of midnight whispers, no residual cologne. For a good minute, I felt satisfied. But then the computer caught my eye, and I realized that while there might not be any physical evidence left, there was still the virtual trail. And for some reason, it was a little harder to rid the laptop of the back and forth messages. Sitting down to do it brought the achy feeling back into my chest, and the tears—which I thought had been washed away with the lime-scented cleaner—threatened all over again.

My finger hovered over the delete button. Brushed it once. Then drew back.

"C'mon, Mia," I murmured. "Like ripping off a Band-Aid."

I pressed my finger forward again, then shrieked as a hand landed on my shoulder. I jumped up so fast that I couldn't quite keep my balance, and my wild leap sent both me and the laptop crashing to the floor. I rolled over, fists up, prepared for a fight. But my whole body sagged when I spotted a familiar blond ponytail.

"Liv!" I gasped.

My dare-dealing, fellow bridesmaid put her hands on her hips and stared down at me. "Whatcha doin', Lu'?"

"Seriously? You just about gave me a heart attack."

"Well, I knocked on the door for, like, three full minutes."

"That usually means someone isn't home."

"Or that they've fallen down, cracked their head, and need help."

"I only fell *after* you arrived," I pointed out. "Because of it, really."

"But you are home," she replied.

"Obviously."

"And not answering the door."

"I was preoccupied."

Liv's eyes flicked to the laptop. "Who's E. B. Burke?"

"What are you…an eagle?" I reached over and snapped the computer shut. "E. B. Burke is no one."

"No one who's got you so distracted that you seem to have forgotten about the final dress fitting we have today," she said.

I groaned. "Shit."

"You really forgot?"

"I was sitting here on my computer, wasn't I?"

She studied me for a second. "Yeah."

"Yeah, what?" I replied.

"I just thought it might be another of your evasion tactics."

"I'm not evading anything."

"Um. The day we spent putting those weird, candied almonds in the boxes? The dinner on Sunday? My calls and texts last night? Pretty sure you somehow evaded every one of those things," Liv said.

"Okay, the only one I'm going to cop to *evading* is the dinner on Sunday. And even then, you wouldn't believe what happened. But I swear, everything else had a legitimate excuse," I told her.

She hesitated. "Lu...are you *sure* you want to do this?"

"Do what?"

"Participate at this level."

I sighed. "Is that your nice way of asking me if I really want to be a bridesmaid?"

"Maaaaaybe," she said.

"Marcelo's my brother. Why wouldn't I want to be a bridesmaid?"

"See...that right there? That wasn't a resounding 'yes,' was it?"

I pinched the bridge of my nose, trying to stave off the beginnings of a headache. "I want to be there for Marc and Aysia. I am very, very, *very* happy for them. I'm just not one of those girls who gets all heart fluttery and googly eyed when I hear the word 'wedding.'"

"I get it," Liv said. "But why agree in the first place? Wouldn't your brother understand?"

"He does understand," I admitted.

It was true. When my life had ruptured, Marc was the one I turned to first. He probably knew more than he *wanted* to know.

"And he asked me anyway," I added. "So it must be important to him."

"Or..." Liv said.

"Or what?"

"He made the offer but assumed you would say no."

That gave me pause. "A pity ask? Did he say that?"

Liv shook her head. "No, of course not! My skills of inference are just that good. And I didn't mean pity, either, Lu. Maybe Marc was putting your feelings first, and just wanted to leave it up to you."

"That's..." I trailed off, considering it.

"Probably true?" Liv filled in.

I blew out a breath, wondering why I hadn't seen it before. Marcelo would never want me to feel excluded from something so important to him. Even if that meant having a shitty bridesmaid in his wedding.

"And I'm repaying his selflessness by sitting in the middle of my living room floor..." I said. "When I should be enthusiastically letting a dress fitter poke me with pins."

Liv reached out her hand. "There's still time to redeem yourself."

I stared at her open palm for a second before grasping it. She was right. I had ten days to transform myself from the world's worst bridesmaid to the world's best bridesmaid. There was still plenty to do. A bachelorette party and a rehearsal dinner. A speech to write.

"C'mon," Liv urged. "Let's go make tulle and sparkles our bitch."

I let out a laugh, closed my fingers on hers, and stood up. "Okay. I'm in. Let me get changed quickly."

She shook her head. "Nope. I'm not taking the chance that you'll fall back into whatever funk you were in and change your mind. Grab a sweatshirt, and let's get the hell out of here."

I rolled my eyes, but did as I was told. As Liv ushered me out the door, I cast a final look toward the living room and my discarded laptop, glad that focusing on my brother's wedding—which I should've been doing all along—would distract me from thinking about Ethan Burke.

Of course, we didn't make it a block from the house before Liv opened her mouth and said, "Hey. It's been a couple of days. Make any headway on my dare?"

And I wondered if it would really be that easy.

Chapter 12

Ethan

One of the bad things about being an efficient, hard-ass of a boss is that when something doesn't go quite as planned, everyone assumes that something is very wrong. Case in point, my arrival home. Sixteen hours late. Plastic bag in hand instead of suitcase.

First came the reaction from my congenial driver.

"Mr. B..." he said. "I was getting worried you drowned in all that Vancouver rain. Did you get sick or something?"

"Not sick, Quincy. Just delayed," I told him through gritted teeth.

I pointedly left the privacy window up and closed my eyes as he drove me home. Which is why I missed the fact that he *didn't* drive me home, and instead took me to the office.

When I expressed my frustration, his response was, "But you *never* want to go home first."

"You and Julie have a real knack for telling me what I never do, don't you?" I muttered.

"What?"

"Never mind. Just take me home."

"Yes, sir."

Thankfully, he took me home without further comment, and I had a completely solitary night. Well. Solitary except for thoughts of Mia Diaz and her cool, parting words. Thinking about them probably should've prompted me to act. Instead, the stinging memory just made me wallow. And the next day brought another issue, this time in the form of the impromptu, midafternoon visit from my assistant.

It was a little after two o'clock when the buzzer at my condo sounded, startling me so badly that I spilled my post-lunch wine, stubbed my toe, and answered the call with a curse.

"Who the hell is this?" I snapped.

Julie's concerned voice carried through the intercom. "Mr. Burke?"

"You know where I live?" I blurted before remembering that she processed all my mail, all my invoices, arranged pickups and drop-offs and God knew what else. "All right. You're getting the raise."

"Uh...Mr. Burke? Are you all right?"

"Fine. Come on up."

"Up?"

"I'm sure as hell not coming down." I pressed my finger to the buzzer for ten seconds longer than necessary, then poured a fresh glass of wine, and waited.

A minute later, Julie was at my door, her face wrinkled up with worry, her generally starched-looking pantsuit slightly bunched up at the elbows. Even her tight, gray curls were a little looser than usual.

"Julie," I greeted. "Now I feel like I should ask if *you're* okay."

Her lips pressed together for a second, then she replied, "You didn't come to work today, and you didn't bring me any paperwork"

"I emailed you and said I'd be taking the day off, didn't I?"

"Yes, but—"

"And I only bring you paperwork when there's paperwork to provide."

"Yes, but—"

"Would you like a glass of wine, Julie?" I said, stepping back from the door.

Her eyes went round and she made no move to come in. "Wine?"

I swirled my glass in her direction. "Liquid joy. You may have heard of it."

"No. I just—does this mean there isn't any paperwork? Literally? What about the jewelry company?"

"Not mine yet."

"I don't understand."

"Yeah," I said. "Me neither."

"You weren't able to acquire it?" Julie's question sounded like an accusation.

I sighed. "That's what 'not yet' means. So if you're not coming in for wine, and you don't have anything else to discuss..."

She took a step back. "Will you be in tomorrow, Mr. Burke?"

"Probably not." I took a hearty gulp of my wine. "I'm anticipating a headache."

She looked at me like I'd sprouted a second head, then backed away like the head in question might bite her. "Okay, Mr. Burke. See you Monday." "See you Monday, Julie!" I replied cheerily. "Maybe."

I closed the door before she could comment. I gulped back the rest of my drink, flopped down on my couch to wallow some more, and wished for some kind of crisis to arise. That was another problem with being so damned efficient. My smooth-sailing ship never rocked. It never tipped. Which meant there was very little to occupy my mind.

"You need to come up with a plan," I said aloud. "And that plan should probably start with a shower."

But five minutes later, I was still sitting in the same spot, staring out at the clear Toronto sky. Brooding now, instead of wallowing. The weather had been temperate since my arrival the previous morning. Not a drop of rain, and barely a cloud. About as perfect as it could get, really. The kind of weather that—if I happened to be home—would usually prompt me to slide open the glass doors to my patio and spend some time enjoying the air and the view. Right then, I just kind of resented it.

With a grunt that pretty much summed up my mood, I made my way to the bathroom, where I set the temperature to just shy of cool. A hot shower had its place. Good for soothing sore muscles. Washing away dirt and worries. This moment didn't feel like one of those. I wanted— needed—a refresher. A shock. But as I stripped down and stepped into the cool stream, I realized something else. The cool water beating down on my head and pouring over my shoulders reminded me of the rain on the night that I met Mia.

Angry with myself, I smacked the nozzle off, then climbed out and toweled dry with unnecessary viciousness.

You hate the rain. You don't miss the permeating damp. And you don't miss a girl you just met.

Except as I tossed on a fresh pair of boxer briefs and stalked back into the living room in search of the final dregs of my wine, the starkness of my living space stopped me in the middle of the beige area rug. I couldn't help but wonder what Mia would think of it. Nothing inside was personalized. It wasn't anything like her little rancher.

The walls were off-white, the leather couches a muted brown. The coffee table had a plain glass top and brushed steel legs. A tall, matching accent table sat on the other side of the room. A brown-speckled vase sat in the center of each.

I turned in a circle, studying the room's lack of personality. I wished I could say that it was just this particular spot that lacked charm. That I'd kept it purposefully plain for the sake of guests with different tastes. It would've been a lie to make the claim.

The kitchen had the same, boring décor. Beige on white. Even the backsplash tiles were desertlike.

The master bedroom—a loft with panoramic views of the city—could've been an oasis. Instead, it held nothing unique. Black and gray. Was there an undertone of masculinity? Maybe. Mostly, though, it looked like it belonged to no one in particular. In fact, the master suite was no more dynamic than the two spare rooms on the main floor. They might as well all be part of some show home. Which is essentially what the whole place was, if I really thought about it.

When I'd bought the condo two years back—cash, and sight unseen—I'd been both too busy and too disinterested to decorate it myself. It'd been in the middle of a particularly big takeover, and I was putting in anywhere between sixty and eighty hours a week at the office. I *still* averaged a six-day, fifty-hour work week. Not because it was necessary. The long days I kept were only required at the start of an acquisition or the setup of distribution. I spent my time there because I wanted to. It was my home away from home, and really…it was *more* home than my condo.

I closed my eyes, picturing it.

I kept a couch in the office, and after years of using it as a place to crash, it had contoured to the length and shape of my body. I had a well-stocked mini fridge and a one-touch espresso maker. My desk was an antique I'd inherited from my grandfather, and a family photo—the only one I had—sat on top of it. I'd hung a map of the world on one wall, and pinned it with all the places I'd like to go, if I ever found the time. There was a mahogany shelf too, covered in mementoes from the places I *had* been, and where I'd like to go back. A jar of sand from Hawaii. A rock from Myrtle Beach, and a stolen pint glass from a pub in Ireland.

I opened my eyes again, sweeping the boring old room with my gaze. *No*, I thought. *This isn't what I'd like to show Mia. I wouldn't want her to think of me as the type of guy who copped out and hired some interior decorator to make things as "basic" as possible.*

I'd far rather have her lift the jar of sand while I told her about how I grabbed it during a storm on Kauai. I'd like to watch her fingers hold the glass, and ask her if it felt warm to her like it always did to me. I'd love to see her face as she opened the blinds and caught sight of the lights of Toronto. Maybe put my arms around her from behind and point out my favorite spots. Then turn her around and kiss her hard. Drop her to the couch and kiss her freckled face. Strip her down, and—

"Holy hell," I muttered as I clued in to just how much denial I was in.

I *did* miss Mia. Every damned thing I'd done since leaving her house had been in the name of avoiding her, or of avoiding doing what had to be done in order to acquire Trinkets and Treasures. Physical distance and actual time weren't going to be enough. I needed a bigger wedge. One I sure as hell wasn't going to find at the bottom of a wine bottle.

Drawing in the miniscule amount of willpower I seemed to have available, I dumped the last of the liquid joy down my sink. I placed a call to my driver while stepping into a crisp suit, and within forty minutes, I was breezing past a very confused Julie into my office.

I hunkered down at my computer, scouring the internet for a means of getting what I wanted. I searched and searched. And somehow—thirtyish hours, a half a dozen calls, and lot of coffee later—I was back home and I had it. An in. The key. All I had to do was pull the trigger. Dial the number and confirm.

A glance at the clock told me it was a little after eleven. That would make it a bit past eight in Vancouver. Friday night too. Not exactly business hours, but a true businessman would take the nighttime call anyway. Especially with the kind of money I was offering up.

So what's holding you back?

I knew the answer, of course. My favorite redhead, and the question that had been hovering around the edges of my mind since her cool send-off. The one I'd been too pissed to think about closely.

Why did she go out of her way to tell me she hadn't wanted me there?

I was already on my way out. We'd made our agreement, and I was a man of my word. If she knew nothing else about what kind of person I was, that much had to be obvious. So why bother?

Unless she needed a wedge too. Something to keep her feelings at bay.

Hadn't she said it was better to end on a fighting note? It sure as hell felt more like a breakup than if we'd just parted ways. So maybe that cool dismissal wasn't quite as easy for her as I'd assumed. Maybe she wanted a reason to be mad at me.

Without being conscious of the fact that I was doing it until Mia's name was right in front of me, I pulled out my phone and scrolled through my contacts. I'd snagged her number from her phone during my morning coffee. Saved it in my address book and added mine to hers. In my head, I'd excused it as a sneaky business maneuver. Staring down at the phone, I knew better. I'd stored it just so I could contact her if I wanted to. Now I *did* want to. Badly. And I hit the call button before I could stop myself.

* * * *
Mia

I wrinkled my nose and took a sip of my too-sweet cocktail, then asked myself for the hundredth time why I'd agreed to come out to the club with Liv, Aysia, and a couple of the other girls from their office at Eco-Go.

Maybe I'd been a little too caught up in the exuberance of the other guests at the wedding shower earlier in the evening. Or maybe I just hadn't wanted to be accused of being evasive again. Either way, I was now stuck inside the ever-loving hell of bass-filled beats and gyrating hips and watered-down booze.

The only thing keeping me sane was the fact that we'd managed to score a table at the far end of the bar where it was quiet enough that my head didn't want to explode. I'd also volunteered for purse guard duty, so I had an easy excuse to avoid the dance floor.

So far, so good, I thought, taking another sip just as Liv appeared at the table.

"Hey!" she greeted, plopping herself down beside me, out of breath and flushed. "Did you see that guy in the gold shirt?"

"Every person in here saw the guy in the gold shirt," I replied dryly.

She laughed. "Yeah. Well. Not anymore. He just got busted for some hanky-panky in the bathroom! Two bouncers dragged him out with his pants around his ankles."

I groaned. "And this amuses you?"

"To no end." She grabbed my drink from my hands and took a giant gulp. "Thanks."

"You're welcome," I said with an eye roll.

"Hey. I was thinking…"

"Oh, great. Should I run?"

"No. Well. Maybe."

I snorted. "Tell me what you were thinking."

She grinned a Cheshire-cat grin. "That tonight would be a good night to follow up on that dare."

My heart flipped in my chest. I still hadn't mentioned a word about Ethan. In fact, I'd been surprisingly successful at avoiding thoughts of him. Which could've had something to do with completely exhausting myself to the point of delirium.

After the final dress fitting on Wednesday, I'd let Liv drag me all over Vancouver in search of shoes, then allowed myself to be roped into some late-night dinner thing that kept me out until one in the morning. One of my part-time employees called in sick on Thursday, so I jumped at the chance to cover her storefront shift. Then I'd hung around until the wee hours working on some new designs. On five hours of sleep, I headed in for my regular workday that morning. When that was over, I'd then occupied myself with the bridal shower, and now the club.

Sure, Ethan pervaded my dreams. And sure, if I held still for too long, his face popped into my mind. But all in all, I'd done an okay job of *not* thinking about him. But at the mention of the dare—something I'd cleverly diverted from on Wednesday, and which Liv hadn't brought up again until now—my heart stuttered in my chest, and thoughts of his soft lips filled my head. And with his soft lips came his warm, strong hands and the feel of his fingers and palms playing over my body.

"What about him?" Liv said, interrupting the blush-worthy memory as she pointed across the bar.

I made myself answer lightly. "If I look over there and see gold-shirt guy..."

"I told you he got kicked out."

"Gold shirt guy is sneaky."

"Yeah. Gold sparkles are totally subtle." Liv pointed again. "But I'm looking at *him*. Blue shirt, dark denim jeans. Hot bod. Looking our way."

"He's looking our way because you're flapping your arm at him," I told her. "He probably thinks you need medical attention."

"Ooh. You think he's a doctor?"

"I think doctors don't hit dollar highball night at a club with the nickname Sticky Floors."

"Yeah, you're probably right." Her face fell, then perked up again immediately. "But it doesn't matter what he does. You're not marrying him. You're just kissing him."

I made a face. "Wasn't I supposed to kiss the next attractive guy I saw? Because that dare was almost a week ago, and I think I've probably already crossed paths with one or two reasonably good-looking guys."

"See...I don't know what to do with that statement. There's too many options. Do I point out that if that's true, then you've already failed in completing the dare? Or do I ask how someone can only *think* they've crossed paths with some hot guys?"

"Neither?"

"Oh, please. You know me better than that. I want to say *both*."

"Fine," I said. "I've been far too busy to give a man more than a passing glance, let alone haul off and kiss one at random. So you win. I lose."

"Yes!" Liv crowed. "But you've forgotten the other part of the game."

"Which is…?"

"If you don't do the dare, you have to answer the truth question."

"You can't be serious. What could you possibly want to know?"

"Just one thing," she said shrewdly. "Who's E.?"

This time, my heart didn't just flip—it stopped. And I had to resist an urge to cast a frantic look around the bar. "What?"

Liv nodded at my phone, which was sticking just out of my purse. It flashed with a missed call, and sure enough, the contact was listed as E. I didn't stop to think about how his number got in in there, I just grabbed the phone and shoved it facedown on the table in front of me.

"E's no one," I said.

"The same 'no one' who was emailing you the other day?" she asked.

I exhaled a sigh. "As a matter of fact."

Liv narrowed her eyes at me. "Uh-uh."

"Uh-uh?" I repeated.

"You only get one or the other. Truth. Or dare."

"I don't remember agreeing to this."

"But you did. Or that's the way I see it anyway." She jumped up, then put her hands on her hips, and surveyed the bar. "Okay, I see him."

For a second, I thought she meant Ethan, and I swayed a little in my seat. Logically, I knew he wasn't there. But I was momentarily light-headed with the idea that he *might* be. He could've flown in. He *was* still coming after Trinkets and Treasures, and his stalking skills were on point, so…

But Liv has no idea what he looks like.

The thought was enough to bring me to my senses. I took a breath, straightened my shoulders, and followed her gaze. I immediately spotted her target. Tall. Thin without being scrawny. Dressed in khakis and a black-on-black shirt and tie. A flop of dirty blond hair, and an easy smile directed toward the man standing with him. He was good looking, no doubt about it. But studying him did absolutely nothing for me. Not even a twinge of attraction.

"Liv…" I said.

"Oh, come *on*," she replied, exasperated. "He's exactly right for you. He's cute. But totally nervous, and doesn't want to be here."

"How can you tell that from way over here?"

"He keeps tightening his hand on the glass he's holding, and when he takes a sip—which he's only done twice since I noticed him—he grimaces. He's also subtly checked his watch four times. So he's twice as interested in the time as in his highball."

"Maybe he's got somewhere to be. Or he's meeting someone."

She shot me a glare. "You're being deliberately difficult, Lu, and I—"

My phone cut her off as it buzzed to life on the table, its vibration sending it skittering over the polished wood surface. I shot out a hand to stop it from clattering to the ground. As soon as it was in my hand, I saw that "E." was flashing across the screen again.

"He's a persistent 'no one,' isn't he?" Liv asked.

I sighed. "Look. He's an asshole, okay? One of those guys who thinks he knows best just because he was born with a penis. You'd hate him. And I'm kind of tired of dealing with him myself. So he's 'no one' because he's no one I want anything to do with. And if he was here in person, I'd tell him to take his calls and shove them straight up his—what? Why are you making that face?"

She pointed down at my phone, which I held out in her direction. And before my eyes could even shift to follow her finger, I knew what I would find. My heartbeat quickened unpleasantly, and the world around me tilted as I forced my gaze down.

Call started, 0:52 seconds, read the screen.

Shit.

I knew I should slam the red key and end the call. Or maybe just drop the phone directly in my drink. Possibly run out of the bar before Liv could read something more in my horrified expression. But at that exact second, Aysia and her two friends came up to the table, drawing my fellow bridesmaid's attention away for a moment. And instead of doing what I thought I should, I did what I knew I shouldn't. I lifted the phone to my ear.

"Hello?" My greeting was almost a squeak.

Ethan's reply—laced with a weird mix of coolness and amusement—came instantaneously. "Shove it straight up my what, Lu?"

"I didn't mean that."

"No, it's fine. If you're into kink, I can get onboard."

My face warmed, and I dropped my voice. "That wasn't a sex thing!"

"Oh, really?" he replied. "Because I generally *so* enjoy being called an asshole in the bedroom."

"I didn't mean that, either."

"Didn't mean it, or I wasn't supposed to hear it?"

"Just…hang on a sec, okay?"

"I've got nothing but time."

I glanced up. Liv was still distracted, laughing at something Aysia was saying, so I decided to take quick advantage and slunk guiltily away before they could notice. For a moment my escape route got me stuck in a throng of drunken dancers, and the loud thump of music almost overwhelmed me. But I spotted a doorway across the bar, and quickly adjusted course. I managed to make it there without getting knocked over or stepped on too badly, but when I entered the space, I realized it was a strangely insulated alcove rather than an actual exit. It would have to do.

"Ethan?" I said into the phone, suddenly worried that he might've hung up.

"Still here, Mia," he said.

Hearing him answer filled me with relief.

"I'm sorry," I said.

"For which part?"

"All of it. I was just trying to get Liv off my back. She basically epitomizes that whole dog-with-a-bone thing. Anyway, she dragged me to this club tonight, and she was going on about truth or dare, then found this guy who she thought would be perfect for me, and I didn't want to tell her that I'd already kissed *you*. And she saw your number and the email, so..." I trailed off as I realized I was babbling kind of incoherently, while Ethan had gone utterly silent. "Hello?"

"What guy?" he said.

"Uh. What?"

"You said your dare-happy friend found the perfect guy. In what way was he perfect?"

I swallowed, not really wanting to answer, and not really knowing why. "Oh. For me to kiss."

"Yeah, I got that part." His voice was a little stiff. "What I want to know is what made him perfect *for you*?"

"I don't know."

"I think you *do* know."

"I already told you the criteria," I said miserably. "She dared me to kiss the next hot guy I came across."

"And *is* Mr. Right hot?" Ethan wanted to know.

My eyes stung, and I felt inexplicably like I might cry, and when I answered, my words quavered a little. "He's good looking, yes."

"So what are you going to do? Kiss him, or tell your friend the truth?"

My tongue stuck to the roof of my mouth. I wanted to tell *him* the truth. That it didn't matter how good looking the guy was, I had no interest in kissing him. In fact, I had no interest in kissing anyone but Ethan.

Which was ridiculous, because we'd had exactly two nights together.

And humiliating, considering the fact that he wanted to forcibly take my business from me.

But I couldn't bring myself to lie.

So I forced out a breath, hoping he couldn't hear the tremor in my evasive reply. "Why are you calling me? Isn't it close to midnight there?"

There was the briefest pause on the other end.

"I want that other two hours," he said.

"You want what?" I asked.

"I asked you for twelve hours. I only had ten."

"Because you left early."

"My flight was changed. Out of my control."

"You can't seriously expect me to give you another two hours of…" I trailed off, a blush heating my face.

"Was it so bad?" His voice fell in timbre, and took on that sex-fueled quality that made me shiver.

I leaned against the wall in the alcove, trying to cool the rush of blood through my body. But pressing my back to the thin panel had the opposite effect, because the pulse of music vibrated through and made my skin tingle instead.

"You know it was good, Ethan," I said. "But putting that aside—and the fact that we agreed that it was over—you're there, and I'm here."

"I'm coming back." His words sounded like a promise.

When? I wanted to say. *Make it soon.*

But I forced a more reasonable reply. "Yeah. Because you're still trying to steal my company, and that's easier to do if you're here."

I waited. Maybe for him to deny it. Maybe for him to retract his threat to my livelihood. He didn't do either.

"Two hours," he said again instead. "And in the meantime, don't kiss Mr. Right."

My temper spiked unexpectedly, and my response came out defensive. "Why shouldn't I?"

"Is my asking not a good enough reason?"

"Not even close."

"Lu…"

"*Mia.*"

"Don't kiss him."

"You have *no* right to tell me what to do," I snapped, hearing the childishness in my voice, but not caring at all. "I'll kiss whomever I damned well please."

"Is that what you want?" Ethan growled back. "To kiss him?"

"Why? Afraid he'll give you some competition?"

"You know as well as I do that he wouldn't compare."

"You arrogant asshole!"

"Monday night," he said. "I'm booking it now."

"Don't bother," I retorted. "Even if I didn't have plans, I'd rather crawl into Mr. Right's bed than spend a minute with you."

"Plans? What pl—"

I slammed my thumb to the phone, ending the call. For good measure, I turned the slim device all the way off. Then I stepped furiously out of the alcove, and lo and behold…smacked directly into Mr. Right. His hands came out to steady me, a pleased little smile showing off a dimple. He *was* hot, dammit. I could see that he was. Cuter up close than from far away, which was kind of a rarity, I thought. And judging from the appreciative way he studied my face, he thought I was attractive too. But being this close to him still did nothing for me. Not even the vaguest tingle.

I tried to imagine myself kissing him. I squinted at his lips. But the thought of getting any closer turned my stomach. I couldn't even listen as he opened his mouth to speak.

"Excuse me," I muttered, then pushed right by.

And I didn't stop moving until I'd reached Liv and Aysia and the two other girls, who were all sitting at our table with fresh drinks in their hands.

Aysia jumped up right away. "Lu, what's wrong?"

"Terrible migraine." It wasn't that far off from the truth; my head was definitely aching. "Will you hate me if I cut out early?"

"Not at all," said my future sister-in-law. "You want us to call you a cab?"

I nodded gratefully, glad to be given a reason not to turn my phone back on. And ten minutes later, I was sitting in the back of a taxi with my forehead pressed to cool window, and thoughts of Ethan pushed firmly to the back of my mind.

Chapter 13

Ethan

I stared across the room at my phone—which had just hit the wall, then bounced to the floor—and wondered what the hell was wrong with me. I didn't lose my temper. I got ice cold when I was angry. I became more effective when I was fired up about something because I channeled my frustration into turning things to my advantage. I'd never in my life thrown something the way I'd just thrown my phone. I was half afraid to walk over and check if it was broken. No way did I want to be that kind of man.

I tore my eyes from the facedown device on my floor, and paced the length of my bedroom.

Why the hell did she have to turn the phone off?

But I knew the answer. The second the line went dead, I'd realized I was being an asshole. A few seconds more, and I realized why. I was *jealous*. Another emotion I hadn't had much occasion to embrace, and one I'd now definitely say didn't bring out my best. Yet there I was, wanting to be a physical barrier between Mia and the unknown man in the club. Something I had no right to do. She wasn't my girlfriend. Even if she had been, the overreaction was totally unacceptable.

Unfortunately, knowing it was true didn't mean I could shake the feeling.

Is she kissing him now? I wondered. *Going home with him?*

I gritted my teeth and tried to fight the green-tinged emotion as it stormed through me.

I *had* tried to set it right. I'd hit redial as soon as I connected the ugly dots, ready with an apology. The first time I got her voicemail, I hung up. I dialed back. It took me two more tries before I clued in. She'd cut me off. It made me angry at myself, which is what resulted in the juvenile phone throwing.

I ran a frustrated hand over my hair, then sank to the edge of the bed. "You've got no claim on Mia Diaz," I said firmly, hoping that hearing it aloud would help.

But maybe you want a claim on her? countered a little voice in my head.

I tried to mentally refute the idea, but I gave up after only a moment. There wasn't much sense in denying it. The proof was in the discarded phone. In the way I hadn't slept properly in days. In the fact that I really had booked myself a flight going out Monday afternoon.

I turned my attention to my laptop, which sat on the edge of the bed with the confirmed flight details still open. I considered whether I should cancel it. Mia was rightly furious with me. I didn't know if I could muster up the energy to fight with her on the business front.

And she also said she had plans tomorrow night, I reminded myself.

What were they? Would they be derailed by the presence of Mr. Right?

My teeth tried to gnash again, and I forced in a calming breath. I glanced at the clock on my nightstand, and was startled to see that it was almost two in the morning already. How had nearly two hours passed already? Not that it mattered. I somehow doubted that I'd be able to get to sleep anytime soon. I was too geared up. Too worried that I was making a mistake.

I flopped back on the bed, thinking about it. *Are you really letting yourself consider making a business decision based on how you might feel about a woman you met a week ago?*

I blinked up at the ceiling. It wasn't that I usually disregarded the human factor in my dealings. I just never doubted that I was right. When I came after a business, I was always sure that what I offered was fair. Sometimes more than fair. The people on the other side weren't my enemies; they were just as driven by profit as I was. Hell. Sometimes they bordered on greedy, and I felt like I was doing the world a favor by taking them out of the equation. It was usually easy to figure out what they wanted from me. It was usually one of two things—more money, or more prestige. Or a little of both. Once I had that pinned down, I was on the path to win.

In the six years since starting Burke Holdings, I'd acquired roughly one business per quarter. Not once had I *not* been able to see what the original owner was after.

With Mia, it was different.

She didn't seem to want money, or need it. I inferred from the lunch with her family that there was some pretty comfortable backing there. Her brother certainly made a pretty penny at Eco-Go. I knew enough about the home development company to be sure of that.

And if Mia was concerned about making her jewelry a household name, she didn't show it. My research told me that her advertising was strictly word of mouth. Three months earlier, a local Vancouver paper had even reported that the company had turned down a celebrity endorsement of some kind.

Yet—like I'd said to her—I had no doubt in regards to her business skills. In the three years since she'd started Trinkets and Treasures, it'd gone from a small-time, home-based hobby to a flourishing company that allowed her to afford the rent on a prime piece of real estate.

So if she didn't want money or prestige, what *did* she want?

"Shit," I said as it suddenly dawned on me.

Mia wanted what I wanted—to hold on for dear life and be her own boss. *And* that's *what really makes her different*, I realized. *She's like me.*

I suddenly felt foolish. She'd *told* me her business was everything to her. Actually, what she'd said was "ditto," when I explained how *I* felt. Somewhere in my head, I'd assumed it was a deflection rather than a sincere exclamation.

I pushed back to a sitting position. What would I do, if I were in her spot? If someone was trying to push me out of Burke Holdings? I sure as hell wouldn't let him or her into my house, no matter what they said at my doorstep. I wouldn't make small talk over lunch with family, or take time out of my evening with friends to explain myself. And if the usurper in question told me to do something—*like not kiss someone, maybe?*—I'd laugh and go out of my way to do the opposite.

"Shit," I repeated, this time a little louder.

I'd probably pushed Mia straight into another man's arms.

Jealousy took a backseat to panic, and I realized something significant. I was a hell of a lot more worried about the thought of losing any chance with Mia than I was about anything else. Even more than getting my slice of her company. It was enough to startle me into immobility.

"This is crazy," I muttered.

And maybe it was. A week, I'd known her. Not nearly long enough to make the risk worthwhile. Except I was an expert at making instant decisions. A pro at assessing whether the rewards outweighed the potential. Why should this be any different?

Maybe because it's your heart, dipshit, not your money?

Unconsciously, I placed my hand over the organ in question. I wasn't a sentimental man, but I believed in instinct. I'd been living by my gut for six years. Successfully.

I had some damned good reasons for caution, but my intuition rarely let me down.

So yeah, it might be my heart. Right then, though, it was thumping out a rhythm that said Mia was worth it. And I needed to tell *her* that. In person.

I glanced at my computer again. There was no way I was giving up the Monday reservation. In fact, I needed to see if I could get into Vancouver sooner.

I jumped up, moved to my closet, then remembered that I'd accidentally let my small suitcase be destroyed by the rain. Annoyed by the delay, I made my way from the bedroom to the storage closet in the hall, sure that I'd stuck my old set of luggage in it. I flung open the door, pushed aside a dusty box, and peered into the dim space.

"Aha!"

I could just see the handle, jutting out from behind a pair of skis. I tried to yank it free. Much to my dismay, it broke off. I rolled my eyes, tossed the stupid thing aside, then bent down and reached in a little farther. My fingers clasped the edge of the suitcase. As I dragged it forward, though, it bumped against the skis, which in turn smacked the bar below the overhead shelf. The shelf rattled. Before I could react, something with a hard, sharp corner slid down and cracked me right over my eyebrow.

The pain and the blood came immediately, and it only took a few seconds of cursing and a look in the mirror to acknowledge that I wouldn't be running off to any airport anytime soon. What I *would* be doing was getting some stitches.

Strangely, after several hours—which included a visit to the ER, and a warning from the doctor to take it easy for the next day or two—I wasn't feeling discouraged. Instead, I felt challenged. Invigorated. Like the universe was presenting the whole situation to me in just the way I liked it—hard, and worth doing.

* * * *

Mia

Unsurprisingly, I slept terribly on Friday night. The fluorescent blue cocktail I'd had at the club didn't sit well. And neither did the last conversation I'd had with Ethan.

I kept asking myself if I'd overreacted. Was it so wrong of him to ask me not to kiss someone else? He'd said please. And had sounded a little desperate.

He doesn't own you, I reminded myself.

But what if I flipped it over? What if he was threatening to kiss another woman? I couldn't lie and say I wouldn't care. The idea of Ethan's lips on someone else's…it made me feel physically sick.

And he was right about there being no comparison. Until Ethan, it had been literal years since I kissed anyone, but I knew it had never been like this before. That it might never be again. It made my heart shrink painfully to think about it.

And yet instead of just agreeing to *not* kiss Mr. Right, I'd blown up. I'd name-called like a kindergartener with a sailor's mouth. I'd threatened to sleep with a stranger. Then I'd shut him out, and when I finally got up the guts to turn on my phone again, the only messages were from Aysia and Liv, checking to see how I was feeling. I'd sent them each a reassuring text, then stared down at the phone for far too long. Like I was hoping I could will a message from Ethan into existence.

Except I wasn't sure that I really wanted to hear from him. Because I was perfectly capable of calling him back on my own. I was an adult who could apologize when she ought to.

But he was still after Trinkets and Treasures, and that threat hung over me like a dread-weighted cloud.

I wanted to ask him to walk away. To explore the possibility of *me* instead of my company. And the desperate desire to do it was what stopped me. I didn't need the humiliation or the heartbreak. And I was starting to think the latter was an inevitability, so I had to avoid the former at all costs.

Heartbreak.

Even the word made me cringe. Knowing someone for a week wasn't enough time to care enough to get heartbroken. But there it was anyway. That sharp ache. The feeling that a chance at something—someone—great was slipping through my fingers. It made me furious with myself. I knew better than to let someone get behind my wall. I wasn't one of those people who didn't know I'd built one. *My* wall was conscious and carefully crafted.

But there I was anyway. Thinking of Ethan. Plagued by him all night Friday, and all day and night Saturday too. Wishing he would call, but knowing that when he did—or when he came into town on Monday, as promised—it would be for all the wrong reasons.

And Sunday was no better than Friday or Saturday. Work went by in a blur, and I tossed and turned all night to the point where I wondered if someone could die from sleep deprivation.

It was so bad that on Monday, when Liv came into my shop to go over the last-minute details for the unique bachelorette party we had planned for that evening, she asked me if I was sick. And when I brushed off her concerns with complaints of plain old exhaustion, she insisted on sending me to the spa for an hour. My protests were met with a plea. People would turn and run at the sight of me, Liv said. And probably assume it was the start of the zombie apocalypse, to boot.

So I gave in. And admittedly, it wasn't all that bad. The twenty-minute power massage actually put me to sleep. The mini-facial took off that freshly-dead hue, and the fresh polish on both my fingernails and toenails perked me up just enough that I felt like a new dress was in order.

But by the time I was actually *at* the party I'd helped plan, the melancholy was creeping up again.

Case in point, I'd been listening to the same woman talk for the last five minutes, but I couldn't even remember her name. Emma? Emily? Ellie? It didn't seem to matter to her in the slightest anyway. She'd been talking for a century about her ex-boyfriend and his new girlfriend, and balancing my reactions equally between nods and cringes had worked so far.

I shifted in my three-inch heels, took a halfhearted sip of my champagne, and nodded sympathetically yet again, then subtly craned my neck to see past the complain-y brunette. Aysia stood on the other side of the room, and when she spotted my glance, she offered me a congenial wave, mouthed a thank-you, then laughed at something the woman beside her said. I was glad she was having fun. I just wished I could manage to do the same.

I stifled a sigh and moved to offer Emma-Emily-Ellie a fresh cringe, but realized a little belatedly that she was gone. I cringed anyway, this time at myself.

Indulging in a moment of self-pity, I lifted the glass and downed the rest of the sparkling beverage. The bubbles popped along my throat, a welcome distraction from the small crowd around me. There were thirty women there, give or take—cousins and aunts and friends and long-lost roommates had all been included on the guest list—but I knew few of them, and I honestly wasn't sure if I could handle another round of small talk.

I clutched the empty glass to my chest and opted for a quick walk around the venue. Modern Grape was its name, and a mix of art and wine were its game. The snappy little gallery was located just a block from my own shop and it was wildly popular—both for local artists looking to make a name for themselves, and for the trendy patrons who walked its halls with glasses full of the crafted-on-site Pinot Noir. For tonight, I'd called in a favor so that we could have the place to ourselves.

It was supposed to bring an element of class to the event. But in under an hour, Liv's contribution to the party would supersede mine, and it would definitely take a turn for the classless. Three male strippers were slotted to begin at eight o'clock sharp. A policeman. A fireman. And a "surprise." Lord knew what that meant. Once that particular bit of debauchery was over, we'd move upstairs for a rooftop party that would include my brother and *his* entourage. Which would mean more dreaded small talk.

"T-minus thirty-eight minutes!"

At the sound of Liv's voice, gleeful with lascivious anticipation, I turned and rolled my eyes.

"You are *far* too excited about the impending flesh storm," I said.

She snorted. "I'll take my excitement over your funeral face. Are you going to join the party, or what?"

"I'm taking a breather. I spent the last five minutes comforting some woman about her horrible ex."

"Oh. You mean Nancy? Yeah, doozy of a breakup."

"Her name is Nancy?" I frowned.

"What'd you think it was?"

"Not Nancy."

It was Liv's turn to roll her eyes. "You can*not* call having a conversation with a woman whose name you don't know being a party animal."

"I'm here, aren't I?" I said. "And I'm drinking."

"Your cup is empty. And you might be *here*. But everyone else is over *there*." She gestured with her own full wineglass. "You might as well be wearing a don't-kick-the-introvert sign around your neck."

"Ha ha."

Overhead, the lights dimmed abruptly, and a bass-filled beat thumped out from hidden speakers.

Liv's face split into a grin. "Ooh. I think the strippers are early! That means your breather is over!"

She grabbed my arm and pulled me back to the main gallery just as the first stripper—the cop—slipped into the room and began gyrating his way over to Aysia. He slapped a pair of plastic handcuffs onto her wrists, dragged her to a chair in the center of the room, then started his striptease. He spun his shirt around over his head, then tossed it aside. When the discarded item landed on the nearby sculptures, I couldn't help but wince on behalf of the absent artist.

Get a hold of your priorities, Mia. Relax. You're here to have fun.

I grabbed another glass of bubbly and took a sip. But I couldn't seem to let go. So when the stripper's tear-away pants came flying at me, I was actually thankful for the fact that they made me spill a little wine down my chest. It gave me just the excuse I needed to slip away.

I stepped from the gallery to the hall, then from the hall to the stairwell. It still didn't give me the reprieve I was craving.

"Fresh air," I muttered.

I took the steps two at a time, pushed my way through the heavy door at the bottom, and burst on to the sidewalk outside the building. For a second, with the air filling my lungs and the openness around me, I did feel better. But as a noisy clang echoed behind me, I realized that my escape plan had a serious flaw. I hadn't planned a means of getting back inside.

I groaned.

The building was locked up tightly. I knew, because as the person responsible for the private rental, I'd made sure that once the last guest had arrived, all the entrances were properly sealed. Exit only. At least until my brother would arrive with the key I'd give him. Then he and his friends would join the women for the rooftop party.

Hoping I was wrong, I turned and grabbed the door handle. It didn't budge, and I knew I was going to have to call Liv to let me back in. I'd never live down the embarrassment.

No other choice.

I reached for my purse. Then groaned again as I realized I'd hung the bag's slim strap over the back of a chair in the showcase room, and in my haste to escape, it hadn't occurred to me to grab it.

The only way I'd get back in was if I tried to scale the side of the building. Which wasn't a real option. Was it?

I took a step back and eyed the brick front. I'd been rock climbing a time or two. Maybe the ridges and dips would be the same. There was even a little balcony on the second floor that looked promising.

Totally a safe and realistic plan.

In spite of the mental sarcasm, I took another step back. Or started to anyway. Because my left heel no sooner lifted from the ground than the right one caught in a groove. But I also no sooner starter to topple backward than a pair of warm, familiar hands landed on my elbows.

Chapter 14

Ethan

For a blissful second, Mia looked pleased to see me. Her honey-browns lit up, her lips parted, and I anticipated a pleasant greeting. My apology might be more eagerly accepted than I'd thought.

Then, as quick as the pleased expression had come, it disappeared. In its place was a guarded look that suited the way she pulled away and took a step back and brushed off some imaginary dirt.

My breath caught as I watched her.

I'd mentally prepared myself to be a little overwhelmed when I saw her again. I'd thought about it on the plane ride—cleared by the doctor this morning—and the whole time I was in the cab too.

I knew the effect she had on me. That luxurious hair. Her gorgeous, freckled skin.

Her all around Mia-ness.

I'd decided it would be like a having the wind knocked out of me. Maybe a little painful, but nothing I couldn't handle.

What I *hadn't* prepared myself for was the fact that seconds after I saw her, I'd have my hands pressed to her skin. Or the way her scent—was it the honey soap I'd given her?—would envelop me. And I *really* hadn't prepared for the teeny, tiny scrap of stretchy pink fabric that would be sheathing her body. I couldn't decide what I wanted to do more—rip it off, or cover it up.

You could start by saying hello.

She beat me to it, her voice as cool as her eyes. "What are you doing here, Ethan? And before you say that you warned me, I don't mean here as in Vancouver. I mean here, as in outside this building. How'd you find me?"

"I tried you at home," I replied. "You weren't there, obviously. So I went by Trinkets and Treasures."

Her mouth pinched. "The closed sign wasn't enough to tell you I was unavailable?"

I ran a hand over my hair. "I already knew you had plans. But I thought maybe—"

"Maybe what? You'd break in and help yourself to some of my trade secrets?"

"Not exactly what my business is about."

"Yeah. Well. Trinkets and Treasures isn't your business, either. But that's not stopping you from invading."

"I'm not a goddamned army, Lu."

"Mia."

"Lu," I repeated firmly. "Stop. Hear me out."

"The last time you said that, you wound up in my bed." She blushed, and quickly added, "Not that there's any danger of that happening again."

"I'm not here to take you to bed. And I'm not here for Trinkets and Treasures."

"Good. Because—wait, what?"

I couldn't stop my gaze from raking over her. "Don't get me wrong. I *would* take you to bed, if that's what you wanted. But I'm just here to apologize. And to tell you that I won't be coming after your business."

She blinked. "You can't seriously expect me to believe that?"

I took a step forward. "You know I'm not a liar, Lu."

She breathed in nervously, but didn't back away. "I *don't* know that, Ethan. I don't know much about you at all. Except that you live and breathe your company, just like me."

"But you *do* know me. At least enough to figure that much out."

"We met a week ago."

"I know. And as insane as it sounds, I've spent more time with you in the last week than I've spent with anyone in years."

"You were in Toronto for more than half that time!"

"Tells you something else about me, doesn't it? I'm not a social man. You know my dating history. You know my commitment level. Knowing these things means knowing the things that make me who I am."

She looked for a moment like she might not argue, but after the briefest hesitation, she lifted her chin. "And what about Mr. Right?"

My hands clenched into fists, but I answered in a respectably neutral tone. "What about him?"

"What if kissing him last night led to a date? What if I made plans with him for tomorrow night?"

"I'd ask to you cancel them."

"And if I didn't want to?"

"I'd be unhappy. But I wouldn't give up."

"You'd just hang around...waiting?"

"Yes."

"We've known each other for a week!"

"I think we've established the timeline."

"Ethan. I don't know what you want from me." Her voice was an ache.

I reached out to touch her cheek, and exhaled with relief when she didn't flinch. "I want you to forgive me for being an ass the other night. And for you to forgive me for wasting time thinking about your company when I could've been thinking about you. I want to tell you why I'm so invested in my work, and to hear why you're so invested in yours. I want to kiss you until you forget about Mr. Right. Until you forget anything but me. I want to look at you in that dress. And to take the dress off. I want sweep you off your feet, and take you on vacation, and sleep in with you on your day off."

"That's a lot of wants," she said softly.

I smiled. "I guess it is. Should I have been more succinct?"

Her mouth tipped up just enough to give me hope. "Maybe."

"Then if I'm being forced to summarize...I guess what I really want is a chance at us."

Her smile faltered. "You're asking for a lot of trust. I don't know if I can give it."

"So try me. Tell me *why* you can't give it. And if you can't do that— yet—then at least give me that two hours to prove I can earn it."

"That kind of trust can't be earned in two hours." She sounded like she might cry. "It takes months. Or years. And even then..."

I inched forward again, bringing myself so close that our bodies were flush against each other. "Give me a chance to get there."

She buried her face in my chest and mumbled something incoherent.

I ran my hands over her nearly bare back, just glad to have her in my arms. "What was that, sweetheart?"

"I didn't kiss him," she said, leaning back a bit. "Mr. Right. I mean. He wasn't actually called Mr. Right. I have no clue who he was. But I didn't kiss him."

"That upsets you?" I asked.

"Yes."

"Why?"

"Because of you."

"I'm not quite following."

"I didn't kiss him because of you!" She said it like it made her furious. "Because he *wasn't* you."

As much as I didn't want to laugh, I couldn't help myself. A chuckle burst from my lips as my heart expanded with pleasure.

"You think this is *funny*?" she asked.

"No. I think it's fan-fucking-tastic." I bent to drop my lips to her forehead. "Take me home with you. Or come to the Memory Motel with me. Or if you want to go somewhere swanky, just tell me where."

"I can't."

My heart dropped again. "Lu, please."

Her eyes widened at my tone. "I just meant I can't right this second."

"Right this—oh. Your plans." I scrubbed a hand ruefully over the back of my neck. "I guess that dress isn't typical Monday-night wear. Not that I'm complaining."

A blush crept up between her freckles. "I'm at my sister-in-law's bachelorette party."

"*At* it?" I repeated. "Now?"

She gestured to the building behind her. "I know it's hard to tell, but there's a whole lot of debauchery going on right now on the second floor. Right between a sculpted tree and something kind of carving. A fish, I think."

"So if the party's in there, why are you out here?"

"I needed a minute. And then I got locked out, and you came along…" She shrugged. "So I guess I got *more* than a minute?"

I smiled. "Maybe it's a sign that you should cut out early."

She shook her head. "I can't. I'm hosting. The two guys who run this place are friends of mine. They're expecting me to supervise. And on top of that, my brother and his entourage are finishing off their night here too."

"Then I guess we'll just have to find a way in." I stepped back and scanned the building.

"How? I was thinking about climbing up—"

"In three-inch heels?" I eyed the sexy-as-hell shoes skeptically.

"Bare feet?" she said hopefully.

"Do you have a death wish?" I asked.

"So what do you suggest?"

"I could try picking the lock."

"You can do that?"

"The key word in the sentence was 'try,'" I replied.

Her face fell. "You've never done it before?"

"Broken into a building? No. My more impressive tricks are strictly legal. But I'm willing to—" I cut myself off as I spied a reason *not* to commit a misdemeanor. "Or..."

"Or what?"

"We could just ask that *really* pissed-off looking blonde to open the door." I nodded my head toward the glass.

Mia turned her head and groaned at the sight of the petite woman who was stepping down the stairs at the other end of the lobby.

* * * *

Mia

As Liv reached the bottom of the stairs, panic hit. She was scanning the lobby, and any second, she was going to move our way. She was going to see Ethan, and know something was up. She'd tell Aysia. Who'd tell Marc. Who'd tell my parents.

Oh, God.

"You have to leave!" I gasped.

"Leave?" Ethan repeated.

"Hide."

"Hide?"

"Stop saying everything that I say!"

"Stop saying—" He cut himself off with a headshake. "If you're trying to hide me, I think it's too late."

"Too late?" I echoed.

"Now who's the parrot?" He nodded toward Liv. "I think she's seen us."

I looked even though I didn't want to. My friend had paused at the end of the lobby with her hands on her hips, and even from the distance between us, I could see that her lips were pursed in annoyance.

"Is it too late to run?" I was only half kidding.

Ethan chuckled. "I'm guessing you've got about T-minus twenty seconds to decide."

"And that's only if she decides not to chase us."

"Would she do that?"

"Undoubtedly."

"She does look determined," he said.

I snorted. "Yeah, that's kind of permanent thing with her."

"T-minus ten seconds."

He pressed his hand to my back, and the contact sent a sharp lick of heat through me. It fanned outward and settled between my legs.

He lowered his head and spoke near my ear. "What do you say, honey? Wanna run away with me? I could toss you over my shoulder and book it up the street right now."

I swallowed. The offer was beyond tempting. But Liv was almost at the door now, and her face was already twisted up with irritation. I cringed at the thought of having to face further wrath.

"You can't tell her who you are," I said quickly.

"Embarrassed by my presence?" Ethan teased.

"It's far more complicated than that."

"So I'm getting."

"Please, Ethan."

"Your secret's safe with me," he said.

"What are we going to say?" I replied desperately

But he didn't get a chance to reply. Liv had reached the door, freed the lock, and was shoving it open.

"What in God's name are you *doing* out here? Someone said they saw you sneak off, and I thought they had to be wrong, but…" she trailed off, her gaze flicking from me to Ethan, then back again, and she let out a relieved sigh. "Oh, thank God."

I couldn't keep the surprise from my reply. "What?"

Liv didn't seem to notice. She was already addressing Ethan directly, her eyes roaming over his body critically.

"What are you supposed to be?" she asked.

"That depends. What are you expecting me to be?" he replied.

"I dunno," she said. "The guy who just went home sick was a little bluer around the collar."

"I've always looked better in a suit than I have in coveralls, I'm afraid." Ethan's tone betrayed no surprise or concern. "Sorry if that disappoints you."

"It's not me you have to worry about," Liv told him. "It's the ravenous horde of women upstairs who're probably expecting a construction worker."

I just about choked on my next breath as I clued into what was going through my friend's mind. She thought Ethan was a stripper. Her eyes swept up and down his body once more. This time in an openly appreciative way that irked me. And I was kind of torn. One half of me—the unreasonable half, apparently—just wanted to step between them so she'd stopped ogling him. The other half of me knew I should find a way to warn Ethan. But before I could even think of a way to do it, he spoke. And it sounded like he'd picked up on Liv's assumption too.

He offered her a cocky smile. "The hordes of ravenous women haven't made a complaint about my abilities. Not lately, anyway."

Liv sighed. "I guess you can pull off the sexy boss look. Or maybe naughty executive? What do you think, Lu?"

Ethan turned his smile my way, a knowing, scorching look in his eyes. "Yes. What *do* you think? Am I a worthy piece of meat? Should I maybe unbutton a few things, give you a little more to go on?"

Heat bubbled through me. "I think I'm okay."

"You think *you're* okay?" he said. "You're supposed to be assessing *me*."

"You're okay too," I muttered.

He lifted an eyebrow, clearly enjoying himself. "Only okay?"

Yeah, I thought. *See how much you enjoy it when you have that horde of women pawing at you.*

But the thought of that actually happening made me want to give Ethan a solid kick in the shins for playing along. If I'd been able to do it without attracting questions from Liv, I might've done it. Lucky for Ethan, my fellow bridesmaid spoke up again.

"Fine," she conceded, finally moving aside so that we could step into the building. "But don't come after *me* for a tip, if anyone feels let down."

"Wouldn't dare," Ethan said back.

"What do you go by?" she asked.

He didn't even miss a beat.

"Mr. Brock Hard," he said easily. "Or 'sir' if you're not behaving."

Liv laughed. "All right, I take it back. You're far better than the construction dude who went home sick."

I glared at her back as the two of them walked side by side toward the stairs.

You could just admit that you're seeing him, I thought. *That would shut down her flirting.*

Except just the concept—seeing someone—made my hands clammy and my jaw tense.

Liv to Aysia. Aysia to Marcelo. And Marcelo to Mom and Dad, I reminded myself, and forced my lips to stay pressed together.

I settled for listening to their conversation and seething internally.

"So," Liv said as we started our ascent. "I didn't see Naughty Boss on the list of themes when I booked. Are you out because of that injury?"

"Injury?" Ethan replied.

"The stitches on your eyebrow."

As Ethan brought his hand up to touch the small, red slash, I cursed myself for not mentioning it earlier. I'd noticed the sealed wound the moment my eyes landed on him. Worry had made me want to reach for it. To run my thumb over it and kiss the edges and ask if he was all right. But I'd fought the urge and won. And now I regretted it.

"Job hazard," Ethan told Liv. "Lots of risks thrusting up against a chair." Liv laughed again. "I guess I'll keep my day job."

"Don't knock it 'til you've tried it."

By the time we reached the second floor, I'd never been so glad to step out of a staircase and into a bachelorette party in my life. Even the squeals of delight from the hopped-up-on-pheromones women were a welcome change from the back-and-forth between Liv and Ethan. But the squeals also reminded me of a few important facts.

Ethan wasn't really a stripper.

But Liv thought he was.

And so would the other women.

Which meant they'd expect him to dance.

I have to get him out of here.

"I'll show Brock the changing area!" The words came out as an embarrassing exclamation, and both Liv and Ethan turned my way.

"You will?" Liv sounded as surprised as she looked.

"I left my purse somewhere near there," I lied.

Her gaze moved between us for a second, then rested on me. "Can you give me a girl-minute?"

I groaned. "Do I have to?"

"Yes." She smiled at Ethan. "This'll only take a second."

He smiled back. "Take as much time as you need. I never like to rush things."

I shot him a murderous look, then let Liv drag me around a corner.

"Not him," she said firmly.

I frowned at her. "What?"

She rolled her eyes. "Oh, please. I saw the way you were looking at him."

I used every ounce of self-control I had to keep from blushing. "I really don't know what you mean."

"The dare! Mr. Hard can*not* be your target."

"He's not."

"I'm not a dummy, Lu. And I'm not saying this for fun. Even if he weren't gay—"

"You think he's *gay*?"

"I know he is," she stated. "The agency I used only hires gay dancers. And they charge extra for out of the ordinary touching. It's in the contract."

"They're strippers surrounded by drunk women," I said. "What, exactly, constitutes out of the ordinary?

"I don't know. But I'm sure grabbing one of the guys and kissing him would be close! So...just don't pick him, okay?"

Too late, I wanted to say, but I made myself nod. "Kissing gay exotic dancers isn't high on my to-do list."

"Good."

"Can I show him where to change now, or..."

"Go. I'll be watching the fireman."

"Enjoy yourself."

Her eyes sparkled. "Oh, I will."

I waited until I was sure she was gone before making my way back to Ethan, who was leaning casually against the wall where I'd left him.

"Okay," I said, "you need to get out of here. Fast."

"But I haven't done my show," he protested with a grin. "And you haven't told me what your funny little friend wanted."

I made a face. "She was warning me not to make 'Brock' the target of that dare."

"Why? Does she want Mr. Hard for herself?"

"Hardly. Brock's not her type."

"Brock's an everyman."

"Yeah. And Brock's also every *man*'s everyman."

"Every..." Ethan's dark eyes widened, and then he laughed. "Ah, shit. Well. At least I know why Brock's so well-dressed and pays so much for his haircuts."

"Shut up," I said. "We need to find a way to sneak you out without causing a scene."

"I'll go as soon as you give me an answer about those two hours."

The cheers from the other room grew louder, and I knew the fireman had to be nearing the climax of his show.

I nodded. "Fine. Two hours. But I'm not promising anything after that."

I'd never seen a grown man's face light up before, but right then, that's exactly what Ethan's did. His smile was pure joy. A boy getting his first bike. And it made my heart thump faster, because I knew the expression was just for me. I had a sudden urge to throw myself into his arms. I even took a half a step forward to do it. But Liv rushed in just then, stopping me from getting any closer.

"Seriously, Lu?" she said. "The fireman's done and Brock's not even *in* the staging area. You're officially fired from babysitting any more strippers we hire."

I opened my mouth to comment on the likelihood of that ever happening again and to point out that technically "we" hadn't done the hiring, but I missed my chance. Because before I could utter a single syllable, Liv had grabbed Ethan's hand and was pulling him away. I stared after them for a second, my jaw hanging loose with unspoken words. My feet wouldn't move. My head spun a little. And I wondered how in God's name I was going to be able to stop Ethan from doing a striptease for a roomful of women.

Chapter 15

Ethan

I stood inside the little space that'd been set aside for the exotic dancers—aka, *me*—for wardrobe changes, and asked myself for the five hundredth time if I was actually going to go through with this insane charade. And if I *did*, how long it would take for someone to realize that taking off my clothes for money wasn't my forte.

Except I couldn't see a way out of it. Not unless I literally ran away.

And you've done that enough times over the past week.

Though if I'd had to pick a situation where I made my stand, this one sure as hell wouldn't have been it. In fact, dancing was way down on my list of favorite things to do.

When I was a kid, twelve years old, my mom put me into a dance class. The Art of Hip-Hop for Boys, it was called. I'd remember that name forever, because it was just so damned pretentious sounding.

At the time, some boy band had just made it big, and every kid around wanted to learn their routine. Not me. I wanted to learn a shit-ton of classic rock on the guitar instead. I cursed my mom every Saturday when she dropped me off. I cursed Byron, the overenthusiastic instructor with the gyrating hips. I even cursed the other guys in the class, who seemed to actually *enjoy* the ridiculous movements. When the twelve tortuous weeks were over, I told my mom it was the most useless thing I'd ever done.

But you did *ask Mia to let you prove yourself.*

And what better way to start than by doing something I hated just to help her save a little face? Because I had a feeling that if I suddenly disappeared, it would somehow come back to bite her in the ass. Her firecracker of a friend would be right pissed off, that much was for sure.

So, yeah. If I had to fake my way through a striptease, then I'd fake my way through a striptease.

"Well, Mom," I muttered heavenward. "I guess I owe you an apology. But please don't watch as I shake my ass for all these women."

"What was that?" a man asked.

I turned and found a dude stepping into the cordoned-off area. He had a stack of clothes over his arm, but was dressed in nothing but a flame-covered G-string. He was also hands down the most ripped man I'd ever seen. Bodybuilder status, probably.

Shit, I thought. *No wonder Liv was worried about my ability to impress.*

I cleared my throat. "Nothing. Just thinking out loud."

"Been there. You new?" he asked, sticking out his free hand.

"Uh, yeah," I replied, taking the offered shake. "Brock."

"I'm Dimitri." He eyed me up and down. "Naughty boss?"

"Something like that," I said.

"Not a bad choice. Definitely some executive women out there. What're you dancing to?"

Shit again.

Dimitri laughed. "Let me guess. You forgot to bring your own stuff?"

I did my best to sound sheepish. "Rookie mistake?"

"You should be glad I stuck around, then. I've got something you can borrow, I'm sure." He stepped over to one of the display shelves, pulled out a hidden music dock, and started scrolling through songs on an iPod. "What're you into?"

"Rock," I said immediately.

"M'kay. Hang on. I might have a few things that work. How long of a set do you need?"

"How long of a set *should* I need?"

He lifted his face and raised an eyebrow. "You seriously are a newb, aren't you?"

"The truth?" I replied. "This is my first show."

"God. A virgin. You poor thing. Well, I usually do a two-song set. And I always have an encore ready if they want it. But I'm a seasoned pro. You might wanna start with a single song, then see how you feel."

"Whatever you think'll work. I trust your expertise."

"Being the boss of the Naughty Boss." He winked. "I like it."

Liv's voice carried in from around the corner. "Knock-knock, Brock! The ravenous ladies are ready for you."

"Am I ready for them?" I asked Dimitri.

He flicked the iPod triumphantly. "Yep. Got it!"

"Thirty seconds," I called to Liv.

"We'll be waiting." Her tapping heels faded away, and I could swear they sounded ominous.

Dimitri squeezed a meaty palm on my shoulder. "Relax. And if you run into any trouble, just think of Channing."

"Thanks."

A beat filled the air—presumably filtered from the iPod to the docking station, then through some speakers in the ceiling—and I straightened my shoulders. I stepped from the makeshift changing area to the short hall. Straight ahead, I could see sparkles and shimmers. I could hear the clink of glasses and not-so-subtle giggles. And the combo was scary as all hell. Far more intimidating than a roomful of bankers and CEOs. I'd never been so fucking nervous in my life.

"Channing!" Dimitri called.

Right, I told myself. *Channing.*

I forced my feet to move forward and chanted at myself in my head the way good ole Byron the instructor used to.

Hip, two-three. Hip, two-three.

When I got all the way into the gallery area that held the woman from the bachelorette party, though, neither Channing nor Byron helped. For the first time in my life, I froze under pressure.

Shit.

Balls.

Channing-shit-hip-two-fuck!

My gaze darted through the room. Pink and blue and purple were everywhere. Then a flash of white caught and held my eye, and my brain—which was working a hell of a lot faster than my body, apparently—told me I had a bigger problem than not being about to move.

The white in question was a veil.

The veil was on a woman's head.

The woman was Aysia Banks, Mia's future sister-in-law.

And she was currently looking at me like she was trying to figure out whether or not she recognized me.

Aysia leaned over and said something to the woman beside her, who shook her head in response, then lifted her face my way. Which clued me in to something else. It was Mia who stood beside her. Her honey brown eyes found me. They held me. And when she mouthed something indecipherable at me, my body finally sprang into action.

My hand came up to my tie. I loosened it, my hips swaying back and forth with the *thud-dum-thud* sound of the bass guitar. One of the women let out a whoop of appreciation as I got the tie free.

I kept my eyes on Mia. I hoped that the other ladies in the room were too inebriated or preoccupied with my hip thrusts to note that I was focusing on her rather than on Aysia.

I undid one button. Then another.

I paused and slid the tie down my arm, then strutted—*thanks, Byron, for that move*—toward the bride-to-be. When I got close enough, I turned my attention to her for just long enough to see that her eyes were glassy with the effects of her champagne, and they didn't show any recognition now. *Thank God.*

I lifted the tie, draped it over Aysia's neck, swished it back and forth, then danced backward, my stare fixed on Mia once again. I had no clue if anything I was doing was remotely sexy, but the look on my favorite redhead's face was enough to keep me going. Even if not one of the other women was remotely turned on, Mia's eyes were full of desire.

I wished like crazy that I had her alone.

I moved down to the buckle on my belt, and undid it in what I thought was an impressive, one-handed move. The leather snapped as I yanked it free, and the whiplike sound made me grin. There was a bit of a cheer from my audience too. More importantly, Mia's expression grew even hungrier.

Want slid through me, and the music suddenly wasn't the only thing pulsing.

Shit, I thought with a pause. *Was I supposed to have an erection like this?*

Maybe I should've asked Dimitri. Hell. I didn't even know if I was supposed to be offering full frontal.

Who knew stripping required so much thought?

I undid the top button of my pants, smiled, did a tease with the zipper, then moved back to my shirt. I undid each of the buttons quickly, then shoved my shirt and suit jacket wide to expose my chest. I heard the cheers from all around the gallery, and I did a spin to indulge those who stood on the other side of the room. But I really only cared about Mia's reaction.

I finished my spin and faced her again. She was watching me, her top lip drawn between her teeth, her breathing visibly quicker than it had been a moment earlier. I smiled and drew my hands over my chest. When I saw that Mia's eyes were following my fingers, I slowed down my self-exploration.

What will it take to make her *squeal like the others?* I wondered.

I suddenly had to know.

* * * *

Mia

I wanted the other girls to leave. Or I wanted to take Ethan by the hand and drag him away. Whatever it took to get him alone so he could finish his striptease in private. Just for me. Because I definitely didn't want him to stop.

I couldn't tear my eyes away from him. I'd never been a fan of exotic dancers. Awkward thrusting. Gross chair humping. Greased-up, waxed chests. And bulges that made me wonder if some kind of surgery had gone wrong. But this was different. I loved everything about Ethan's understated movements.

The way his long, strong fingers slid over his well-defined abs.

The way his eyes were fixed on me and only me.

The way his hips undulated with just the right rhythm.

And the longer it went on—second by slow, agonizing, shiver-inducing second—the less I cared that anyone else was watching. The less I cared that they might notice how his smolders were directed my way.

He danced forward and slid his jacket and shirt back off his shoulders, glanced around like he was surprised to find an audience, then shrugged the clothes back into place. It was a ridiculously coy move. Especially factoring in what *I* knew about his confidence in bed. But the crowd ate it up. And so did I.

Take it off, urged a voice in my head.

Like he could read my mind and wanted to torment me, Ethan started to do his buttons *up*. The move brought a chorus of complaints as the women in the gallery started to protest. And I heartily agreed with their sentiment.

No, no. Take it off!

Ethan smirked, just shy of cocky, put up his hands in defeat, and undid the buttons again. Then he slid out of his jacket, twirled it around on his finger, and tossed it toward Aysia. Which was really toward me. And as my future sister-in-law caught it in the air, Ethan's heady scent enveloped me. My mouth went dry. My panties grew damp. I *squirmed.*

God, how I wanted him to come closer. I wanted to be the one slicking my hands over his body like he was doing now. I needed to feel his rock-hard muscles under my fingers. To lick off the little beads of sweat I could see forming across his abdomen.

A gasp escaped my mouth. I knew Ethan saw it, even if he didn't hear it. His eyes were on my lips, the smirk growing into a self-satisfied half-smile. He moved his hips in a circle, thrusting them into the air each time he reached the center of the circle. The bachelorette party replied with shrieks of encouragement that intensified as he dropped his shirt down to his elbows.

Take. It. Off!

And a heartbeat later, he complied with the silent order. The shirt pooled to the ground at Ethan's feet, and he strutted forward, his unbuttoned pants flashing the waistband of his charcoal gray underwear. He was close enough to touch. Close enough to smell. My mouth itched to be on him, my palms ached to rub him.

Take.

It.

Off.

I dropped my gaze to his fingers, which traversed the edge of his boxer briefs. It wasn't fair that he got to touch himself. Not when I was near enough to be able to do it for him.

The music picked up, and so did Ethan's grinding. He matched the driving guitar with enthusiasm. One part stripper, one part rock god. And still wearing too many pieces of clothing.

"Take it off." It slipped out in a whisper, but Ethan's eyes homed in on my face like he'd heard it perfectly.

He inched the pants down.

"Take it off," I said again.

Another inch.

The pants hit his knees, and suddenly I was squealing like the rest of them. Bouncing up and down on my heels with anticipation, begging him to strip, and giggling like a crazy person as he complied. I wanted him naked. I was salivating to get him that way, the rest of the room be damned. When his fingers found his waistband, I knew I was the loudest screamer in the bunch.

"Take it off!"

But just as he was about to go full frontal, chaos erupted. The gallery filled with men's voice, and the women's shrieks took on a different quality, and for a second, I was afraid we were under some kind of attack. But then I spotted a familiar face—my brother's—and I realized that the bachelor party had invaded early.

A moment after I figured it out, a warm hand slipped into mine, and Ethan's rumble filled my ear. "C'mon, baby. Let's get out of here before your brother sees me mostly naked."

I didn't argue. I let him pull me away from the group and out into the hall, then to the stairwell. We raced down the steps, pausing at the bottom to catch our breath. Only when we stopped, the wind went out of me completely. Because while Ethan *was* mostly naked, he'd somehow managed to grab his shirt and pants. The latter hung over his arm. But he'd slipped the former back on, and now it hung open. His chest and abs were on display, still covered in light sweat that trailed down the V to his low-hanging underwear.

God.

I was sure I'd never seen anything sexier in my life. And just like that, the animalistic urges that had been building since the second he undid his tie—or maybe since the second his hands landed on me outside, if I was being honest—took over in an explosion of need.

I launched myself at him. And clearly he wasn't expecting the amorous assault. He stumbled into the wall behind him and pressed his hands back to stabilize himself.

Perfect, I thought.

It left him exposed.

I dropped to my knees and pressed my mouth to his bare stomach.

"Lu, what're you—shit. Yes. Lu. God, please—Lu, I—" His words cut off into a mumble as my tongue flicked along the elastic of his underwear.

I reveled in his lack of ability to speak coherently.

My hands came to his knees, then slid up to his thighs. His muscles were tense under the attention, the thrum of his pulse palpable under my palms. I didn't want to rush, but I couldn't seem to help myself. I brought my fingers to the bottom of his boxer briefs and tugged. He groaned as his rigid manhood sprung free. I was sure I let out a moan too.

My own need pulsed through me with increasing intensity. And as I parted my lips to take him in, my knees spread on the ground, welcoming the throb.

I widened my mouth and drew him in even farther, both for his pleasure and mine. And he was definitely enjoying it. Each breath was a hiss or growl. His body bucking lightly against me with each suck. And a few moments later, his hands gripped my hair. I loved the way they held so tightly, like they were the only thing that kept him from going over the edge.

But I wanted him to go over the edge.

And I did. So badly. I wanted to possess him. To give him this and to take it from him at the same time. *My* sexy, dark-eyed stranger. *My* phony exotic dancer. *My* Ethan.

Mine.

The word circled through my mind, feeling so right that it almost hurt. Mine, and I needed to prove it.

I sped up my attention, deepening it as if I could devour the length of him. He dropped a curse, and another incoherent mumble, and then my name. "Hell. Shit. If you don't—I'm going to—Lu. Oh, God, Lu. Mia. Please, just...ah."

I didn't stop. Wouldn't. Couldn't.

His fingers moved through my hair with desperation. I knew he was close. So close. My own body was unbelievably near as well. Unconsciously, my hips rocked back and forth in time with my sucking, though they met only air. And as much I enjoyed the way Ethan throbbed in my mouth, it was a shoddy surrogate for the need between my thighs.

And then he spoke, giving me my out.

"Touch yourself, Lu," he groaned. "Please."

I obeyed. I slipped one of my hands down to my thigh, then up under my dress. I pushed aside my panties, and I thrust my fingers to my clit. Pure, autoerotic pleasure shot through me. I ground against my own hand and sucked Ethan impossibly deeper into my mouth.

And I couldn't hold on. Not for a heartbeat more.

I moaned over the length of him as I found my release.

And moaned harder when he cried out my name and found his at the same moment.

Chapter 16

Ethan

As the last wave of satisfaction rolled from me, my fist unfurled and I sagged weakly against the concrete wall. The world came back into focus slowly. The first thing I realized was that Mia was still on her knees in front of me, her hand invisible under her dress. It was sexy as hell. But I wanted her close. Summoning what little strength she'd left me, I dragged her up and crushed her against my chest. I drew in a deep breath, noting that she smelled like sex and honey.

Perfection.

I hugged her tighter, wishing I could come up with an appropriate string of articulate sentences to express the way the explosion of warmth between my ribs made me feel. But I couldn't think of damned thing, so I just settled for pressing my hands to the small of her back.

"Ethan?" she said.

"Sorry." I loosened my hold. "Not trying to squish you."

She laughed against my bare skin. "You're not. Well. Not in a bad way. I just wanted to ask you something."

"Ask away."

"Your place or mine?"

"I've heard that somewhere before."

"I know. But it was such a good idea that I stole it."

I grinned into her hair. "All right, my little thief. I just so happen to have a room at the Memory Motel. But I also have some fond memories of your house, so…"

She wriggled against me, then placed a warm trail of kisses up my collarbone before pulling away to look up at me. "The motel's closer."

"In a hurry?" I teased.

"Definitely not." She blushed as she said it, then quickly added. "But two hours is going to go fast."

My heart lurched unpleasantly. "Oh, no. You're not getting off that easy."

"What do you mean?"

"I'm rationing those hundred and twenty minutes."

"Rationing them how?"

"For starters, I'm splitting the time into four, thirty-minute sessions," I said. "And each time a thirty-minute session ends, if you decide to stick around, I'm not counting that."

Her expression was a mixture of amusement and amazement. "You've really thought this through, haven't you?"

I shook my head. "Nope. This is all on-the-fly shit. And while we're at it, I'm not counting any time we spend around other people. So if we're in a group like we just were, anything that happens for next twenty minutes or so is void."

"Void? You're calling what just happened *void*?"

I lifted a finger to trace the pink stain of her cheeks. "No. I call that fucking amazing. But if I'm only getting two hours, then you can be damned sure I want to use them wisely."

She leaned in to my touch. "So what do we do now?"

"Think you can get out of supervising the rest of the party?" I asked.

"My brother has a key to lock up. And I'm sure Liv would *love* to be the boss," she replied.

"Good. That means I can take you to the Memory Motel and get my first thirty-minute interval. After which, you can stay or go as you please."

"Gee, thanks."

I kissed her nose. "Oh, you're so very welcome. Should we get a cab?"

She gave my waist a squeeze. "How about you put on your pants, I take off my heels, and we take a shortcut on foot?"

"There's very little I'd like more than that."

I reluctantly let her go, and scooped my pants from the ground. As she bent too to slip out of her heels, I caught a glimpse of the smile on her face. It was small. Satisfied. Completely pleased. And there was something about it that made me sure I wasn't supposed to see it. Like she was smiling to herself about some closely guarded secret.

I wanted to ask her to turn the smile my way. To tell me what was going through her head that made her glow like that, and to ask if it had anything to do with me. I hoped like crazy that it did. By the time I'd finished buttoning and zipping, though, the little smile was gone. There was another in its place, but wasn't anywhere near the same.

I resisted an urge to ask her why, and instead extended my arm. "You ready?"

"I don't think anything could make me quite ready for Mr. Brock Hard," she teased.

I pulled her in for another kiss, then led her out of the stairwell, through the lobby, and out into the cool evening. It wasn't raining, but dampness permeated the air, and I thought it might start up again soon. The thought didn't seem quite so unpleasant with my and Mia's fingers threaded together. Hell. I might even like walking through a downpour with her. I glanced at the sky, almost hoping to see clouds.

Mia bumped my shoulder, drawing my attention back to the earth.

"It's nice, isn't it?" she said. "That almost-rain smell."

I inhaled again. "It's not bad."

"You don't like it?"

"I do. I just didn't know it until I smelled it here with you."

"For a big, bad businessman, you say some pretty sappy things."

"Well. The two things aren't necessarily mutually exclusive." I squeezed her hand. "You're a business owner too. Don't you have the odd sappy moment?"

"I learned not to be sappy a long time ago." She pulled her fingers away, then looked down like she was surprised to see that she'd let go.

"You wanna tell me about it?"

"No," she said softly. "Not yet."

We reached the end of the first block then, and Mia paused to look back at the building we'd abandoned.

"Worried they're going to miss you up there?" I asked.

"Worried? Not really. I mean, I probably shouldn't have abandoned my hostess duties. But Marc and Aysia will be all over each other and might not even notice. If they do, they'll just assume I ducked out early, and I'm sure Liv wouldn't be thrilled to hear I ran off with a 'stripper,' but then again..." She pressed her palm back into mine and starting walking again, tugging me along. "She's the one who dared me to kiss you in the first place, so tough luck for her."

"Not me," I reminded her. "Some random, incredibly hot guy."

"Don't let your ego get the better of you. I *had* just fallen from a tree."

"How'd you get roped into that, anyway?"

"The tree?"

"No. The dare."

"Oh. You probably don't want to know."

"I kinda do, actually. Or. We could go back to discussing what led to your de-sappiness." Part of me hoped she'd actually deflect to the last thing.

"Fine. But if you *really* want to hear it, I have to tell you about my childhood." She said it like it was supposed to be a threat, but I was immediately eager to hear every detail.

"Good," I replied. "Tell me."

"Really?"

"Yes."

"Okay. Well. We moved around a lot because my dad was just starting out in property development, and he liked to be close to whatever he was overseeing. My brother is a couple of years older than I am, and he was always really good at making friends. He had the whole small talk thing mastered from, like, birth, and every time we went somewhere new, he'd be like the shiny new toy."

"I think you're pretty shiny yourself," I interjected.

"I was a freckle-covered, redheaded brace face," she informed me. "And don't you dare say I was probably adorable, or I'll drag you down to California to go through my mom's photo albums."

"Is that an option?"

"Do you want to hear the story?"

"Desperately."

She rolled her eyes and went on. "*Anyway.* Marcelo was always the cool new kid, so I needed to find a way to keep up, and the one thing I had going for me was that I was pretty much fearless. I already knew I was awkward and kind of nerdy, so what did I have to lose by being a little crazy too?

"And out of this, the dare was born," I filled in.

"Exactly. Marcelo was always happy to play along, because I'd do whatever he told me to. I became a part of his party tricks. But when we got older, I got more reckless. I did some dangerous things, and my brother went away to college..." She shrugged. "Let's just say that ages sixteen through twenty weren't my finest hours."

She sounded ashamed, and my heart hurt at the thought that she was living with some cloud of regret hanging over her. I stopped walking and pulled her around to face me.

"We make lots of bad decisions when we're young," I said. "Then we grow up and pass that torch on to the next generation. I'm sure as hell not the same man I was ten years ago."

"I know. But I'm not talking about a tattoo I wish I hadn't gotten, I—" She cut herself off, and her eyes dropped to her hands before she took a breath and added, "It doesn't matter."

"It obviously *does* matter, honey," I argued gently. "Whatever it is—or was—you can tell me. I'm not going to judge you for it."

There was something close to anguish in her eyes as she answered. "Here's the whole trust thing again, Ethan. The things that happened didn't just shape *me*, they ruined other people's lives too."

"Okay," I conceded. "Take whatever time you need. When you get there, I'll be waiting."

She looked up at me, hope overtaking the sorrow, and I made a silent promise to make sure I was worthy of that hope.

* * * *

Mia

I stared down at Ethan's stubble-dusted jaw for another long moment, then glanced at my phone to check the time. It was nearly ten a.m., and it was Thursday. I had a couple more hours until I had to go to work.

But...Thursday.

I bit my lip.

I'd really, *really* meant to go home on Monday after the allotted thirty minutes was up. Really. Even if just to prove that I could. But Ethan had successfully turned more than a few parts of me—my legs, my brain, and pretty much anything between my belly button and my knees, for example—to jelly. So even if I'd truly wanted to, I might not have been capable.

And how does that explain how Monday became Tuesday and Tuesday became Wednesday and Wednesday became now?

It didn't. There wasn't much of an excuse other than that I didn't want to be anywhere else. Of course, I did go somewhere else. To work. Then back to the motel. And home to get some clothes. And back to the motel again. Where Ethan told me I didn't *need* clothes. And showed me that he was right. The whole time, he claimed that he'd only used up a single half-hour interval too.

Sneaky bastard.

I sighed, smiled, and dropped my eyes to the even rise and fall of Ethan's chest.

He'd been nothing but kind and patient for the last few days. He'd abided by my request to steer clear of Trinkets and Treasures. He hadn't complained that my usual "weekend" was spent working in exchange for the *actual* weekend off for the wedding. He'd kept silent while I dealt with last-minute bridesmaid duties over the phone, and hadn't asked again about my so-called de-sappiness.

But there was more than that. He was attentive. Insatiable. Thoughtful. So incredibly warm and sexy and all things good.

And the conversation was as fantastic as the sex. And that was really saying something.

I liked talking to him. Listening to him too. There were no awkward pauses or uncomfortable moments. At even the hint of lag, Ethan would make me laugh. Or kiss me. Or both.

He'd told me all about his business, not holding back about the number of smaller companies he'd pulled under his umbrella. It was as interesting as it was impressive.

But what I'd enjoyed more was hearing the personal things, like his childhood. I'd loved learning about it. His face was animated when he talked about the tiny apartment in Toronto where he spent his early years, describing in detail the horrors of no air-conditioning in the summer and unreliable heat in the winter. Growing up in a lower-class neighborhood— the only son of a struggling mechanic and a chronically ill mother—had given him a deep appreciation of hardship. He'd explained that part of what spurred him to work so hard to achieve his goals was never wanting to have to worry about money again. But he never had gotten around to telling me about the other things that inspired him to do what he did.

I frowned, remembering that I'd asked. He'd easily diverted the conversation. First to tell me an anecdote about an impromptu snow day, then to ask about my college years. I hadn't really noticed at the time, but thinking about it now, he'd also changed the subject when I asked if his family still lived in Toronto. It made me wonder.

Did he do it on purpose?

I dragged my eyes up from his chest to his face. Was there something he was holding back? I had a nagging suspicion that there might be. But what?

Like you have any right to complain, I said to myself.

I was still keeping my own secret tightly under wraps. Although it was admittedly getting harder to do. I actually *wanted* to let it all out. To throw my usual caution aside and leave myself vulnerable. Maybe it would even spur him to divulge whatever it was that he was keeping hidden.

Assuming there is *something.*

But as I studied his features—already familiar, already capable of making me smile just by existing—the belief that he was covering something up grew stronger. I didn't do hunches. And it was impossible to get to know someone completely in mere days. My parents had told me and Marcelo plenty of times that they were always discovering new things about each other, and they'd been married for three decades. Yet something in my gut told me I was right. And as crazy as it seemed, I *did* feel like I knew Ethan well enough to wade through the hints and draw the conclusion.

"Are you watching me sleep?" His voice made me jump.

I cleared my throat. "Uh…"

One of his eyes opened, and it was full of amusement. "Don't worry. I can admit that I've done the same thing to you a few times."

"You have?"

"Yes. But try not to look so horrified. You only drool a tiny bit."

"I do *not* drool."

He laughed, then slid sideways, flipped me to my back, and covered my body with his own. "Tell yourself what you have to."

I wriggled a little in a futile attempt to free myself from his strong grasp. All my effort did was create a bit of friction that brought my nipples to attention. They rubbed against Ethan's chest. Which drew a light growl from him, which in turn immediately heightened my desire.

He dropped his lips to mine, and flicked his tongue along the inside of my mouth. Tasting. Promising. Making me ache.

My legs spread in an automatic invitation, and he released my wrist to slip a hand between us. The wetness between my thighs didn't need any coaxing whatsoever. I was eager and ready the moment his fingers slid into me. I moaned and lifted my hips to meet the attention. But his hand wasn't really what I wanted. What I *did* want was wedged against my thigh, just a few inches shy of where I needed it.

I wanted *him*. Quick and hard. And now.

Luckily, I wasn't above begging. "Please, Ethan…"

"I'm sorry, honey."

"Sorry?"

"I think we might be out of condoms." He said it like he'd just announced the impending apocalypse, and I might've laughed if it hadn't half felt like it *was* the end of days.

"You can't be serious," I replied.

"I'm pretty sure we used the last one at two this morning."

"But it was such a big box."

"And your, um, *appetite* is voracious."

I started to blush. And to argue. But couldn't muster up a denial. Especially considering just how badly I wanted to indulge in my voraciousness at that moment.

"This is bad," I said. "What do we—my purse!"

"Your purse?" he repeated.

"When I picked up my stuff, I stuck a condom in," I explained. "You know. Just in case."

"In case, or in hope?" he teased.

"Do you, or do you not want to—oof!"

Ethan shot to the side, practically pushing me out of the way as he reached across the bed and snagged my handbag from the nightstand.

Maybe all the rushing and the joking should've been a turn-off. Or at least dialed down the urgency. But the sight of Ethan's perfectly sculpted ass hanging over the bed tipped the scales back to rushing. I barely gave him a chance to get back into the bed properly before I tore my purse from his hands and dumped the contents onto the sheet. I found the condom— just one, but thank God it was there—and tore it open, then pushed Ethan back and rolled it on to him. He was just as ready as I was, and it only made me more eager.

I straddled him and held myself poised over him for a heartbeat. Then I sank down, plunging him into me. His hands came up to my thighs, and his eyes closed. I let myself watch him for a moment. But only *a* moment. And then I lost myself in the rhythm, letting the motion rule the *rest* of the moments.

It wasn't slow lovemaking. It wasn't drawn out and full of romantic undertones.

It was frenzied and perfect. It was raw and satisfying.

Full of wordless moans and gasps.

And the orgasm that overtook me was the same. As fulfilling as it was quick. I rode the waves all the way to the end, and opened my eyes just in time to see Ethan throw back his head. He murmured my name and tightened his grip on my legs, then pulsed inside of me.

But when I extricated myself from his body and wiggled into a sideways embrace, the frantic mood changed in an instant. Mostly because of Ethan's next words.

"I think you should go on the pill," he said.

My pulse did a weird little pause, then jumped and doubled. "The pill?"

"Small, round, white thing. You take it once a day so you don't get pregnant. Unless you want to get pregnant. In which case we can—"

"No!" I took a breath. "I mean, no. No, I don't want a baby right now."

He shrugged far too casually. "Okay."

"Ethan."

"What?"

"The *pill*?"

"If you're worried about catching something, I give you my word that I'm clean. But we can go get tested." He said that too casually, too.

"It's not that," I replied. "It's...the *pill*!"

"You keeping saying it like it's a dirty word."

"The pill..." I couldn't fight a slight wince. "It's...I dunno. Permanent." He chuckled. "It's not permanent. You can stop taking it anytime."

My wince became a serious blush. "I should've said long term. And I meant the relationship part, not the pill itself."

His went silent for a minute, his fingers trailing up and down my arm. "Didn't I say that was what I was after?"

"I don't know if you *said* it, in explicit terms."

"Oh, it's like that, huh?" His hand slid up my arm to my chin, and he tipped my face up so that we were eye to eye. "Lumia. I want a long-term relationship. With you. Just in case you needed clarification on the last bit."

I stared at him. "Is this real?"

"Is what real?" he replied.

"Any of it. You. Me. Us."

"I damned well hope so." He chuckled. "Although, if my imagination is this good, I might quit my day job and find a more creative outlet for my talents."

I didn't laugh, and instead insisted, "But it'll *have* to end."

"Why?"

"Logistics."

"Since when do passion and logistics mix?"

"They don't. That's my point."

He leaned back. "Tell me what, specifically, you think the issue is."

"Well, for starters, there's the distance thing," I told him.

"We're skin to skin. Pretty much zero distance."

"Would you quit making jokes? I'm serious." And I was, so serious that my heart wanted to burst with sadness at the idea of the space that separated us.

He sighed and smoothed my hair back from my face. "Okay, fine. Look. Yes, my office is in Toronto, and your store is here in Vancouver. But I can commute."

"You can commute from Vancouver to Toronto?"

"Yes."

"That's insane."

"My work only requires me to be at the office a few times a year. I spend a big chunk of time traveling across Canada for acquisitions. There's no reason to not have a home base in Vancouver. And you can join me in Toronto—or anywhere—any time you want."

I blinked. "Okay. I take it back. *That's* not insane. *You're* insane."

"The only thing I'm crazy about is *you*." He kissed my forehead, then my nose, then my lips. "You don't have to say yes right away. Just think about it."

"I don't even know what I'm saying yes to."

"To me."

"I…" I trailed off, unsure what to say.

But it came to me just a second later. And I started to talk, the words tumbling out so fast that I couldn't stop them.

Chapter 17

Ethan

The first words in Mia's story filled me with dread.

"He was forty-three," she said, "and I was eighteen."

My gut clenched unpleasantly, both at the statement itself, and at the fact that her tone was laden with guilt. Like whatever happened was her fault. I wanted to cut her off and reassure her that whatever the hell it was—*eighteen and forty-three for Christ's sake?*—she'd been barely more than a kid. I resisted the urge to interrupt. Her voice was already so small and uncertain that I knew the slightest disruption would probably stop her altogether. I settled for circling my hand on the small of her back in silent comfort, and let her talk.

"I was still doing the whole girls-gone-wild thing," she told me. "My friends and I were at club with a couple of fake IDs, when one of them spotted this group of older dudes in the corner. Nice suits. Gold cards. One of the girls bet me a hundred dollars that I couldn't seduce one of them. I took the bet, of course. And succeeded. Of course. Me, in my shitty cut-off jeans, and him, in his designer suit."

She paused to take a breath, and went so quiet that I thought she might not actually start talking again. But after a few seconds, she cleared her throat and went on.

"His name was Gary," she said. "A property investor. My friends teased me that I'd somehow managed to fall into that whole 'marrying your father' thing."

"Marrying?" The surprised response slipped out before I could stop it.

Mia swallowed and let out a nervous laugh. "I'm getting ahead of myself, I guess."

"Take your time, love."

"Whatever my friends said, he was *nothing* like my dad. Gary was flashy. The expensive suits. Fancy car. Swanky apartment. My dad wouldn't be caught dead near any of that. But I was the rebel, right?" She shook her head. "And the fool. For two entire years, I cut myself off from my family because they hated the man I thought I loved."

She stopped again, her eyes closing. I closed my eyes too, trying to picture it. To picture *her*. A younger Mia. A little crazy, a lot less in control. For some reason, all I saw was vulnerability. A tough exterior covering a scared little girl. Steeling herself against the outside world the same way she steeling herself now to tell me her story.

She breathed out. "It was all a lie."

"What do you mean?"

"I ran around with him for two years. I worked retail jobs or not at all. I stayed in his apartment or with friends. He traveled a lot for work. But finally, after all that time, *he* convinced *me* that I should reconcile with my parents. He suggested bringing them some tangible proof of just how good we were together. He gave me a ring. And an investment opportunity."

My hand pressed to her back. I could sense what was coming, and I could feel her genuine pain.

"He ripped you off," I said.

"More than that," she told me. "He ripped my *dad* off. He came in all charm and big plans. And he cost my parents their life savings. *I* cost them that money. My parents put their trust in Gary because I asked them to."

"How'd you find out the truth?"

"Three days before the wedding—a small, private thing, thank God—I came home to an empty apartment. Before I could even make a guess at what happened, the landlord was at the door, demanding six months of back rent. It didn't take long to figure out that Gary wasn't even Gary. He was an experienced con artist. Patient, dedicated. A real piece of work with a half a dozen identities and a decent record."

My jaw twitched with anger. I wanted to throttle the man, and I'd never even met him. Ridiculously, I hated that I didn't know her then. Hated that I couldn't go back in time to protect her from the past injustice. It was a futile anger, and I hated the helpless feeling nearly as much as I hated Gary the con artist.

I had to force myself to speak calmly. "The police?"

She sighed. "Yes. Well. It got complicated. I lost it. I went after him myself, and I was a little too efficient. I found him living in the suburbs and I drove my car straight through his living room window."

My jaw twitched again, this time with dark amusement. "The sonofabitch deserved it."

"He did," she agreed. "But his wife and kid didn't."

"Shit."

"Yes. To put it mildly. I'm thankful—so unbelievably thankful—that no one got hurt."

"That's a hell of a burden."

"A burden," she repeated. "Yes, that's probably the best word to describe it."

"So what happened after?" I asked.

"His wife left him, but they didn't press charges and neither did we. Our lawyers did some fancy paperwork. A friend of the family—Marcelo's boss, actually—helped my parents climb out of the financial hole I created. I got some much-needed therapy, and I figured out who I was and what I wanted," she said. "The end."

"I don't think that's where it was supposed to *end*, honey."

She kissed my chest. "Okay. A new beginning, then, if you want to get cheesy. I went back to school, and found out that I was pretty good at it. I got my four-year business degree in two and a half years. I did the jewelry stuff on the side, and it took off. Like, *really* took off. So I put the two things together, and voila. I had seed money and know-how, and Trinkets and Treasures was born. When my brother moved up here, I decided to take it to the next level. My therapist signed off on it, and here I am. A really great business, a family who worries about me constantly but doesn't say it aloud, and some pretty serious trust issues."

I pulled her in a little closer. "And a man who's asking you to go on the pill. Just to complicate the already complicated."

"And that. It scares me."

"It does? Or I do?"

She met my eyes. "I don't know."

My ribs squeezed hard in my chest. "I don't want to scare you. Tell me what you want from me, Lu, and I'll do it. Or get it. Or be it."

"That's an awfully big offer."

"And a genuine one."

Her eyes dropped, and her fingers moved gently over my stomach. "I just want one thing, from you, really."

I clasped her hand in mine. "Name it."

She looked up again. "Don't fuck me over."

"I promise I won't."

I tipped my head down and brushed my lips over hers. When I pulled back, the smile I'd glimpsed on Monday—the one I'd been sure she didn't want me to see—was back, and this time it was it was directed unabashedly my way. I lifted my thumb and ran it over her lips. Warmth bloomed in my chest.

"When you look at me like that..." I trailed off, embarrassed by the sudden roughness in my throat.

Her smile widened. "Like what?"

Like you might be falling in love me, I wanted to say.

But I had a feeling I'd pushed her about as far as she could go for right that second. I kissed her again.

"Do you want me to kick Gary's ass? Find a way to make him pay?" I asked.

She sat up, her eyes wide, but when she caught sight of my face, she gave my chest a shove. "That is *not* funny."

I lifted my hands and put them behind my head. "You're right. It's not. A scumbag like that is no joke. But what kind of boyfriend would I be if I didn't make the offer to beat him up?"

The label slipped out before I could stop it, and Mia picked up on it right away.

"Boyfriend?" she said.

"Bed buddy?" I offered.

"Um. No. That's *far* worse."

"Significant other?"

"I think that's what my grandparents call each other."

"Gentleman suitor?"

"Really?"

"I think you're missing the point," I said. "I'm willing to commit a crime for you."

"Noted," she replied dryly, then swung her legs over the edge of the bed. "I have to go to work."

I grabbed her hand. "Because I called myself your boyfriend, or because you really have to go?"

"Maybe a bit of both." She wrinkled her nose at me, then freed her hand and grabbed her clothes from the floor, but sighed a little as she dressed. "The only boyfriend I've ever had was more than twice my age and stole my parents' retirement money, then turned out be one shade shy of a bigamist. So you'll have to forgive my hesitation."

I frowned. "What do you mean your only boyfriend?"

"Gary."

"Yeah, I got that—oh. Shit, Lu." I sat up and ran a hand over my hair. "That's *not* what it's supposed to be like. That asshole isn't a good example of what a boyfriend should be."

"I know that," she replied. "Really. I've had examples of great men surrounding me since I was born."

"But?"

"I got a little lost along the way. But I promised myself never again." She paused at the end of the bed and gave me a too-serious once-over. "So if there's anything you want to tell me..."

I stared up at her, disliking the renewed guard in her eyes. It made me uneasy, even though I had nothing to hide. I didn't want her to have reservations. I wanted her smile. *The* smile. And the trust that let her tell me everything she just had.

"Is there something specific you want to know?" I asked.

She shrugged, and I knew she had something on her mind. I reached out for her again, and tugged her between my legs, pressing my knees to her outer thighs to hold her in place.

"No secrets, Lu. I swear." I slid my hands down her arms to clasp her wrists. "If you have a question, all you have to do is say."

Her gaze hung on me for a few moments, the guard slipping a little more with each second. I didn't look away. And finally, she did smile. Not quite the one I wanted, but close enough.

"We can talk more later, right?" she said.

"We can talk forever," I agreed. "It takes a lifetime to get to know someone as well as I want to know you."

And there's the smile.

"Sappy," she said, but bent down and kissed me anyway.

* * * *

Mia

I expected my day to pass slowly. Mostly because the second I left Ethan and the Memory Motel, I wished my work was done for the day.

But surprisingly, the time passed quickly. I got started on a whole new design, and the sketches just poured out of me onto the paper. I might've even kept going if Chloe hadn't come up to tell me that she was closing shop for the evening. At the sound of her voice, I looked up, and was startled to see that the sky was already starting to dim.

"You cutting out soon too, boss?" my assistant manager asked.

I stretched a little, then nodded. "Pretty quick, yeah."

"We barely heard from you today. Working on something good?"

"A concept for a new line."

"Ooh. Can I see?"

"Sure." I slid the drawings toward her.

She flipped through them, her face brightening with each one. "These are fantastic! Some of your best yet. They're almost…I dunno…whimsical. And very romantic."

I took them back from her and smiled. "You think?"

"I know."

I looked down, admiring my own handiwork. They were definitely different from my usual stuff. Simple. Silver chains, semiprecious stones in varying colors. Pink. Pale blue. Heart-shaped.

"What are you going to call the line?" Chloe asked.

"*A Lifetime*," I replied immediately.

Chloe just about squealed. "That's perfect! It's going to be amazing. It'll blow any competition out of the water."

"Thanks."

"*A Lifetime*," she repeated, then gave me a little squeeze. "I can't wait."

"Me neither," I replied with more feeling than I meant to.

"Enjoy your wedding weekend, okay?"

"I will."

I waited until she slipped out of the office before giving the drawings another once-over. Then I grabbed my pencil and scrawled the name on top of the first one.

The words—the concept, really—had been floating around in my head ever since Ethan said it. It'd stuck around all day, making my heart race and flutter. Making my hands shake at odd moments, so hard that I'd have to put down my pencil. Making me smile and sigh.

It was crazy. I knew that. Maybe just sex-fueled infatuation. But it felt so right. Like so much more than that.

A lifetime.

It *was* the perfect name for the new line. And I couldn't deny that it was inspired by the emotions that bubbled just under the surface every time my mind drifted to Ethan. Which was every few seconds, really. And as quickly as my day had gone, I was eager to get back to him. Even just to hear about his day in person. As many jokes as he made about being little more than my secret concubine, he'd been exploring the city on his own while I worked, and his play-by-play texts about his experiences were hilarious. There was a lot of complaining about the rain. A lot of comments on the organic coffee and the plaid. And according to him, every second person was in socks with sandals.

But his stories were better when punctuated by kisses.

Smiling again, I pushed my chair back from my desk and stood up. As I grabbed my purse, my phone rang from inside, and I yanked it out, fully expecting it to be Ethan.

I answered without checking the call display. "Hey."

But instead of Ethan's voice, it was my landlord's that greeted me. "Ms. Diaz! It's Charlie Cho."

I slung my purse over my shoulder and grabbed my sweater from the back of my chair, replying as I made my way out of the office. "Oh. Hey, Mr. Cho. Everything all right?"

"Perfect on my end," he said. "Just wanted to check with you whether or not the new owner had been in touch?"

I moved down the stairs. "The new owner of what?"

"The building."

"What building?"

"*My* building. Your shop."

I paused in the middle of the store, my mind filling with unease. "You sold it? Just like that? I didn't even know you were thinking about it."

"I wasn't," he said. "The buyer came in and made me an unbelievable offer."

"When?"

"Just this last weekend. My lawyer said the offer was far too good to pass up. Happened so fast that I'm still in shock."

My pulse was moving at a cold, sluggish pace. "Who?"

"Owner of some big distribution company," my landlord told me.

"Who?"

"Something...Holdings. The guy's name is Ethan...uh...Bark?"

"Burke," I corrected woodenly.

"Yeah," agreed Cho. "You've heard of him?"

He continued on for another minute, telling me just how great the purchase was. How he could retire. Adding that the new owner had put in a clause about letting Trinkets and Treasures—and the other stores in the row—stay where they were for a minimum of three months. It mostly sounded like underwater gibberish to me. And when I finally managed to get him to hang up, almost all of it went out of my head anyway. Because Ethan had bought my store.

The reality of that statement played on repeat in my head, the emphasis a little different each time.

Ethan bought *my store.*

He bought my *store.*

Ethan. Bought. My. Store.

And with each replay, it grew a little more real. A little more infuriating. And a ton more sickening.

Overwhelmed, I ran from the sales floor to the counter. I bent down, grabbed the trash bin from behind the register, and heaved until my stomach was empty, and every muscle in my body felt like it'd been worked over by an angry personal trainer with something to prove. And when I was done, I felt no better.

The sonofabitch.

He hadn't been able to talk me into getting what he wanted. He hadn't been able to seduce it out of me, either. So he'd simply gone behind my back.

I closed my eyes and tried to find a way to ease the achy, shattered feeling in my chest. Why had he bothered to come back? Why bother saying all the things to me that he'd said?

Because he's a narcissistic bastard.

Who I'd trusted. After not even two weeks. When I knew better than anyone just how untrustworthy people could be.

I pressed my fingers to my chest and cursed my own naivety. My own stupidity. I cursed that fact that it *hurt.*

In my hand, my phone buzzed to life again. This time, I took a careful look at the screen.

E.

No way in hell was I indulging in his game by answering. Who knew how long he thought he could keep his sneaky purchase a secret? I wouldn't take the chance that he'd pick up on my tears, either. The asshole didn't deserve my sorrow.

I let it go to voicemail.

But—of course—it rang again immediately. I swallowed against the thickness in my throat, and I pressed the button to ignore the call. I doubted he'd take the hint.

But he'll figure it out quickly enough.

The real question was what I was going to do about it. Short term and long term. Three months minimum, Cho had said. But I wouldn't put my hard-earned dollars into Ethan-the-asshole's pocket. That much was for sure. No doubt his intention was to make it impossible for me, anyway. Drive up the rent. Force me to sell to him.

"Not a chance in hell," I muttered.

I'd sooner sell my product out of my living room. I wondered how the staff would feel about that.

The staff.

My stomach churned a little more. Hadn't Ethan cared at all how this obsessive acquisition of his would affect *them*?

"Of course not."

You should confront him, urged a little voice in my head.

But I couldn't stand the idea of letting him think he'd *won*. Of gloating over it. Of reminding me that he'd played my body as well as he'd played my business.

No wonder you thought he was hiding something, I thought. *Lying, two-faced, disgusting jerk.*

My phone erupted with another ring, and I automatically moved to silence it. But as I lifted it, I saw that this time it was Liv calling. I stared at her flashing name, and realized that I *really* needed a short-term plan. Because Ethan knew where I worked. Where I lived. My brother's name. And speaking of Marcelo, I had the wedding to think about.

I breathed in, then made myself answer the phone in a calm, rational voice. "Hey, Liv."

"Oh, thank God!" she replied immediately. "Aysia's got a dress crisis, and she's freaking the fuck out. The wrong-shaped pearl on the bodice. What the hell does that even mean? Can you come? Pretty, pretty please?"

"Where are you?"

"My place."

Perfect. Ethan has no clue where that is.

"Yeah, for sure," I said. "How would you feel about a sleepover, actually?"

There was no pause. "That would be *so* amazing. We could take care of this stupid pearl thing, have a few calming drinks, and—"

"Sold," I said.

"Really?"

"Yes."

Now she hesitated. "Is something wrong? You *always* fight me on this stuff."

I shook my head even though she couldn't see me. "Not tonight. I just figured something out, and this is the perfect excuse to down a margarita."

"Sweet. See you soon."

I hung up, called a cab, then switched off my phone completely.

Chapter 18

Ethan

It took me a half hour after Mia's expected arrival time to start to worry. It took me ten minutes more to call, and ten seconds more to try again. A third call. A fourth call. A fifth. Straight to voicemail, and I knew something was off.

Another fifteen minutes went by before I decided I should do something about it.

I started with the obvious. I called Trinkets and Treasures. Though I wasn't expecting an answer, it still made me grit my teeth with concern when the line just rang and rang.

I paced the room at the Memory Motel with my phone in my hand. "C'mon, Lu. What's going on?"

I waited another half hour. Mia had made it clear she wasn't yet ready to let her friends and family know about us. She'd specifically asked me not to come by the store. It was all fine with me. It really just gave me more time alone with her.

But that was before she was kidnapped. Or crashed into a ditch. Or was maybe abducted by aliens.

I paused pacing to question my sanity. Mia was a grown woman. An incredibly competent grown woman. Just because she'd turned up within twenty minutes of the end of her workday both Tuesday and Wednesday didn't mean she *had* to turn up in that timeframe now. Things came up.

If she was late, there was a reason. If she couldn't take my calls, there was an even *better* reason.

I hoped.

I started pacing again. Stopped again. Paced again.

"What the hell am I doing?" I growled as I spotted myself in the mirror. My face was a ridiculous mask of distress.

You're overreacting.

I took a breath and stepped to the edge of the bed, then made myself sit down. The problem wasn't that I couldn't reason through a scenario that would take her away from our room at the hotel. She could've stopped at home. Run into a genuine issue at work. Or been needed for something related to her brother's wedding. I could posit something similar for the lack of phone contact. She might be in some kind of meeting where she couldn't pick up. Or left the device somewhere. Broken it. Had it stolen, or just let the battery die by accident. Any of those things was more likely than the whole alien abduction bullshit my mind had only kind of been kidding about. But like I said. A valid excuse wasn't the issue. What *was* the issue was that familiar kick in my gut.

It was the same one I used in business. The same one I'd used to conclude that Mia was more important than her store. Now rearing up, telling me something wasn't right.

Deciding to give it yet another try, I grabbed my phone, selected her number, and muttered, "C'mon, sweetheart," as the line clicked.

Voicemail.

I slammed the phone off.

"Fuck."

What the hell was I supposed to do now? Sit and wait while my instincts screamed to go tearing out of the hotel in search of her?

"Double fuck."

I took a breath, and attempted to do something *sane*. I dialed her. Again. This time, to leave a nice, normal message.

Which is probably what you should've done the first time.

"Hey, Lu. It's me. And in case you don't recognize my voice by now, I mean the man who saw you naked this morning. And if *that* doesn't narrow it down. Well." I cleared my throat, thinking that the joke sounded as forced as it felt. "Anyway. I was expecting to see you over an hour ago, and just wanted to check if everything was all right. I know how society frowns upon stalking, and I'd hate to be *that* guy. So give me a call and let me know you're alive."

But I did become that guy. Because she didn't call. Or show up. Or answer a single one of my increasingly worried texts.

I swung by Trinkets and Treasures numerous times, and walked the area on foot in search of some clue as to her whereabouts. I had a cab drop me at her place, and sat on her porch for so long that one of the neighbors called the cops. It was actually my pathetic conversation with the Vancouver constables that finally sent me back to the Memory Motel.

"All right, Mr. Burke of Toronto, Ontario," said the female cop as she handed back my ID. "It's just about midnight. You want to tell us why you're sitting on this porch here in a province that's not your own?"

"My girlfriend didn't come home," I told her, hearing the slightly hollow ring to the label—Mia hadn't yet confirmed she actually wanted to be called that, after all.

"Your girlfriend," repeated the male cop. "You staying here with her?"

"No," I replied.

"She expecting you?" He sounded like he knew full well that she wasn't.

"It's more complicated than that," I said.

The female cop narrowed her eyes. "Complicated how?"

"She was supposed to meet me at our hotel after work, but she didn't show up. Her phone's off. Or broken. And I haven't heard from her, so I got worried." I tried to smile. "So here I am."

The male cop shifted on his feet and exchanged a look with his partner. "You're here from Toronto, visiting your girlfriend, but staying in a hotel?"

"Complicated," I repeated. "Maybe you guys could look into where she is? She's got a brother in town. He might have some idea of where she is."

The female cop shook her head. "Mr. Burke, you said she didn't show up and turned off her phone. Is there a possibility that she doesn't *want* you to contact her?"

"No." As soon as the word was out of my mouth, I realized I'd said it a little too emphatically.

It was the thing that my gut wanted me to acknowledge, but that my heart had refused to consider until that moment. Maybe Mia *didn't* want to see me again. Maybe her protest about the boyfriend and girlfriend labels was more than a passing bit of discomfort. My chest compressed. What the hell was I going to do if that were true? Less than two weeks I'd known her, and I somehow couldn't imagine my life just picking up where I'd left it before she literally fell into it.

Shit.

"You know what?" said the female cop. "We're going extend you an unusual courtesy, Mr. Burke. We'll do a bit of follow-up for you. And *if* we find something wrong, we'll give you a call. Have you got a number where we can reach you?"

I tugged one of my business cards from my pocket, handed it over and started to thank her. Then I realized her promise had an edge. A couple of edges, really. If something was wrong, they'd have someone to question. If something *wasn't* wrong, they'd have a suspected stalker's phone number.

"In the meantime," added the male cop, "we'll also call you a cab. What hotel did you say you were at?"

I resisted an urge to tell them I *hadn't* specified, and instead offered my most winning smile. "The Memory Motel. Room one-o-one."

And thirty minutes later I was back in that room, slumped in a chair as I battled an increasingly hollow feeling in my chest.

She would've told you if she wanted to end things, I reasoned. *At the very least, sent a text or an email.*

Except both mediums remained woefully devoid of incoming messages. Mia's cell phone was still off. Cops were probably running down my mundane rap sheet—a single speeding ticket and case of poor judgement that resulted in a teacher's house being toilet papered—just in case. And not a damned clue as to why I was being left out in the cold.

At some point, I must've drifted off, because the ring of my cell phone jarred me awake. I grabbed it right away, sure it had to be Mia. Instead, my assistant greeted me cheerily from the other end.

"Did I wake you, Mr. Burke?" she said. "It's after six there, isn't it?"

I fought a snarly answer. "Guess I slept in, Julie. To what do I owe this early-morning call?"

"I just wanted to congratulate you."

"For?"

"Trinkets and Treasures."

My stomach rolled. "What about it?"

"Acquiring it!" she replied. "I was starting to think something was wrong, but then the owner called me this morning, and—"

"Mia called *you?*"

"Lumia Diaz, yes. She called the office."

"What did she say?"

"That she was happy to hear you were taking ownership, that Charlie Cho had called to confirm that transfer of property, and that she hoped you were going to be very happy."

"Charlie Cho?" I repeated, the name striking a vaguely familiar chord.

"That's right," Julie confirmed.

My mind struggled to find a connection. *Ownership of—damn. Damn, damn,* damn *it all to hell.*

"Did something come through from the lawyers?" I asked.

"Didn't you read your emails yesterday?" she replied.

"Skimmed them." It was a lie; all I'd done was flip through, hoping to find something from Mia.

Doesn't it make you wonder how the hell you succeed in business at all? asked a snide voice in my head.

"Mr. Burke?" said Julie.

I cleared my throat. "I'm here. Just tell me what the emails said."

"Your purchase of the property in Vancouver went through," she told me.

Shit on toast.

Hadn't I still had a final call to make?

I didn't realize I'd asked the question aloud until Julie answered it.

"Sort of," she stated. "The lawyer said that the last offer you made had your preapproval."

"Cho rejected that offer," I muttered.

"He changed his mind," Julie replied. "Mr. Burke, I hate to ask this again...but are you okay?"

"Fine. But I've gotta go."

There was a pause. "Should we expect you back before the weekend's over?"

"I'm afraid not. I've got a wedding to crash." And I hung up before she could question my sanity.

* * * *

Mia

I couldn't say that I managed to completely erase Ethan from my mind. But I could say that I managed to fold him up, shove him into a box, duct tape the lid shut, then move him and his boxed-up self to the back of my mind. It helped that all the last-minute plans for Marc and Aysia's wedding were now in full swing. It helped even more that I'd moved in temporarily with Liv, and she didn't give me a spare moment to think about anything but fluffy dresses and winged eyeliner.

I left my phone off. I didn't check emails or voicemails or sneak a peek at my social media. I knew I'd have to deal with my new "landlord" eventually, but it could definitely wait until Monday. Then I'd begin my relocation search. Because no way in hell was I letting Ethan use this little trick to win.

It was bad enough that coming into my own store—where I'd stupidly left the jewelry for the wedding party—made me feel like a thief. I'd actually had to talk myself into coming in to get it. I'd avoided talking to the staff as I breezed through and made my way upstairs. But now that

I had the little velvet bags in my hand, I didn't seem to be able to move. I'd been standing with the jewelry clutched in my fingers for a good five minutes, watching the rain pelt the window across from my desk. I wanted the bad weather to end in time for my brother's wedding, but right now, the premature darkness and soggy sky suited my state of mind perfectly.

This is still your office. Still your view, and still your store. He might own the building, but he doesn't own you.

The affirmation should've been reassuring. But right then, it made my throat scratch unpleasantly. Because in spite of Ethan's underhanded dealings, and in spite the mental box where he currently resided, I couldn't change the fact that he'd gotten under my skin. I couldn't stop myself from wishing more than a little that it hadn't been a game for him. And it kind of broke my heart.

Kind of?

I swallowed and stared at the storm, willing it to wash away the thick, terrible feeling in my rib cage. It wasn't fair that it hurt like it did. It wasn't fair that I couldn't lash out. And it *really* wasn't fair that the reason behind that was I was too scared to face him because I didn't trust myself to be near him.

I was furious at Ethan. But I was way angrier with myself.

So much for keeping him in the box.

I took a breath and slammed the desk drawer shut. So long as I didn't have to see him, I'd be fine. And I was sure that once he got my message—his office assistant sounded more than competent enough to give it to him— he'd figure out that I knew what he'd done. He wouldn't have to keep up the ruse any longer, and I'd be able to breathe again.

But right that second, I had a rehearsal dinner to get to. To get *through*.

I fixed a somewhat plastic smile on my face, stepped down the stairs, waved to the two girls working in the store, then pushed the door. Before I could even get it all the way open, a gust of wind blew it straight out of my hands and slammed it to the building so hard that I was surprised it didn't shatter. I had to grab it and force it shut. And I got soaked immediately. The rain wasn't just coming down now. It was hammering from the sky, and somewhere overhead, thunder rolled ominously. Even though it was only five in the evening, it looked like midnight.

"Great," I muttered, squinting through the sheets of rain toward the street in search of my taxi.

I'd asked the cab driver to come back in ten minutes, but I couldn't see him yet. I was about to give up and wait inside when the familiar yellow car rounded the corner. He pulled up right in front of me, and I didn't wait for him to get out and help me with the door. I climbed right in, wiping the rain from my face and pulling a compact mirror from my purse as I settled into the seat.

"We should probably hurry," I said breathlessly. "I think taking the side roads through the Brampton subdivision will save about five minutes."

I flicked open the little mirror and examined my face. Aside from a tiny bit of smudged mascara, my makeup remained intact. I ran the edge of the tissue over the corner of my eye, expecting the car to start moving. But we just stayed where we were.

"We really should go," I stated as I wiped away the last hint of wayward mascara. "I have somewhere to be in a little under an hour, and I'd prefer to be on the early side."

We still didn't budge.

Mildly annoyed, I lowered the compact. Surprise immediately overrode my irritation. The keys were in the ignition and the meter was running. The cabbie sat in his seat, his head tilted my way, his mouth open and his brows pressed together like he didn't quite know why I was there.

"Hey. Um. What's the hold—" My words cut off as a familiar voice carried from the other side of the backseat and clued me in too late to the fact that I wasn't actually alone.

"You trying to steal my cab?"

Ethan.

His tone was teasing, but strained too.

I turned. Slowly. Full of dread and terrible, hopeful anticipation. And seeing him hit me with about as much force as I expected. His dark eyes and stubble-covered jaw took my breath away. Unwanted, unwelcome heat licked through me. It felt like a lifetime since I'd seen him, and it'd barely been a day and a half. And in spite of everything—in spite of what he'd done and continued to attempt to do—my treacherous body wanted to pull itself closer to him. I actually had to grip the seat beneath me to keep from inching over.

"Well?" Ethan prodded.

"Um." It was all I could manage to get out.

"My cab," he repeated slowly. "Is this an attempted theft?"

"I…" My gaze accidentally landed on his lips, distracting me.

C'mon, Mia. Have some self-respect.

I cleared my throat and tried to make myself sound more like my normal, articulate self. Infused with cool indifference, of course.

"No," I said. "I'm not trying to steal your cab. In fact, if you're still using it, I'll get out."

I started to move toward the door, but his hand came out and landed on my wrist. "There's no reason we can't share."

"There are probably a hundred reasons we *shouldn't* share," I replied. "But the only one that matters right now is that this discussion is going to make me late."

Ethan flicked his attention to the cabbie and issued a nod. "Go ahead. I believe the Regent Inn is the destination."

My mouth worked wordlessly for a second, and the driver clearly took my silence as agreement, because he settled into his seat, then pulled the car on to the road.

"I'd prefer to be on my own," I stated stiffly.

"But stopping and getting another cab would add time," he replied. "And like you said a second ago, you don't want to be late."

I glared at him, hating that any argument I made would come across as petulant. I fixed my gaze straight ahead instead. But Ethan wasn't going to let things go quite so easily.

"We have unfinished business, Lu," he told me in a low voice.

I refused to turn his way. "You're wrong. We have *no* business, Ethan."

"We both know that's not true," he replied. "At the very least, you owe me a brief conversation."

"I owe you nothing."

"I just want to talk. To explain."

"Less than nothing."

"In private," he said.

"That's never going to happen." I made sure my reply was icy.

"Lu."

My temper flared. "You are so damned entitled, aren't you? You think the whole world owes you something. You want to have a conversation? Fine! Acknowledge that you're selfish, self-centered, egotistical *bastard* of a man, and maybe I'll consider talking to you for the five seconds it's going to take our driver to find a safe place to pull over."

His head swiveled away from mine, and his jaw went so rigid that it looked like it might hurt. Or shatter, if it got bumped. And in spite of the way I willed myself not to, I felt bad for lashing out. I wanted to reach over. To *apologize*, for crying out loud.

Dammit.

Feeling sorry for the asshole was most definitely *not* on the agenda.

I dropped my gaze to my lap just for the sake of not having to see him suffer, and I did my best to keep my eyes pointed downward for the rest of the ride.

I wished desperately that I could rewind the last few days and start them over. Undo the dare. Forget that his mouth had been so perfectly firm and tasted like heaven.

I couldn't stop my gaze from drifting back to him. My head was bursting with questions.

Why was he still in town?

Why was he in the cab outside my store?

Why, in God's name, did he want to talk to me in private?

You have what you want, I thought. *You own my building. What more do you need?*

I snuck yet another glance at his face. Still stiff. Still pained. *Why?* I took a breath. I opened my mouth ask. But the sudden jerk of the car as its tires screeched to a halt cut me off.

Chapter 19

Ethan

My arm shot out automatically to protect Mia from slamming forward, and I tossed a furious look toward the driver for his reckless stop. But the curse I had ready for him never made it out. The chaos outside the front windshield was more than enough of an excuse for the hard braking.

One of the wide, tall trees that lined the road sat at a crazy angle, its trunk shattered near its base, the length of it blocking passage. The entire street ahead was shrouded in darkness, all the lamp standards black, all the businesses an inky blur. Two police cars and a fire truck sat in silence, their lights flashing and their occupants in the street directing people around the destruction. At the very end of the block, the Regent Inn had somehow managed to maintain its power, and it glowed cheerily.

The taxi's radio squawked to life, and a woman's voice crackled through. "Hey, uh, Jeff? If you're still en route to the hotel, you might wanna rethink it. Just got word that there's a downed tree blocking access."

The driver—Jeff—thanked the dispatcher for the belated warning, then turned to us. "Guess you folks need to rethink your destination."

Mia shook her head. "I *can't* rethink it. Bridesmaid duty doesn't end because of a fallen tree. I'll sneak around on foot."

The cabbie sighed like it was a personal offence. "I won't be able to give you service to the front door."

"I think we can manage," I interjected.

"*We?*" Mia repeated.

"I've got a room booked," I told her.

"For the love of Pete. *Why?*"

"I said I wanted to talk."

"And I said no."

"Which is why I took the liberty of booking the room."

"So you're stalking me? Again?"

The cabbie cleared his throat. "Do you need some help, ma'am?"

"I'm fine. He might be a thief, but he's not as tough as he thinks he is." She glared at me, then reached for her purse. "How much is the fare?"

"Not necessary," I told her.

"I'm not taking your money," she snapped.

"You're not," I agreed. "But the driver is. I've already given him my credit card info."

For a second, she looked like she might argue, but she just shook her head, then swung open the door and slid out, pausing just long enough to say, "It still doesn't mean I owe you anything."

Then she slammed the door hard and turned to battle the rain and the wind at a run. The cabbie stared after her, then raised an eyebrow my way.

"Must be a hell of a woman," he said.

"I think she's the one." The words were out before I could stop them, but as soon as I'd said them, I realized just how much truth they held, and I smiled. "Now all I have to do is convince her of that. Pop the trunk so I can get my bag?"

"You got it. Good luck, buddy."

"Thanks."

I pushed my way out, grabbed my suitcase, and squinted into the driving rain. It only took me a second to spot Mia. She'd already made it past the first responders, and she stood near the end of the cracked tree trunk, her tan rain jacket flapping in the wind and her high-heeled shoes clutched in one hand. Her legs—bare and flashing creamily even in the dark—made me want to shiver. Then she looked up, and even though I couldn't see her expression, I knew what she was planning.

"Oh no you don't," I muttered. "You are *not* climbing over that thing."

Careful to avoid drawing any unwanted attention from the fire fighters and the police, I hurried over the cold, wet ground. The puddle splashed up, soaking the bottoms of my legs, but I cared a hell of a lot less about my own discomfort that I did about the idea of Mia scaling the splinter-laden, broken-leg-waiting-to-happen mess of a tree.

Thankfully, the universe tossed a little luck in my favor.

The moment Mia lifted her foot was the moment before I reached her. It was also the moment she slipped. Her arms windmilled, and she tumbled forward. Her hands hit a branch on the tree, which protested against the assault, then bounced back and sent her straight into my outstretched arms. It felt damned good to have her body pressed to mine, even if it was only a matter of necessity. I had to force myself not to tug her even closer.

"You all right?" I asked as I reluctantly released her.

She stared up at me, her gaze momentarily unguarded and warm. Like she'd forgotten that she was furious at me. It buoyed my hope. Even when she quickly brushed off her jacket and took a step away. Knowing that the hint of want was there under the surface was enough. My eyes couldn't help but rake over her. Even sopping wet, with her hair plastered to her face and her makeup starting to run, she was the most beautiful woman I'd ever seen.

"Lu…" I said. "Can we grab a coffee? Or a glass of wine? Hell. I'd take a water."

"For what purpose?" she replied coolly. "So you can tell me you didn't buy my store out from under me? Because I'd rather not waste time with any more lies."

"I want to explain what happened."

"So you're *not* denying it?"

"If I did, you'd just call me a liar again, wouldn't you?"

"Because you *are* one!" she snapped.

"You know that I bought your building," I replied.

"No shit."

"I'm not lying about it."

"Do you think that makes it *better*?"

"The truth tends to do that, yes. I bought the building with bad intentions. But I made a mistake."

"I—" She looked momentarily confused and a little curious too, but she just shook her head. "No. Save it. There's really no need for us to talk to each other. The cab ride is over. The hotel is a few hundred feet away. I've got things to do, and I'm sure you do too. We can just pretend we've never met."

"That would be impossible to do."

"Maybe try banging your head against something hard. I hear that can induce memory loss."

She started to spin back toward the tree, but I grabbed her arm and stopped her.

"Be reasonable, Mia," I said. "If you try to climb that thing, you're going to get hurt."

"Yeah, well…that's up to me, isn't it?" she snapped.

"Not if you have a death wish it isn't." I paused, trying to come up with a way to convince her. "Look. If you won't do it for your own sake, then at least think of your brother."

"My brother?"

"His wedding photos. I'm sure skinned knees can be digitally erased, but..." I trailed off and shrugged.

She made an exasperated noise. "Fine. You create a diversion by getting arrested. I'll walk straight in, and we'll both get what we want."

I bit back an urge to tell her the scenario wasn't even close to what I wanted, and an even stronger urge to list—in detail—what I *did* want.

"Or. We could walk *around* the death trap, and sneak between that fence and that coffee shop over there." I nodded to the spot I meant. "And in a minute, we'll both be inside the warm, dry hotel."

She eyed the path in question, pursed her lips, then nodded and started walking. I didn't have time to be satisfied by the fact that she went along with my plan. The second we crossed onto the Regent Inn's property, chaos reigned. A throng of people crowded the covered entryway, huddled together in small groups. There were buses and cars parked haphazardly across the space, and a sense of frenzy surrounding the whole area.

"What the hell's happening?" I muttered.

A soaking-wet kid in a hotel uniform paused beside us. "Power's out at three other hotels. They started busing people in right before that tree came down."

"Shit," I said.

"Completely," the kid agreed, then took off again.

From where I stood, I could see that the inside of the hotel was just as crazy. Dozens of unhappy guests were jammed into the lobby. Hotel employees flitted around frantically. A crowd lined up at the desk. Checking in was going to take an hour.

More than hour, I thought.

I turned to make a comment about it to Mia, but she no longer stood beside me. My heart dropped. I craned my neck and searched through the crowd. A flicker of red drew my attention.

There.

She was inside already, moving through the lobby toward the elevators with the little blonde who'd mistaken me for a stripper.

Liv, I remembered. *The darer.*

I stepped forward, intent on catching up with the two of them. I only made it a few feet into the hotel before being stopped by a harried employee.

"Sir," she said as she blocked my way. "Are you checked in? Do you have a key card?"

"Not yet," I replied, trying to see around her.

"I'm sorry. But the management has asked that only registered guests go past this area."

"I've got a reservation."

"Have you checked in, sir?" she asked.

Shit. I'd lost sight of Mia.

Gritting my teeth, I dropped my gaze to the woman in front of me. "No, I haven't. Look. Could you make an exception?"

She pointed to the enormous line and shrugged apologetically. "I'm sorry. I'd like to make an exception for pretty much everyone, but it's just not worth losing my job."

"Right."

"Sorry," she said again.

"Not a problem," I lied.

I eyed the elevators once more, yanked my bag toward the front desk, and told myself that at least the amount of time I'd be stuck standing there would be long enough to come up with a plan.

* * * *

Mia

I breathed out, gave my appearance a final check in the mirror, and told myself I was fine. That being stuck in a car with Ethan for a few minutes changed nothing. Accepting his suggestion for getting past the tree and the blockade was just convenience. Hearing him label his purchase of my store as a mistake wasn't an apology I had to accept.

And leaving him in the crowd does not *make your heart hurt a little, right?*

"Right," I said to my reflection. "His own fault for being a jerky, stalking maniac who didn't have the foresight to check in ahead of time."

I wrinkled my nose and sighed. I knew perfectly well that he couldn't have predicted the disastrous weather and ensuing disorder. But I also knew perfectly well that I shouldn't feel bad for him being stuck down in the crowd, and I couldn't seem to cast off the feeling.

At least I no longer looked—as Liv had put it—like I'd just had sex in a mud puddle. The black satin dress was probably a little over the top for the impending rehearsal and dinner. I'd actually only thrown it into my bag at the very last second because of a panicked moment where I thought the floral wraparound I'd picked might be a little *under* the top. If that was a thing. But I was glad to at least have the option to put on something else.

My hair was still damp, and the rain had washed away most of my makeup. I couldn't muster up the energy to do a complete reapplication, so I'd settled for a quick swipe of eyeliner and a light coat of lip gloss. Not glamorous. But serviceable.

I picked up my phone and glanced at the time. The power outage had caused a bit of a delay, so I still had almost thirty minutes until the start of the rehearsal.

And a good opportunity to be early, I told myself.

I dropped the phone into my clutch, then snapped the clasp shut.

I certainly didn't want to spend the next half hour alone in my room musing over Ethan. Wondering why he didn't flat out deny his deception. Or make more excuses.

It doesn't matter what *his reasons are,* I thought firmly. *They won't change a thing.*

But as much as I tried to fight the niggling doubt, it wormed its way back in as I stepped into the hall. It built up even more as I got into the elevator, and it had me sucking in my lower lip nervously as I got out.

I wasn't naïve enough to think it was all some big misunderstanding.

Because you were fooled. And you enjoyed *being fooled, so you want to find some excuse...some reason to go back.*

"And he's not worth it," I muttered.

I paused in the crazy busy lobby to check the sign that listed all the special events happening in the hotel, just in case the chaos had caused a change. But as I confirmed that we were still in Ballroom One for the rehearsal and the Regent Lounge for dinner, Ethan's familiar voice carried to me and stopped me from going any farther.

"Unless there's another Regent Inn in Vancouver that caters to Hotel Platinum members," he was saying, "then I *must* be booked in here. Top floor, turndown service, executive brunch tomorrow, all confirmed by email this morning."

A woman answered, "Can I be honest with you, sir?"

"I'd prefer it, actually," he said.

"Every one of our rooms is booked," replied the woman. "Every cot is in use. We've shuffled around as much as we could, and even the rooms we hold for our overnight staff have been reallocated to hold guests instead. Anyone who isn't already checked in...won't be. It's the worst possible time for a reservation to be lost. We're calling around, trying to find alternatives, but the last customer had to take a room in Coquitlam."

"Coquitlam?"

"It's a neighboring city. A good forty minutes away."

"Christ."

"I'm sorry, sir."

I closed my eyes and willed myself not to look. Not to give in to the need to see his face. But I couldn't seem to walk away, either. Unconsciously, I took a step closer. Then another.

Ethan sighed, sounding frustrated and apologetic at the same time. "I'm sorry for the language."

"It's not the worst thing that's been said to me all night, trust me," said the woman.

"Not surprising under the circumstances, but I know it's not your fault. Just give me the best-case scenario."

"Being honest again?"

"Yeah."

"The guys from hydro are due here to assess the downed tree sometime in the next hour. The hotel is lucky enough to own two shuttle buses, which are ready to go the second that tree is out of the way. We're prioritizing the higher-need guests first. Families with young kids and the elderly."

"So I'll be at the bottom of the list."

"Yes. I'm sorry, sir."

I turned in slow motion, but the words that slipped out of my mouth came out in a rush. "You can use my room. I've got a dinner, and I'll probably be out late anyway. So if you want to shower or lie down..."

His dark eyes traveled the length of my body, then settled on my face. "Is that a serious offer?"

No! screamed a voice in my head. *Don't do it. This is a bad idea. Very bad. Rescind it while you still can.*

But I nodded. "Yes. Like I said, I won't be there."

"Trust me. The thought of being in an actual room has a hell of lot more appeal than being stuck in this glorified sardine tin with fifty strangers," he said with a wry smile. "But if you're going to change your mind..."

"I won't. Unless you don't want to use it."

"I could stand to get a little dryer and a little cleaner."

"There's a minibar," I told him.

"Also not unappealing," he stated. "Unless you're planning on using those tiny bottles to poison me."

I fought—really fought—a smile. "If only my planning were that good."

The concierge cut in. "Sir?"

She had a pen poised over a pad of paper, and her eyes darted from me and Ethan to the line of people who were still waiting their turn for bad news.

"Really," I said. "It's just a room."

He shrugged and stepped out of the line. "Okay, then. I'll accept."

I was as relieved as I was anxious.

Stop it, I ordered silently. *You're just being the bigger person.*

Which was all well and good until I remembered a small, annoying fact.

"The key card," I said with a groan.

Ethan frowned. "What about it?"

"They were having a problem with them earlier, and it was just *me* checking in, so I only got one."

"So we'll go back and get another."

I pointed to the surge of people around the desk. The concierge was already invisible again.

"You want to stand in line again?" I asked. "Or take a chance that the guy who looks like a pro boxer won't kick your ass for cutting in?

He followed the direction of my finger. "Is there an option 'C'?"

"I'll have to take you up to let you in." *Another bad idea.* "I've only got about five minutes to spare, but if you want to go out later or whatever, you can swing by the Regent Lounge to grab me again." *An even* worse *idea.*

But Ethan was nodding. "Sounds like a plan."

"Okay."

I took a breath and led him through the lobby to the elevators, not speaking until we'd actually stepped through the sliding doors. And what I did say came out sounding weak, even to my own ears.

"It's just a room," I blurted.

"Yeah, you mentioned that," he replied.

"Oh. Well. I just want to be clear."

"You know I'd never take anything from you without your permission, Lu," he said.

I started to point out that was *exactly* what he'd done, but the elevator doors slid open, and a wizened, hand-holding couple stepped in, interrupting me.

"Evening," greeted the older man.

"Evening," Ethan replied easily. "Going up?"

"Floor eight," the older woman confirmed.

Ethan pressed the button, then leaned back against the car. A weighted silence hung in the air, and strangely, the older woman broke it.

"You two have a fight?" she asked.

"You know that's none of your business, Darla," scolded her partner.

"Oh, please, Chuck," said the woman. "She's clearly upset with him, and the sexual tension in here is thicker than it was at Woodstock."

The man chuckled. "You weren't at Woodstock and you know it."

"Not that *you* know of," Darla teased, then fixed me with a stereotypical finger waggle. "Mark my words. You don't want to waste a precious moment being mad at the man who loves you just because he did a stupid thing."

"Men do a lot of stupid things," her companion agreed. "Takes us a while to get there. Nearly sixty years ago I let this one slip away, and it took me all this time to talk her into taking me back."

The elevator dinged again, and Chuck gave Darla a playful swat on the rear end before following her out. The second the doors slid shut, I turned to Ethan.

"Don't even bother," I said.

"With what?" he replied innocently.

"That couple. They weren't some sign from above."

"Well..." he started.

"Well, what?"

"Technically, they did get on *above* us."

I rolled my eyes. "That's not what I meant. And they got off *below* us. So there."

He inched closer. "Give me a chance, Lu."

The plea in his voice was as obvious as the desire in his voice. And I wanted to give in so desperately that it hurt. But I'd given him a chance. More than once, it felt like. And each time, I got closer to falling. Closer to letting myself believe that after only two weeks, I'd found the man I was meant to be with. But that also meant I was that much more at risk for heartbreak.

"Lu?" Even the way he said my name made me want to throw myself into his arms and sob.

I stiffened my resolve. "It doesn't matter, Ethan. Whatever your reason was for buying the building, and whatever you think we need to talk about. it's not enough."

The air around me was suddenly stifling, and as the elevator finally reached our floor—*not* our *floor,* I corrected silently, *my floor, the twelfth floor, anything but* our *floor*—I couldn't get out fast enough.

Chapter 20

Ethan

For the first time, it occurred to me that I really might not be able to win her over. And it just about broke my fucking heart.

I breathed out, and I thought my rib cage might crack as I watched Mia stumble in a seemingly blind way up the hall. I followed behind, feeling a little blind myself. I was almost surprised when she reached into her tiny bag and managed to let herself into the room without any trouble.

"This is it," she said over her shoulder, but she didn't look at me.

Crack, crack, went my ribs.

I hurried forward, barely making it to the room before the door closed all the way. And I no sooner got inside that Mia turned to leave.

"So this is it," she said, stepping wide around me. "The rehearsal is in Ballroom One downstairs, and the dinner's being catered in the private section of the Regent Lounge. Like I said before, feel free to use the shower or crack open the minibar. Go ahead on order something from room service if you're hungry."

Crack.

"Lu."

"Don't."

Cr-r-raaaack.

"Don't what?" I sounded like a man on the edge.

Her throat moved up and down. "Look. Just…everything's on me."

"On you?"

"It's my room and you're my guest, so…"

My jaw clenched painfully. "All right. Have a good time."

Pretending I was burning from the inside out, I flopped backward on the bed and stared up at the ceiling as I listened to her open the door. Listened to her open it and exhale a soft, nearly inaudible sigh.

But in the end, I couldn't let her go quite so easily. I slid my legs over the edge of the bed, strode across the room, and closed my hand on her shoulder.

She gasped and spun. "Ethan!"

Maybe it was her surprise that made her drop her guard. Or maybe it was the sudden, palpable current that ran from my fingers into her bare skin. Either way, when she looked up at me, I knew that whatever she said, there was a part of her that wanted me. Maybe just physically, but it was something. It was how things started, which made me think that maybe I could get them started again.

The pain my chest eased a little, and as I stared down into her eyes, I forgot what I was going to say. If I ever knew.

I wanted her too. I ached to take her. To kiss her. To hold her for an eternity.

The one.

She exhaled a warm, sweet breath that whispered across my lips as she said my name, this time softly. "Ethan."

"Do something for me, Lu," I replied.

"I can't—"

"Just a small thing."

"Which would be?"

I had to beat back the hope in my heart so I could speak normally. "Don't decide yet."

Her perfect, tempting mouth worked a second before she shook her head. "I have to go, Ethan."

"I know. I'll wait."

"I might be late."

"I'll still wait."

"And I'm tied up with the wedding all day tomorrow."

"I'll be here."

She opened her mouth again, then closed it, then opened it once more. "So. I'm really going to leave now."

"Okay," I said.

"And you aren't going to try to stop me this time."

"No."

"Well. Good."

And this time, I did let her go.

Not because I wanted to. Just the opposite, in fact. As the lock clicked shut, I wanted to throw it open again. I wanted to drag her back—caveman style, if necessary—then toss her onto the bed and make her forget the wedding rehearsal altogether.

I pushed to my feet and stared at the blank wood panel. As much as I was sure of *my* heart, and as much I thought she was just protecting hers, none of it mattered if she wouldn't let me past her wall.

You need an in.

I ran a frustrated hand through my hair, then paused as my reflection caught my eye. I looked like hell. Crooked tie. Dirty suit and soaked shirt. Even my hair had flecks of mud caked in it.

"What you need is a cold fucking shower, Ethan," I said to my ragged self. "For more reasons than one."

With a resigned sigh, I bit back my need to do otherwise and set myself up to get clean and clear my head. I undressed, wrapped myself in a towel, cranked the shower—deciding on scorching hot rather than cold—and let my mind work for a solution.

I didn't want to approach her friend Liv. Even though I had her to thank for Mia in the first place, I got the feeling it would just create more of a problem.

I lathered my hair with the hotel-issue shampoo, then stuck my head under the tap for a thorough rinse.

Who else could I ask for help? Even though she spent most of her time and energy at work, she didn't talk about her employees like they were friends.

But she's close to her family.

And they were all in the hotel.

I paused in my washing to cast a look toward the bedroom. There was a phone on the nightstand. A hotel operator at the ready.

I couldn't. Could I?

I twisted the tap into the off position, then grabbed a towel from the rack and stepped out into the bathroom. My gaze flicked to the bedroom again, and before I could get into a more in-depth argument with myself about it, I strode to the phone and grabbed the handset. I dialed zero, then greeted the operator cheerily.

"Who am I speaking with?" I asked.

"This is Lise. How can I help you?"

"Hi, Lise. This is Ethan. I think your name's a little prettier than mine."

She let out a laugh. "Charm will get you everywhere, Ethan."

"I know you're completely swamped down there, so I won't bug you too much. I'm with the wedding party that's here this weekend, and I've got a small problem that I'm *really* hoping you can help me with? Please?"

"I'll see what I can do."

"Lovely. The groom's name is Marcelo Diaz. I'm trying to sneak him a message, and was hoping you could put me through?"

She laughed again. "So long as you're not planning on hijacking his bride."

I laughed too. "Hardly. I'm actually looking for a tip on how to get his sister to fall a little more in love with me."

"Well, that's the best, sweetest thing I've heard all night, Ethan. Hang on for one second, and I'll put you through."

"Thanks, Lise. Much appreciated."

I leaned back as the line clicked, then rang on the other end, and waited for the answering service to come on. Instead, Marcelo's voice startled me into sitting up again.

"Hey," he said. "Whoever this is, it better be good, 'cause I'm about to practice getting married!"

I cleared my throat, unusually nervous. "This is, uh, Ethan Burke. I wasn't actually expecting you to pick up."

"Ethan! Hey, man, yeah. Just forgot something in the room and had to sneak back up."

"You remember me from a few days ago?"

"Can't say I thought you'd be calling me *here*, but yeah, I remember. How could I forget? First date my baby sister's had in literal years. Thought she was becoming a nun. Hoping she was, maybe."

I tried to force a laugh, but couldn't quite manage it. "That's why I'm calling, actually."

"You're starting a convent?"

"Hardly."

Marcelo went silent for a second, then sighed. "All right. I was being deliberately flippant because I don't want to hear about Mia's love life."

"Sorry, man." I scrubbed a hand over my chin, but made no offer to hang up. "I just wasn't sure who else to ask."

"Okay. Bearing in mind that this *is* my sister we're talking about, tell me what you're after. No bullshit."

I took a second to organize my thoughts, trying to find a way to say things nicely. Appropriately. Using words that wouldn't get me a black eye and a bruised kidney.

"No bullshit," I finally said. "I met your sister two weeks ago, but it feels like two years. She kissed me, and the world kind of shifted. It sped up. Then she decided not to kiss me anymore, and the world stopped. I'm in an unpleasant, zero-gravity free fall, and I'm desperate to undo it."

"I can't believe I'm going to ask this," he muttered. "But *why?*"

"Why?" I repeated.

"Why'd she decide not to kiss you?"

I took a breath, then launched into the most succinct version of events, skipping over the best parts and highlighting the worst. Telling him why I'd come to town and about how my business worked, and how I was sure things with Mia weren't work-related in the slightest bit.

"Am I totally fucked?" I asked at the end, closing my eyes and waiting for the worst.

It didn't come. Instead, Mia's brother sounded sympathetic.

"With Lu, it's all about trust," he said.

"I know."

"It's not an unfounded fear, either."

"I know that too."

There was a pause on the other end. "She told you."

"About Gary," I confirmed. "And about the money and about what happened after."

"She probably *didn't* tell you that she still feels responsible for all of us. She thinks she let us down, obviously. And all that counseling she had… it made her so cautious that she doesn't fully trust *herself*, or something. That's the best way I can put it." He exhaled heavily. "None of us blame her for a single damned thing. We sorted our shit out. Our parents and I both know the entire blame lies at that bastard's feet."

Something clicked. "She thinks it's her."

"Isn't that what I just said?"

"No. I mean, yes, you said it." *And if I apply it to us and our situation…* "I need to make sure she knows she's not a liability to herself."

"Yeah, man. That pretty much sums it up. She probably needs to be told in black and white that it's okay to, uh—" He cleared his throat. "Fall in love?"

The question sounded almost like a threat, and in spite everything, I smiled. "That's my end game."

"All right. I've gotta hang up. Marriage rehearsal and all. But one other thing, Ethan…"

"What's that?"

"If you hurt her, I will personally kick your ass all the way from here to Timbuktu."

"Noted."

I hung up the phone then, and swung my feet back up on the bed, feeling infinitely more settled.

"Thank you, Marcelo Diaz," I murmured.

I closed my eyes, thinking about grand gestures and declarations of love and how best to use them. What words would work? What would make my favorite, honey brown eyes light up and fill with the trust I needed? I could think of exactly three. They were the right ones. But would they be enough? I damned well hoped so.

Unexpectedly, exhaustion took over, and I drifted off with visions of red hair and freckled skin lulling me to sleep.

* * * *

Mia

I stared miserably into my untouched gin and tonic and waited for Liv to say something. Anything, really. Though I was expecting something critical.

The rehearsal and dinner had gone off without a hitch.

My brother and Aysia were set to be blissfully happy.

But I couldn't get my mind away from Ethan. Away from the ache in my heart. In my soul. Which is why, in desperation, I'd asked Liv to join me at the hotel bar for a drink. I'd poured out the whole story to her. I started with the kiss. I gave her the syncopated version of Gary-the-con events. And I ended with the fact that I'd left him in my room. Yet Liv just sat there. Silent.

"Say something," I finally urged.

"Ethan Burke."

"Not his name."

"No, but…really. Ethan Burke, aka E. B. Burke."

"All the letters make my head hurt. But yes. Him."

"The owner and operator of Burke Holdings"

I made an exasperated noise. "Isn't that what I said? You're making me feel like I'm ridiculous for not knowing who he was in the first place."

"You're not ridiculous," she replied, "but there was the magazine article about him one time. One of those most eligible bachelor things. You know I'm always on the hunt. Let me see if I can find it." She pulled out her phone, typed away furiously, but stopped abruptly and lifted her eyebrows at me. "Whoa. Wait. *This* is Ethan Burke?"

I glanced down, my throat tightening at the sight of him on her phone. It was him. Expensive suit. Small smile. Dark, unreadable eyes.

"Yes," I said. "That would be Ethan."

"But...he's the stripper!" Liv exclaimed.

"Oh. Right. I guess I left that out. He's not actually a stripper. Obviously."

"Hell of an oversight. Of course, now *I* feel ridiculous for not recognizing him."

"Can we please focus on the problem?" I pleaded.

"I don't know what the problem *is*, exactly," she replied. "He's a multi-millionaire! Probably a billionaire, actually. Like...top twenty richest men in the country!"

"I know. Because he steals people's companies."

"I don't think reputable businessmen go around stealing companies."

"Did you hear *nothing* I just said?"

She nodded. "Yeah, I heard all of it. He tried to buy you out. You said no. He became insistent, you became defensive. There was some hot sex, and now you're sitting here with me instead being upstairs, boinking him."

"Boinking? Seriously?"

"Making crazy, uninhibited love," she amended with an eye roll.

I groaned. "He bought my damned building, Liv."

"And he said it was a mistake."

"How does that make it any less underhanded?"

"Back the truck up a second. Let's just assume he's as crazy as you are. He's totally desperate to *not* admit that he wants your company more than he wants your *company*. So he goes that extra insanity mile, only to realize afterward that he's essentially screwed himself over. It's kinda too late, so all he can do is apologize."

"There are so many assumptions in that scenario," I replied.

But something about it seems plausible, anyway, doesn't it? Ethan doesn't do things halfway.

I shook off the thought and added, "That doesn't make him any less of a ruthless bastard, though, does it?"

"Are you trying to convince me, or yourself?"

"I don't know," I admitted, dropping my gaze back to my drink.

"Okay. Hang on. The article. It might sway your opinion a bit." She clicked the phone screen a few times, then read aloud. "In the world of distribution, E. B. Burke is king. Half a decade ago, he resolved to do something to save small business in Canada. When asked if his umbrella company might be counterproductive to that ideal, Burke claimed that he sees himself as nothing more than a middleman. He also states that his own family's loss is the inspiration for forming Burke Holdings After giving in to pressure to sell to a large corporation, Burke's father lost his life and his business in a suspicious fire."

My heart flipped in my chest. "What?"

Liv held out her phone. "Read it yourself. The guy's not a jerk. He's a motivated businessman with a heart of freakin' gold."

Not really sure I wanted to, I took the cell phone and scanned the rest of the article. The writer talked about how Ethan didn't like to talk much about the rough years between losing his father, then his mother, and the time he started his business. How he wanted a clean slate and worked hard to get it. He was driven. Determined never to let someone else go through what his dad had been through.

"I thought..." I trailed off, unsure what I *had* believed.

That he was hiding something damning at the very least.

"Oh, God," said Liv as she took the phone back. "You're so blind."

"I am?"

"He's in love with you."

I swallowed. "Impossible."

"Really, Lu? It's the night before your brother's wedding, and you're here..." She waved her hand around the bar. "Talking about Ethan Burke's terribleness. While Ethan Burke himself is upstairs in your room. Waiting for you. For an eternity, apparently."

"I have to go up there, don't I?"

"No shit."

"I'm sorry for dragging you out here to whine."

She snagged my gin and tonic and hopped up. "No worries, I know how to make the best of it."

I jumped up too, gave her the briefest hug, then scurried out of the bar, hope making me move with quick enthusiasm. But the buoyed feeling in my chest didn't last quite as long as it should. By the time I was actually in the elevator, self-doubt had crept back in. My feet dragged as I reached the hotel room door.

Liv might be right. Ethan might be in love with me. But was I even capable of accepting that? Was I capable of trusting someone? He'd asked me for a chance. But what made me so sure that he'd take one on me?

I stuck the key card into the slot, then pushed open the door. It was so still and quiet that I thought for a second that I was too late. That maybe Ethan *hadn't* waited.

Trepidation made me cold.

But then I spotted him sprawled across one half of the king-size bed, and relief slammed into me so hard that I swayed.

I stepped closer and let myself stare down at him.

How did he manage to scatter my thoughts and make my heart thunder, even when he wasn't awake?

I studied the familiar lines of his body, searching for an explanation.

His face was heartbreakingly handsome. I'd established that the moment I laid eyes on him. The ever-present, five-o'clock shadow. The strong jaw and thick lashes. I didn't even have to think about them, and the dark brown of his irises filled my mind.

My gaze traveled down the rest of his shiver-inducing body. He'd obviously taken me up on my offer of the shower, as evidenced by the fact that he wore nothing but a towel. The smallish piece of terrycloth staying on at all was a minor miracle, considering the way he was splayed out. But there was something just as endearing as there was sexy about his arm thrown back over his head. Like he hadn't meant to fall asleep like that, but hadn't been able to help it.

It made me want to smile and cry at the same time. It was completely unfair to be made to feel this way about him. To have my heart expand to the point of bursting but to be unsure that I could have what I so desperately wanted.

Swallowing the tears that threatened, I lowered myself to the edge of the bed. I lifted my fingers and held them over his chest, shaking a little.

I craved contact, and he wouldn't turn me away. I was a hundred percent certain of it. But I also knew I wanted more than physical satisfaction.

I tried to draw in a steadying breath and started to stand, but his heady, masculine scent made me sway again. It was just enough time for Ethan to shift on the bed too. His hand came up and landed on my bare thigh. Then tightened. Heat zapped through me. And as much as I tried to keep it in, a want-tinged gasp escaped my lips.

Ethan's lids fluttered, then dragged open. When his eyes fixed on me, they were filled with desire. Affection. Need.

And his voice was the same. "Mia?"

"Why didn't you tell me about your parents?" I blurted.

He blinked sleepily. "I did."

"I mean the hard stuff. The fire."

"Ah. You finally looked me up on Google."

"No. Well. I mean, I looked you up before, but I didn't see anything about that."

He gripped the towel, then turned and propped himself up on his elbow. "That article's not my favorite. The guy who interviewed me caught me on the anniversary of the fire."

I stared down at him, sudden understanding sweeping in. "You think it makes you weaker."

He did a single shoulder shrug. "I've got more than my share of pride. And softness is what got my dad killed, so..."

"What happened?" I asked softly.

Ethan rolled to his back. "Things were rough, financially. I told you that before. So when this so-called businessman came in and offered my dad a substantial sum for his shop—I was out of town when it all happened, but the last call he made to me, he told me he'd accepted the offer for love. He wanted time with my mother before she passed. But he no sooner signed the paperwork than the new owner burned it down for the insurance money. The firefighters said my dad must've come by for something and tried to put out the fire. Smoke inhalation killed him."

"I'm so sorry, Ethan."

"Me too, honey. Which is why I decided to make sure that shit never happened to anyone else. No bad deals."

"You're a good man," I said.

"I want to be."

A further truth hit me. "I'm a source of weakness. Of softness"

He rolled back and grabbed me so quickly that my breath caught.

"You are *not* a source of weakness," he said. "I always believed that I understood why my dad sold so quickly and without properly looking into things. But it wasn't until you kissed me and those literal fireworks went off that I truly knew what he meant."

His words should've made me happy. Instead, they brought inexplicable tears to the surface.

Ethan reached out to wipe one away. "Lu, what's wrong?"

"It turns out it's me."

"What's you?"

"I'm the liar, Ethan."

"You're not a liar."

"You're wrong. I'm so completely full of shit. The second I fell out of that tree and landed on you, nothing else mattered."

"I don't know if that's a compliment or not, but I'll take it." He smiled, but it quickly turned a frown when he realized I wasn't smiling too. "It's *not* a compliment. You're not happy that you want me?"

"Because I'm not *supposed* to want you. Not more than I want anything else, anyway. My business. My life. Those are the things that make me *me*!" The words burst out in a furious rush of untethered emotion, and I dropped my gaze, embarrassed.

He paused, then said, "Look at me."

"Why?"

"Please."

I made myself lift my face, sure that shame was written all over it. He brought up his hand and dragged his knuckles along my cheekbone.

"I don't want it," he said.

For a single moment, I thought he meant me, and my heart threatened to shatter. But as I drew in a ragged, pain-filled breath, my brain caught up with my ears.

He said it. *Not* you.

I exhaled. "You don't want what?"

"Your store," he replied.

"Don't just—"

"Lumia. I mean it. I don't want it. In fact. Hang on."

He rolled over, grabbed his phone from the nightstand, clicked it couple of times, then handed the device over to me. I squinted down at what appeared to be a tiny, legalese-filled document.

I gave up trying to read it, and sighed. "Why don't you just tell me what it is?"

"It's the deed to your building," he said.

I swallowed against the immediate lump in my throat. "And you're showing it to me because...?"

"It's yours."

"Mine?"

"If you want it, Lu."

"You want to *give* me the building." I blinked. "It's gotta be worth—"

"A lot," he agreed. "You'd be your own landlord. And some other people's landlord too. But we can work that out if it's not something you want to take on. There are property management companies, and—why are you looking at me like you're going to say no?"

"Because I can't take this! And even if I could...it doesn't change the fact that I feel like I'd just walk away from it all to have you. That's not normal. Or reasonable."

He chuckled. "I'm pretty damned sure that's how love it supposed to be. Being willing to give everything up for the other person, but not actually having to do it because the other person feels the same way."

I met his eyes. "You'd walk away from Burke Holdings?"

"If you really wanted me to."

"That's insane."

"That's what love does."

"Ethan..."

"Lu."

"Are we really making this leap?"

"Already jumped." He kissed my forehead, then my lips. "Just waiting for you to catch me."

"You're sappy," I breathed. "But I love you anyway."

"I have been waiting a lifetime to hear you say that."

"We met two weeks ago," I reminded him.

"I know. And I've loved you since the second you knocked me flat on my ass. Love at first sight makes it feel like a lifetime. I love you too, Lumia."

"Then come here and prove it."

And he did. Several times.

Epilogue

The Wedding

Ethan

Every eye should've been on the bride. But for all I cared, Mia's sister-in-law could have shown up in a hot pink tutu and go-go boots. I was only interested in Mia in her purple satin dress. In the way it hugged her ample curves and contrasted with her red hair. I couldn't really understand why no one else just wanted to stare. I was thankful, though, because I also wanted her all to myself. Which is why I was glad when the ceremony and dinner were through. And more glad when the dancing started and I could find an excuse to get her alone.

I grabbed her hand and tugged her into the hall, then kissed her until I was sure she needed to gasp for air.

"What?" she teased breathlessly when I released her lips. "Did you get tired of being a spectacle?"

"Being paraded around and awkwardly introduced to your family, you mean?" I replied. "How could I ever get tired of that?"

Her eyes sparkled. "I meant being referred to as 'the stripper' by Liv. But that other stuff too."

"It's all right. Being 'the stripper' gives me street cred." I leaned down to give her lower lip a nibble.

"Would it be wrong to ditch my own brother's wedding?" she asked.

"Wrong times a million."

"Damn it."

An overhead speaker fizzed to life, and the DJ's voice carried in. "Ladies, in case you missed it. The brand-new Mrs. Aysia Diaz is about three seconds away from tossing the bouquet. Get your butts in here for your chance to grab it."

Mia shot me a mischievous grin, then slipped out of my grasp and ran back toward the dance floor.

* * * *

Mia

I dived into the fray at the last second, my hands outstretched just in time to snatch the bouquet from the air. The girls around me squealed and congratulated me, but it was Ethan who held my attention. He stood just outside of the group, his mouth tipped up in that half-smile I loved so much. And it widened when I stepped in his direction.

"Well," he said, "at least this solves one problem."

"What problem's that?" I replied

"That whole labeling thing."

"What do you mean?"

"That dreaded b-word." He winked.

I frowned, thinking about it for a second before realizing what he meant. "You mean boyfriend?"

"That's the one," he agreed.

"How does it solve the problem?"

"We can skip it altogether and go straight to the f-word instead."

"The f—oh."

"I promise I'll buy you a ring. But first I have a confession." He smiled sheepishly.

I groaned. "What?"

"Darla and Chuck."

"Who?"

"The old couple in the elevator."

"What about them?"

"I paid them."

I stared at him, waiting for the punch line. But he just looked incredibly sheepish.

"Their story was true, though," he said. "I heard them telling it in the line at the desk, and I was desperate to give you a nudge."

"So you *paid* them to tell it in front of me?" I asked, incredulous.

"Yes. I told them if they saw me again, and I happened to be with the world's most beautiful redhead, to find a way to share."

"How much?"

"Two thousand dollars."

I blinked. "You can't be serious."

"Worth every penny," he said sincerely.

A laugh burst from my lips. "You're such a manipulative bastard, E. B. Burke."

He grinned. "I know. And now that *that's* out of the way..."

Before I could come up with a clever retort, he bent down and kissed me breathless. Again.

THE END

Don't miss Marcelo and Aysia's story. Look for AFTER HOURS, on sale now.

AFTER HOURS

By Melinda Di Lorenzo

Six foot two. Lips to die for. And boy, can the man fill out a suit. The gorgeous stranger sending Aysia Banks steamy looks from across the bar is the perfect way for her to take her mind off her high-stress job, and maybe even forget about her ex.. An invitation to dance leads to a smoldering night, which turns into a weekend of uninhibited, toe-curling, blow-your-mind passion. Things are starting to look up for Aysia—until Monday morning...

Another city, another company to save. It's nothing new to executive Marcelo Diaz, who's used to calling the shots and getting what he wants. But what is different, is Aysia: the vixen he spent the weekend rewriting the entire playbook with. But before Marc can take things any further he's shocked by what he discovers...

Marc was hired to keep his employer's reputation squeaky clean.

Part of Aysia's job is to enforce her department's strict no-dating rule.

And they work for the same company.

Now, with their red-hot connection doused by office policies and politics, Aysia and Marc try to put their fling behind them. It should be easy. But when a behind-the-scenes power play threatens their careers, they'll have to bring their hearts to the table...

Business or
Pleasure

L
Y
R
I
C
A
L
&
C
A
R
E
S
S

MELINDA DI LORENZO
After Hours

About the Author

Amazon bestselling author **Melinda Di Lorenzo** lives on the beautiful west coast of British Columbia, Canada, with her handsome husband and her noisy kids. When she's not writing, she can be found curled up with (someone else's) good book. Visit the author at melindadilorenzowrites. blogspot.com, find her on www.facebook.com/MelindaDiLorenzo, and follow her at twitter.com/melindawrites.

Printed in the United States
by Baker & Taylor Publisher Services